Praise for the Novels of
Jack Caldwell

"*Caldwell writes in the spirit of [Jane] Austen, with the same wit that cemented Austen's novels as literary classics.*"

– SOS Aloha's Reviews

PEMBERLEY RANCH —
"*Something truly original for fans of Jane Austen and fans of historical fiction. It's* Pride & Prejudice *meets* Gone with the Wind—*with that kind of romance and excitement.*"

– Sharon Lathan, bestselling author
of *Miss Darcy Falls in Love.*

THE THREE COLONELS —
"*Achingly romantic and breathlessly paced, it ate me alive with alternating feelings of dread, mirth, tears, and joy … just what a great read is supposed to do.*"

– Austenprose

MR. DARCY CAME TO DINNER —
"*This is a wonderfully clever, witty, and laugh-out-loud book! I highly recommend it to anyone who wants a good laugh—I was laughing from start to finish!*"

– Laughing with Lizzie

The Companion of His Future Life

JACK CALDWELL

WHITE
SOUP
PRESS

THE COMPANION OF HIS FUTURE LIFE

For information, address Jack Caldwell, 2724 Regatta Drive, Sarasota, FL, 34231.

http://www.cajuncheesehead.com
http://whitesouppress.com/
http://austenauthors.net/

ISBN: 978-0-9891080-1-0

Layout & design by Ellen Pickels

Dedication

To Barbara,
the joy of my life.

In Appreciation

To Amy Robertson, Sarah Hunt,
Debbie Styne, and Ellen Pickels,
for their endless hours editing this work.

Chapter 1

The Proposal

The Reverend William Collins of Hunsford paced the grounds of Longbourn in the early hours of the day. He was a tall, heavy-looking young man of five-and-twenty. His air was grave and stately, and his manners were very formal. Mr. Collins was not a sensible man, and this deficiency of nature had been but little assisted by education or society. The greatest part of his life was spent under the guidance of an illiterate and miserly father, and though he belonged to one of the universities, he had merely kept the necessary terms without forming any useful acquaintance. The subjection under which his father had brought him up had given him great humility of manner at first, but it was now a good deal counteracted by the self-conceit of a weak head and the consequential feelings of early and unexpected prosperity. A fortunate chance had recommended him to Lady Catherine de Bourgh when the living of Hunsford became vacant, and the respect he felt for her high rank and his veneration for her as his patroness, mingling with a very good opinion of himself, made him altogether a mixture of pride and obsequiousness, self-importance and humility.

Having now a good house and sufficient income, Mr. Collins intended to marry. In seeking reconciliation with the Bennet family of Longbourn, he had a wife in view, and he meant to choose one of their five daughters if he found them as handsome and amiable as they were represented by common report. This was his plan to atone for inheriting their father's estate. He thought it an excellent one, full of eligibility and suitableness and excessively generous on his part.

His plan did not vary on seeing his cousins. Miss Bennet's lovely face confirmed his views, and for the first evening, she was his settled choice. The next morning, however, made an alteration, for in a quarter hour's tête-à-tête with Mrs. Bennet before breakfast, amid very complaisant smiles and general encouragement, he was cautioned against the very Jane he had fixed on. Her eldest daughter, Mrs. Bennet felt it incumbent to hint, was likely to be very soon engaged. As to her younger daughters, she did not know of any prepossession.

Mr. Collins had only to change from Jane to Elizabeth, and it was done in the time it took for Mrs. Bennet to stir the fire. Elizabeth, next to Jane in birth and beauty, succeeded her of course.

Now, after his marvelous success at the ball at Netherfield where he had made the acquaintance of the nephew of his most esteemed patroness, Mr. Collins steeled himself to make his declaration. There was no time to waste, for his leave from Rosings Park extended only to the following Saturday. As was his wont, he began to practice his suit.

"My dear Cousin Elizabeth…" *Is that too flowery? No.* "My dear Cousin Elizabeth, almost as soon as I entered the house, I singled you out as the…companion of my future life." *Yes, yes, that is well.* "But before I am…I am"—*hmm*—"run away with by my feelings"—*Yes!*—"on this subject, perhaps it will be advisable for me to state my reasons for marrying—and moreover, for coming into Hertfordshire with the design of selecting a wife, as I certainly did." *Yes, I should make clear to her my reasons for marrying as well as how my choice must most agreeably settle the concerns of the Bennet family.*

Mr. Collins had no misgivings on the prospect of matrimony—not for himself. He prided himself on the quality of his abode in Hunsford, so improved by the attentions of his most exalted patroness. Surely, no lady could be other than overjoyed at the prospect of such a household! However, Lady Catherine had advised him to choose *properly*.

Choose a gentlewoman for her sake, she had said, and for his own. "Let her be an active, useful sort of person, not brought up high, but able to make a small income go a good way."

Mr. Collins was not impressed with the manner in which Mrs. Bennet kept house, though it was a pleasant surprise that they did have servants.

Elizabeth Bennet was a lovely woman with sparkling eyes, an agreeable smile, and quite the lush form. *Stop it! Beauty is only skin deep, and I should not be tempted by the ways of the flesh!* But her mode of expressing herself was worrisome. Her wit and vivacity would be acceptable to Lady Catherine, he thought, when tempered with the silence and respect her rank would inevitably excite. *Yes, Cousin Elizabeth must know that rank is important!*

His musings were interrupted by a movement in the small bit of wilderness near the house.

MARY FRANCES BENNET WAS WALKING from the bit of wood near Longbourn, reading her copy of Fordyce's *Sermons to Young Women*. She was attempting to divert herself from the apparent romantic successes of her two eldest sisters. Mary was no expert in the ways of the heart, but no one with two eyes could mistake the admiration Mr. Bingley held for Jane, and it was becoming a certainty that Mr. Collins would settle on Elizabeth.

It would be an understatement to say that Mary Bennet had conflicted feelings. Her life-long study of matters spiritual had only partly offset that she was Fanny Bennet's middle daughter. She longed for the attentions of a man—a good, righteous man, of course—as much as any of her sisters did. But who could compete with the beauty of Jane or the wit of Elizabeth? Mary might as well as have been wallpaper, so she lost herself in music and reading, waiting for the day God would reward His servant.

Today was that day, but God works in mysterious ways.

So engrossed was she in her book that Mary never saw the tree root, but her foot did not miss it. The only fortunate result of her subsequent fall into a mud puddle was that her book remained undamaged.

Carefully rising from the muck, Mary quickly made her way to the rear of the house, where Mrs. Hill was taking in the laundry.

"Oh, Miss Mary!" the good woman cried. "Look at your dress! You poor dear! And breakfast is just served!"

Mary hated being late for breakfast, as her mother was quietest early in the day. "Oh, Hill, I must quickly go change my—"

The housekeeper stopped her with a smile. "Oh, Miss, that is not necessary. Do I not have a nice clean gown for you here? Come, no one is about. Out of your things."

Mary was scandalized. "Hill! Outside? Do I dare?"

Mrs. Hill shook her head. "Enough of that! Let me help you."

MR. COLLINS PULLED HIMSELF BACK behind the tree, his hands over his eyes. Surely, he would burn in hell for spying on his cousin! He silently berated himself as he waited for the ladies to return to the house. Minutes later, he peeked around the tree to find he was quite alone. A very abashed clergyman made his way into the house. Try as he might, however, he could not clear the image from his mind: his comely Cousin Mary, standing in her shift and waiting for the housekeeper to exchange her dress.

The Bennet family members were their usual, unruly selves during breakfast. Mrs. Bennet expounded at length on Jane's fitness to be mistress of Netherfield Park. Her eldest lowered her head in embarrassment, and Elizabeth was clearly mortified for her. The two youngest, Kitty and Lydia, were giggling at their latest plans for meeting militia officers. Only Mary seemed to notice that Mr. Collins was out of sorts.

As the toast was passed to Collins, his eyes caught those of his young cousin. Turning red with remembrance—*who knew what a fine, full figure she hid under those dresses of hers!*—Collins contemplated his intentions. He glanced at Elizabeth.

Yes, she is lovely—almost as beautiful as the eldest—but will she make Lady Catherine happy? He had wished, in his brief time at Longbourn, that Elizabeth had shown the piety exhibited by her younger sister. Collins was a man and, of course, preferred a pretty face to a plain one.

But his misadventure that morning had given him pause. He had to admit that Miss Mary was agreeable—yes, *very* agreeable indeed. It would not do to declare himself to Miss Elizabeth until he knew Miss Mary better, he decided.

As breakfast ended, Collins turned to the young lady. "Miss Mary, might I enquire whether you would be agreeable to a discussion of some of the views of Mr. Fordyce?"

Mary blinked in confusion, surprised that he was addressing her. "That…that would be delightful, Mr. Collins."

THE NEXT DAY, MR. WILLIAM Collins successfully proposed to Miss Mary Frances Bennet. Thus, our story begins.

Chapter 2

The Wedding

Elizabeth Bennet sat in the pew of the Meryton Church, trying to understand what was going on. There, before the altar, was her sister Jane, a participant in a wedding ceremony but not as the bride. Jane was the bridesmaid. For her sister Mary. Who was getting married. To William Collins.

What has happened?

Six weeks earlier, Jane was enjoying the attentions of Mr. Bingley, Elizabeth was enjoying her contempt for Mr. Darcy, and both were trying to avoid Mr. Collins. Now, Mr. Bingley and his annoying sisters and friend were gone from the neighborhood. Mr. Wickham, the soldier who had been so entertaining to the Bennet ladies, was paying exclusive attentions to Miss King. And Mary was uniting herself for life with Mr. Collins.

What has happened? No, no, this is wrong. It should be Jane marrying Mr. Bingley. Perhaps this is a dream. Perhaps if I close my eyes very tightly and open them, this will all go away.

Mr. Collins was repeating his vows. "With this ring, I thee wed. With my body, I thee worship."

Elizabeth tried. It did not serve. *I believe I shall be ill now.*

Eventually, the ceremony was over, and Elizabeth found herself alone in the church with Jane. Her sister reached over to pat Elizabeth's hand.

"Lizzy? Are you well?"

Elizabeth shook her head. "I have a mind amazed at its own discomposure, Jane. I cannot believe that Mary has married Mr. Collins. It is just…wrong!"

"Well, it has happened, and we are all returning to Longbourn for the breakfast. You must come along now."

Elizabeth grasped her sister's hand. "Oh, Jane, if only we were going to *your* wedding breakfast!"

Jane smiled a thin smile. "Mr. Bingley is perhaps the most amicable man of my acquaintance, but I am sure you apprehend too much about him. He is a very pleasant sort of person, and I enjoyed his company. That is all. Now, come along."

Elizabeth chose not to challenge her sister and walked out of the chapel. At the door, she turned back and looked at the sanctuary one last time.

William Collins is my brother. I cannot believe it!

The new Mrs. Collins approached her elder sisters as she prepared to leave.

"Mary, let me wish you joy again," cried Jane as she hugged her.

"Thank you, Jane." Mary turned questioning eyes to Elizabeth. "And you, Lizzy? Do you wish me well?"

"Of course! All the joy in the world, my dear sister." As much as she tried, Elizabeth's sentiment sounded false, even to her own ears.

Mary was clearly not deceived, but she did not challenge her sister. Instead, she grasped Elizabeth's hands most fervently. "Please, you must promise me, both of you, that you will visit me as soon as may be."

Elizabeth was taken aback to see the apprehension in Mary's face. "Of course, we shall! Shall we not, Jane?"

"Oh, yes," Jane assured them both.

Elizabeth smiled. "There, it is settled! Write to us when you are ready."

Mary was visibly relieved. "I shall—perhaps at Eastertide. I shall ask Mr. Collins."

Elizabeth was almost overcome by the look of fear and trepidation on Mary's countenance. "Oh, Mary, take care! We love you so!" She embraced her trembling sister.

Mary was in tears. "You do? Oh, I love you, too! Both of you!"

Jane joined in, and the three held each other until they were interrupted by a pompous voice.

"Ah, what a picture of sisterly felicity! Would I could but stand here to admire it for the rest of my days! But, Mrs. Collins, we must be off if we are to make Hunsford before nightfall." To Elizabeth's disgust, Mr. Collins was actually dancing from foot to foot, so fervent was his desire to leave.

Mary closed her eyes and took a deep breath. "Yes, Mr. Collins, you are right. Give me your arm...husband."

Elizabeth blanched. *I believe I shall be ill now.*

The remainder of the leave-taking took no little time as Mrs. Bennet was in full rapture over her now-darling daughter being the first to leave Longbourn after entering the state of Holy Matrimony. Finally, the farewells were accomplished, and the couple ascended the waiting carriage. As it pulled out of the drive, Mary leaned out.

"Jane, Lizzy, do not forget your promise! Goodbye all! Goodbye!"

WE HAVE ARRIVED, THANKS TO God's grace, to the most charming house. Hunsford Parsonage is a very comfortable place with well-designed rooms and a lovely little garden. Lady Catherine de Bourgh has been most attentive to the needs of the parish, and Mr. Collins assures me that no expense was spared in the improvements to the house. No detail is beneath our patroness's notice.

Elizabeth set down Mrs. Collins's letter to gaze at Jane, who was occupied with reading a letter of her own. Mary's letter was full of information about Hunsford, but there was little in it that spoke to the feelings of the writer. Was she happy? Elizabeth could not tell and because of that, she was worried.

She caught Jane's eye. "What does Miss Bingley say, Jane?"

A small sigh escaped from her lips. "More of the same—how

wonderful Town is, how excessively they are in demand for balls and parties and other entertainments, and how occupied Mr. Bingley is in London. I believe she is trying to tell me that Mr. Bingley shall not be returning to Netherfield soon, if ever."

"Surely, she is mistaken!"

Jane put on a sad smile. "It is all right, Lizzy. I am in no danger. Mr. Bingley shall do as he pleases. I have no claim on him."

Elizabeth snorted. "No claim? After the attentions he paid you? Jane, if he should not return to Netherfield, I shall never forgive him!"

Jane smiled more happily. "Tell me of Mary's letter."

"You shall read it for yourself." She handed her the missive. "She tells of many things—of the house and gardens and village— but nothing of import, nothing of her feelings."

Jane looked up from the letter. "Not everyone thinks as you do."

Elizabeth tossed her head. "That is unlikely, for I believe my feelings to be the most natural things in the world. *You* would certainly not write such a letter, I am sure."

"True," Jane conceded, "but I am not Mary."

"But she is our sister. She is a Bennet." Elizabeth frowned. "Oh, Jane, I am worried."

Elizabeth's dire tone did not disturb Jane's calm countenance. "In a few weeks, we shall be there and see for ourselves."

"En garde!"

The match continued. The foils touched tentatively before the taller of the two gentlemen made an aggressive move forward. The other participant parried and attacked, but he was easily countered. There was a rush of movement and...

"Touché!" called the referee. "Match!"

The winner whipped off his fencing mask. "Charles! What are you about, man? Five to nil? You fight like a rank beginner."

Charles Bingley put down his épée. "Forgive me, Darcy. My mind is elsewhere."

Fitzwilliam Darcy grimaced at his best friend. Since he made Bingley his sparring partner, his skill had improved to the point of making Darcy work for his victory. But today, he had performed badly. It was understandable, of course, but it was painful to observe.

Poor Bingley. It has been months, so he must have had true feelings for the girl. If only she returned them! Ah well, it is better that he suffers now rather than after it is too late—trapped in a marriage of unequal affections, especially with such relations! He then recalled one of Jane Bennet's sisters, and his mood darkened.

He needed to work out his confused emotions, but Bingley was not up for another match. Darcy looked about his London fencing club, but no one would meet his eye. Few wished to be Darcy's next victim—not Knightley, not Willoughby, certainly not Hurst—as he was regarded as one of the best in the club. The men most widely considered to be Darcy's equal were Richard Fitzwilliam and—

"Tilney! Are you available for a set, sir?"

Captain Frederick Tilney gave Darcy a lazy smile. "A moment, Darcy, and I am your man." A few minutes later, both men had taken their positions on the mat. A crowd gathered to watch the cream of the club do battle.

"Loser buys dinner, Darcy?" asked Tilney.

"Agreed."

"En garde!"

MRS. GARDINER WAS IN ELIZABETH'S room a month later, helping her to pack. "I can understand Mary wanting her two eldest sisters to visit her new home, but I am disappointed that I shall not have the opportunity of entertaining two of my favorite nieces in London this Easter."

"Jane and I wished to be with you and my uncle in Town above all things," Elizabeth assured her, "but Mary asked for us particularly. In fact, she had us promise most faithfully before she and...*he* left for Hunsford."

"Lizzy!" Mrs. Gardiner scolded. "He is your brother! Surely you can say his name!"

"Must I?"

"Lizzy!"

"Very well—*Mr. Collins.* He sent us a letter as well, extolling the delights we are sure to find at Rosings Park. Four pages it took to describe its attractions!" Elizabeth's eyes danced with mischief.

Jane entered the room as Elizabeth was speaking. "Our new brother does go on at length. I trust it is because of the uncommon kindness Lady Catherine de Bourgh has bestowed on him and my sister."

Mrs. Gardiner embraced the girl. "I am sure you are right, my dear. And are you well? I must say you look a bit pale."

"I am well, Aunt. I am looking forward to seeing Mary. That is all."

ELIZABETH AND JANE WENT TO their father's library to take their leave of him.

"Ah, my dears," Mr. Bennet exclaimed as he embraced them, "I shall not forgive you too quickly for abandoning me to the care of your mother and two youngest sisters! I shall not hear one sensible word uttered in this house for the next six weeks!"

Jane answered as Elizabeth giggled. "You shall be quietly amused, as you always are, by the exuberance of my mother and sisters."

"Indeed, sir," added Elizabeth. "And when you get your fill, you shall retreat to the sanctuary of your library."

Mr. Bennet chuckled. "Are you looking forward to your visit to Hunsford? Mr. Collins writes at length about the grandeur of Rosings, and Mrs. Collins has remarked about it, too."

"Have you received a letter from my sister, sir?" asked Jane.

He pulled a letter from the pile on his desk. "Yes, it seems our Mary has been well received by Lady Catherine and has developed an acquaintance with Miss de Bourgh. She writes very complimentarily of her—all kindness and attention, even though she is in ill health."

Elizabeth frowned. This did not sound like the lady described by Mr. Wickham. Could Mary be deceived?

Mr. Bennet looked at Elizabeth from the corner of his eye. "She also writes of our friend Mr. Wickham."

"Oh, sir? What does she have to say?"

"Here, read what she writes." He handed the letter to Elizabeth. She leaned close to Jane so that they could read together.

Mr. Wickham's name was mentioned as Miss de Bourgh and I
discussed what other acquaintances we may have in common, knowing
that I have met her cousin Mr. Darcy. I must say that Miss de Bourgh
was very disinclined towards the gentleman. The son of the Pemberley
steward, W. was raised at that family's expense and was a favorite
of the late Mr. Darcy. But there has been a falling out between him
and Mr. Fitzwilliam Darcy, who was once his childhood friend. Miss
de Bourgh does not know all the particulars, but she is under the
impression that W. has ill-used the son of his benefactor after the elder
Mr. Darcy passed away. Some money was settled upon W. before he
left Pemberley, it seems, and Miss de Bourgh knows nothing else, save
that his name is not to be mentioned in Lady Catherine's hearing.

As I hold Miss de Bourgh, to be a kind and well informed person, I
feel I must warn you and my sisters against W.'s tales. Although she
will not say so, it is my opinion that Miss de Bourgh feels that that
gentleman is not to be trusted.

Her father grinned as his daughters looked up at him. "Well, Lizzy, what say you to that?"

Elizabeth blustered. "It is beyond belief! It is as if the entire of Mr. Darcy's family is set upon blackening Mr. Wickham's name! How cruel!"

Mr. Bennet laughed. "That was my impression too. Quite the family, are they not?"

Jane frowned as she considered the letter. "Perhaps there is some grave misunderstanding between the two. Mr. Wickham is a very agreeable person, but Mr. Darcy, while proud, is a very respectable gentleman. I cannot see how Mr. Bingley could be friends with someone who has treated a childhood friend with the dishonor you describe. And I must give Miss de Bourgh's views some credence, though she would only know of these matters from Mr. Darcy's side."

Mr. Bennet shook his head with affection at his eldest. "You may think that, Jane, if it gives you comfort. As for myself, I will hold to my opinion of the gentlemen in question, and their families too, until proven otherwise."

"I agree with you, sir. Mary has not been out in society as we have been, Jane. We have been to London while she has not. She is sure to have been overwhelmed by the attentions paid to her by Miss de Bourgh."

Jane was shocked. "Lizzy! Do you not trust your sister's judgment?"

How can I, when she agreed to marry that odious Mr. Collins? "We shall see, Jane, when we arrive in Hunsford."

Chapter 3

A Trip to Rosings Park

When Jane and Elizabeth left the high road for the lane to Hunsford, every eye was in search of the parsonage, and every turn in the road expected to bring it in view. The palings of Rosings Park were their boundary on one side. Elizabeth smiled at the recollection of all that she had heard of its inhabitants.

At length, the parsonage was visible. The garden sloping to the road, the house standing in it, the green pales and the laurel hedge—everything declared that they had arrived. Mr. Collins and Mary appeared at the door, and the carriage stopped at a small gate which led by a short gravel walk to the house. In a moment, they were out of the chaise, rejoicing at the sight of each other. Mrs. Collins welcomed her sisters with the liveliest pleasure.

Elizabeth saw instantly that her new brother's manners had not been altered by his marriage. His formal civility was just as it had been, and he detained her some minutes at the gate to hear and satisfy his enquiries after all her family. They were then, with no other delay than Mr. Collins pointing out the neatness of the entrance, taken into the house, and as soon as they were in the parlor, he welcomed them a second time to his humble abode with ostentatious formality and repeated his wife's offers of refreshment. When Mr. Collins said anything of which his wife might reasonably be ashamed, which certainly was not infrequent, Elizabeth involuntarily turned her eye to Mary. Once or twice, she could discern a faint blush, but in general, Mary wisely did not seem to hear.

After sitting long enough to admire every article of furniture in the room, from the sideboard to the fender, Mr. Collins invited Elizabeth and Jane to take a stroll in the garden. It was large and well laid out, and Mr. Collins remarked that he saw to its cultivation himself since to work in his garden was one of his most respectable pleasures. Elizabeth admired the command of countenance Mary displayed when she talked of the healthfulness of the exercise and her frequent promotion of such activity.

Here, leading the way through every walk and cross walk, every view was pointed out with a minuteness that left beauty entirely behind. Mr. Collins could number the fields in every direction and could tell how many trees there were in the most distant clump. But of all the views his garden could boast, none were to be compared with the prospect of Rosings afforded by an opening in the trees that bordered the park, opposite the front of his house. Rosings Park was a handsome modern building, well situated on rising ground.

From his garden, Mr. Collins would have led them round his two meadows, but the ladies not having the proper shoes to encounter the remains of a white frost, turned back, and Mary had the opportunity of showing them the house. It was rather small but well built and convenient, and everything was fitted up and arranged with a neatness and consistency for which Elizabeth gave Mary all the credit. Jane remarked that she found the house delightful, which brought a smile to Mrs. Collins.

"Yes, Lady Catherine has been very generous in her additions and improvement to the parsonage. I could not be more satisfied with my situation."

"A very generous person, I should think," said Jane.

Elizabeth blushed at the reminder of her own father's neglect of the Longbourn living.

Jane continued, "I would like to meet Lady Catherine."

Mary opened her mouth to answer, but Mr. Collins joined in. "Yes, you will have the honor of seeing Lady Catherine de Bourgh on Sunday at church, and I need not say you will be delighted with her. She is all affability and condescension, and I doubt not but you and your sister, too, will be honored with some portion of her notice when service is over. I have scarcely any hesitation in saying that she will include you and my sister Elizabeth in every invitation with which she honors us during your stay here. Her behavior to my dear Mary is charming. We dine at Rosings twice every week and are never allowed to walk home. Her ladyship's carriage is regularly ordered for us. I should say, *one* of her ladyship's carriages, for she has several."

"Lady Catherine is a very respectable, sensible woman indeed," added Mary, "and a most attentive neighbor."

"Very true, my dear, that is exactly what I say." Mr. Collins's head bobbed in a most amusing way. "She is the sort of woman one cannot regard with too much deference."

Suddenly the curate held up his hand, for he had heard a familiar noise. Silencing his wife and new sisters, he quickly stepped to the window as fast as his long legs could carry him, looked out, and breathless with agitation, cried out, "Oh, my dear sisters! Pray make haste and come outside, for there is such a sight to be seen! I will not tell you what it is, but make haste, and come out this moment!"

Elizabeth asked questions in vain, for Mr. Collins would tell her nothing more, and the party ran out to the lane in quest of this wonder. It was a small carriage handled by a slim, pale-faced young woman of about three and twenty. Mary's face broke out into the widest smile Elizabeth had ever seen.

"Miss de Bourgh!" cried Collins. "You honor us, madam!"

"It is nothing, I assure you, sir," said she. "Your wife mentioned that today was the day of her sisters' arrival, and as I happened to be on my road, I took this chance to welcome them to Rosings. Would you do the honors?"

Introductions were made all around, and Miss de Bourgh continued. "I bring news that you are all invited to Rosings tomorrow for tea." Miss de Bourgh's voice was lost in a fit of coughing, which alarmed them all.

"Miss de Bourgh, will you not step inside? Some water—may we fetch it for you?" Mary was clearly concerned.

"Excellent suggestion, my dear," said her husband. "Please, Miss de Bourgh. Our cottage is far too humble, I know, but allow us to repay our gratitude to your esteemed mother by aiding you in your hour of distress!"

The girl waved them off. "No, no, I am well, I assure you. It is always bad during the spring. Shall you come tomorrow?"

"Nothing shall prevent it!" promised Collins.

THE PARTY WALKED UP THE lane to Rosings Park the next day, Mr. Collins having decided that to use the offered carriage would be too great an imposition to his noble patroness. As the Bennet sisters were fond of walking and the distance involved was neither too great nor the weather too intemperate, there was no opposition to the parson's plan. As Mrs. Collins and Jane were involved in conversation, it fell to Mr. Collins to entertain Elizabeth.

"Is it not the grandest house you have ever laid eyes upon?" He waved in a majestic way to the edifice before them. "But, of course, it is," he answered himself. "Such beauty, such refinement and elegance! Lady Catherine de Bourgh has the most excellent taste!"

Elizabeth could only look upon the place with stupefaction. Many houses improve upon closer inspection, but Rosings Park did not have the fortune to be counted among that number. As a matter of fact, the closer one got to the building, the more overdone it seemed.

"It is a wonderment, sir." *A wonderment, indeed, that anyone could spend so much to achieve so little!* "I am sure I have never seen the like." *Thank goodness.*

Mr. Collins continued to prattle on about the imposing residence until his knock upon the door was answered by a footman dressed in a costume that would be too much in St. James's Court, much less a country estate. Once the party entered the house, Mr. Collins became unusually quiet.

Apparently, the man was overwhelmed by the décor. Elizabeth

certainly was. *Why, the interior of the house is worse than the exterior! Does the woman believe that gold leaf is so desirable that it must cover nearly every surface? I am amazed that the servants do not wear it.*

They were escorted into a salon decorated in a style to complement the rest of the house. In other words, it was overdone. There, standing by a sofa, was Miss de Bourgh. Next to her by a large chair was a tall, elegant woman of a certain age, as overdressed as the wallpaper. She wore a look that Elizabeth perceived the lady intended to be reserved yet welcoming but was condescending instead. She did not wait to be introduced.

"Good afternoon, Mr. Collins, Mrs. Collins. I can see that you are in good health. As I have always enjoyed the most excellent health, it is nothing to me, but others must look to their diets. Vegetables! You must continue to eat as many vegetables as you may. Peas and squash are particularly healthful."

"Vegetables are of the first importance on our table, my lady, thank you," answered Mary. Something hidden in her tone aroused Elizabeth's notice, but before she could consider it further, the grand dame turned in her direction.

"That is well, Mrs. Collins. These young ladies must be your sisters."

"Lady Catherine, allow me to introduce my sisters, Miss Jane Bennet and Miss Elizabeth Bennet. Sisters, I have the pleasure of introducing Lady Catherine de Bourgh and her daughter, Miss Anne de Bourgh." As the Bennet sisters declared their delight at being introduced to such fine company, Elizabeth wondered at Mrs. Collins's actions.

We met Miss de Bourgh yesterday, yet Mary acts as if we did not! And Miss de Bourgh says nothing! In fact, there was no sign of recognition in the young lady's face or any apparent inclination to correct Mrs. Collins. Mr. Collins said nothing either. Jane was confused as well, but only Elizabeth, who was blessed with such intimate knowledge of her sister's feelings, could be aware of it. *Miss de Bourgh acts as though she and Mary are only indifferent acquaintances. How strange! Are they keeping their true relationship from Lady Catherine's notice? Of course, such a friendship would be beneath her. What insufferable pride!*

Lady Catherine began again. "Mrs. Collins tells me there are five of you—all daughters. As I told her, I cannot know what your mother could have been thinking. The estate is entailed to Mr. Collins, I understand. It must be a comforting thought to know that he is your brother and will care for your mother after your father goes to his reward."

It was now time for Mr. Collins to enter the conversation. "Yes, I could not ask for a finer family or more grateful sisters. Of course, the Bennets are nothing compared to the de Bourghs or Fitzwilliams, but I am happily resigned to my good fortune."

"But five daughters!" Lady Catherine continued as if the parson had said nothing. "Should I have had more children, they would certainly have been boys. But it matters not, as the de Bourghs have done away with that foolish tradition of inheritance along the male line. Rosings Park is destined to go to Anne upon my demise." She gave a smile to her daughter, who simply nodded in return, no other expression crossing her face.

"A far superior arrangement, you may be sure, madam," Collins simpered.

"I cannot but remember what Ecclesiastes says, my lady."

All eyes turned to Mary Collins. "What was that? What did you say?" demanded Lady Catherine.

Calmly, Mary returned, "Ecclesiastes says, *Vanity of vanities, said the Preacher, all is vanity. What profit has a man of all his labor which he takes under the sun? One generation passes away, and another generation comes: but the earth stays forever.*

"*Lo, I am come to great estate, and have gotten more wisdom than all they that have been before me in Jerusalem: yea, my heart had great experience of wisdom and knowledge...I perceived that this also is vexation of spirit. For in much wisdom is much grief: and he that increaseth knowledge increaseth sorrow.*'

"However, we are in England, not Judea, and it is written to *'Render unto Caesar that which is Caesar's,'* so I can say nothing further upon the matter."

Lady Catherine spurted, but said nothing in return. Mr. Collins's face was very red, but as her ladyship allowed the matter to pass without comment, he was spared the agony of choosing between the views of his wife and his patroness. Miss de Bourgh covered her mouth to cough, but Elizabeth thought she saw a smile upon the young lady's lips.

"Miss Bennet, are all your sisters out?" asked the grand dame.

Jane turned to her. "Yes, madam."

"Your sister has said so, but I thought that she must have been mistaken. That is very singular!"

"I assure you, your ladyship, my mother knows well her duties."

"Indeed," Elizabeth was compelled to add, "with one sister married and two older ones out, it would not be a source of sisterly affection to strictly follow the dictates of propriety."

The mistress of Rosings turned her gaze upon Elizabeth. "You certainly express your opinions freely, Miss Elizabeth Bennet! What is your age?"

Elizabeth colored. "With an older sister unmarried, you certainly cannot expect me to own it."

"Come, come, Miss Elizabeth, you cannot be more than one and twenty! Miss Bennet, while certainly of age, is in the full bloom of her beauty and cannot be considered anything but an agreeable young lady. I am full aware of Mrs. Collins's age, and you are but a year or two her senior."

Elizabeth hesitated but answered, "I am not one and twenty."

"And your accomplishments, Miss Bennet? Do you play, sing, and draw?"

Jane nodded. "I do not play, your ladyship, but my sisters, Elizabeth and Mrs. Collins, do. I enjoy embroidery."

Lady Catherine was not done with her inquisition. "Do you not all sing and dance and draw? Did not your governess teach you? Surely your education was deficient."

Elizabeth seethed at the woman's rudeness, but Jane never lost her composure. "We did not have a governess. My mother saw to our education. We sought the talents that interested us. We all dance tolerably well, and my sister Kitty draws."

"Humph! Your mother has coddled you. You should have learned all. I assure you, Anne would have been a great proficient had her health permitted it." The young lady in question began coughing again. After a glance at her daughter, Lady Catherine turned to Mary. "Mrs. Collins, have you taken advantage of the pianoforte in Mrs. Parks's rooms?"

"Indeed I have, my lady. I thank you."

The mistress of Rosings nodded. "I told your sister that she will never play well unless she practices frequently and on a good instrument. I have given her permission to use the pianoforte in the housekeeper's rooms. She shall disturb no one there."

Mr. Collins interjected, "Oh, my lady, she does practice—almost every day! You are so exceedingly kind to offer such a boon to us! And I can say that your advice is most correct. Such music that flies from Mrs. Collins's hands! I am the true beneficiary of your generosity, my dear Lady Catherine!"

The old lady nodded. "Mrs. Collins, you may bring your sisters to practice, as well." This was announced as if the greatest gift in the world was bestowed.

Elizabeth was astonished at the smile that graced her sister's features. "You are too kind, my lady." Elizabeth looked again, and she could swear there was a look of triumph in Mary's eyes.

After the party returned to Hunsford, Elizabeth sought out Mrs. Collins. After expressing her pleasure in visiting Rosings, she asked, "Mary, how is it that Miss de Bourgh was so cool towards you? I must say that, had I not met her yesterday and witnessed your apparent affection, I would think her a most indifferent acquaintance."

"Yes, I can understand your confusion. I will say nothing now, but perhaps after you and Jane retire, I might speak with you both."

Nothing more was said, and Elizabeth had little choice but to accept the scheme. Sure enough, after the Bennet sisters had gone to their room, Mary's soft knock soon followed them.

"Sisters," she began after gaining entrance, "I must explain the strange behavior you witnessed today. You noticed, I am sure, Miss de Bourgh's decidedly withdrawn countenance while we were at tea."

"Indeed we did," said Jane, "and we cannot but wonder at it. Yesterday her behavior indicated a more intimate relationship. But perhaps we were mistaken in her courtesy and kindness."

"No, Jane, you were not at all mistaken. Anne—Miss de Bourgh—is more than the daughter of my husband's patron. She is my dearest friend. Indeed, she is like a sister to me."

"She must be if you can refer to her by her Christian name!" exclaimed Elizabeth. "But how do you account for her behavior today? Does Lady Catherine object to such a friendship?" Elizabeth did not doubt the answer, knowing who her nephew was.

Mary looked away as if to gather her thoughts before responding. "That is partially the answer, Lizzy. We both fear Lady Catherine's displeasure and are worried she would demand that her daughter abandon the relationship as one that is below someone of her station—"

"Below!" cried Elizabeth. "The daughter of a gentleman? Wife of her own parson?"

"Lady Catherine likes to have the distinction of rank preserved, Lizzy. But that is not the only reason. Anne and I have become fast friends because of our enjoyment in activities that would not meet with Lady Catherine's approval. We do not want to endanger Anne's freedom by having our activities discovered."

The two Bennet girls looked upon their sister in disbelief. "Freedom! You speak as if Miss de Bourgh were a prisoner in her own house!"

"In some ways she is, Lizzy—a prisoner of her mother's suffocating protection."

"Should you continue this friendship if her ladyship objects?" asked Jane.

Mary's eyes flashed. "Anne is my dearest friend! I shall never give her up!"

Jane continued in her soothing voice. "Can you share with us what this activity portends? Surely it is not disgraceful, is it?"

Mary held her head high. "I do not find it disgraceful, but Lady Catherine, and even my father, may disagree. However, as my husband does not object, I wish to do as I please!"

"Mary! Tell us what this activity is. We shall judge you fairly.

Trust us."

"I do not know. You have not thought so of my participation in the past!"

The two girls shuddered in horror. "Mary!" Elizabeth pleaded. "Tell us! We beg you!"

Mrs. Collins drew a breath. "Music."

Silence descended upon the room.

"Music?" asked Jane.

"Yes," Mary sniffed. "I have been teaching Anne to play the pianoforte."

"Oh, fie on you, you horrid girl!" cried Elizabeth. "How can you tease us so? Such thoughts were going through my mind—and Jane's too, I should not wonder!"

Mary gave her a puzzled look. "What thoughts were those?"

"Yes," added Jane, "What were you thinking?"

"Never mind," equivocated their sister, blushing furiously. "It is of little importance."

Jane turned back to Mary. "But why must you keep this secret from Lady Catherine? Surely, she could have no objection to music." Elizabeth voiced her agreement with Jane's observation, but Mrs. Collins shook her head.

"She has put much stock into the belief that her daughter is of weak constitution and suffers ill health. It is why she has not allowed Anne to learn music or riding. If Anne cannot be a master of her talents, then she must not suffer to be exposed as a mere enthusiast. In fact, Anne only uses her carriage when her mother is occupied. She is supposed to be driven by others."

"Mary," said Jane, "are you saying that Lady Catherine would be displeased to learn that her daughter is not as unwell as she fears?"

"Anne does not enjoy perfect health, that is true, but she is capable of more than her mother believes. Lady Catherine, however, is not a person to be gainsaid. She means well. She is concerned lest her daughter overexert herself."

Elizabeth asked, "So you and Miss de Bourgh practice in secret?"

"Yes, in the housekeeper's rooms. As you know, Lady Catherine has kindly allowed me use of the pianoforte there, and Mrs. Parks is in our confidence. Her ladyship would never enter those rooms, so we are safe."

"And Mr. Collins—does he approve of this activity?'

Mary said carefully, "He does not object is more accurate, Jane. He is uncomfortable in keeping something from Lady Catherine's notice, but he realizes that Miss de Bourgh will one day become mistress of Rosings, and he does not wish to offend her. He is very pleased that she has bestowed such attentions upon me. He is caught in the middle, you see, so he closes his eyes and tends his gardens. We have convinced him that what Lady Catherine does not know will do her no harm."

Elizabeth nodded in approval. She had taken a liking to the heiress and wished her the same pleasure from music that she herself enjoyed. This image of Anne de Bourgh was in stark contrast to the description of the lady she had heard from Mr. Wickham, but Elizabeth convinced herself not to be troubled. The girl was obviously a person of secrets, and if she could deceive her own mother, it was no surprise that others would so misconstrue her true character. And, Elizabeth smiled to herself, Mr. Collins's gardens were truly beautiful, evidence of his constant care.

Jane, however, was troubled by Mary's story—disguise being abhorrent to her—but she soon brightened; her character was ill suited to unhappiness. She comforted herself with the expectation of Lady Catherine's happy surprise when the full extent of her daughter's accomplishments was finally revealed.

THE NEXT AFTERNOON, ELIZABETH WAS given the opportunity to gain a greater insight into the marriage of her sister. After shutting himself in his study for most of the morning, working on that Sunday's sermon, Mr. Collins entered the sitting room for tea.

"What will be the scripture reading, Mr. Collins?" asked his wife as she handed him his cup, prepared exactly to his liking.

The vicar smiled. "Our Lord cleansing the temple of the money-changers and the like." He sipped his tea. "Ah, perfect, as always! You see, my dear sisters, how Mrs. Collins fairly dotes on me!"

"Thank you, my dear. And what will be the topic of the sermon?"

"The responsibility of all of us to cast out from society those who are unfit. Lady Catherine was most insistent that we remind the people that the dregs of society are a danger to the social order and the preservation of rank."

Elizabeth blanched.

"But Mr. Collins," said Mary in a concerned voice, "this sounds very like the sermon from last week! Will not Lady Catherine be offended? We cannot let her think her pastor is without imagination. It will not do to so submerge your talents, my dear. What is the subject of next Sunday's sermon—Easter Sunday?"

"Why, the Resurrection, of course."

"Of course, how silly of me. Hmmm…" One delicate finger tapped Mary's full lips. "Perhaps it might be wise to prepare the congregation for that holy day, to remind them that Our Lord foresaw his sacrifice."

The clergyman rose and paced about the room. "You know, I did have it in my mind to do just that very thing."

"Oh, how sensible of you, Mr. Collins! Christ was very brave to challenge the Sanhedrin, knowing that would provoke them to act against him."

"Indeed, indeed. I recall a lecture in seminary on that very subject. I can remember it still!"

"And shall you share such a mighty memory with the people of Hunsford, Husband? How generous of you! Lady Catherine would be pleased, I am sure."

He stopped his pacing, slapping a hand to his cheek. "Yes, yes! I shall write it this instant while it is clear in my head! Sisters, excuse me!"

Jane spoke up. "Mr. Collins, shall you not take tea?"

"No, I must strike while my muse is upon me! I shall go! If you seek for me, look for me nowhere but in my study!" He strode quickly to the door, and as he flung it open, he looked back at his wife. "Mary, my dear, may I ask that you look over my manuscript once I have done an acceptable draft?"

She nodded. "I am at your disposal, as always, my dear."

"Excellent! Wonderful woman! Your sister is an invaluable assistant. She often finds misspellings and other mistakes in my prose. Once she finishes her purview, my words truly sing to heaven! Never has my writing flowed so well!"

"It is a little thing, Mr. Collins," Mary simpered. "I know your intentions, and I know your ways. Your ideas flow so fast your pen cannot keep up. I am glad I do justice to you talents."

"Indeed, I am the most fortunate of men. Until later, ladies!" Blowing a kiss to his wife, Mr. Collins left the room.

Mary refilled her astonished sisters' cups and gave a wink to Elizabeth. "Shall we go to Rosings tomorrow?"

THAT NIGHT ELIZABETH FOUND IT difficult to sleep, so she perused Mr. Collins's library. As she expected, it was meanly stocked, and the few volumes in evidence were of a pious nature. Finally settling on the least offensive book at hand, she left to return to her rooms when she had yet another insight into the Collins's relationship.

She espied her sister and her husband in earnest conversation in the sitting room as she walked towards the stairs. As she was a quiet walker, they had no idea of her presence, and Elizabeth was in a quandary. She knew she should either withdraw or make her presence known. But like an onlooker to a terrible carriage accident, she moved closer, the shadows of the hall concealing her.

Collins was holding Mary's hand and looking at her most earnestly, almost dancing in his impatience. "My dear, dear Mrs. Collins, might I come to you tonight?"

Elizabeth covered her mouth. *Oh, my lord!*

Mary took on a thoughtful expression and then asked her husband, "You do recall our agreement?"

"Oh, yes! Not a sound shall escape my lips."

"Silence is very agreeable, for our marital duties are a holy thing. But Mr. Collins, you forgot yourself last time."

The tall man seemed to shrink. "But, my loveliness, I could not restrain my amour. Forgive me!"

Elizabeth covered her ears. *Oh, my lord!*

"That is all very well," said Mary, "but my most innocent sisters are in the house. It would not do to…expose them to our activities."

"You are right; you are very right! I shall redouble my efforts. I shall not fail you, oh mistress of my heart! Please say that you will receive me!"

Mary looked up at him and then faintly smiled. "Very well. Shall we say in an hour?"

Never had Elizabeth seen Mr. Collins more pleased. "Oh, thank you, my little Mary-kins!" He bent to kiss her on the cheek.

Elizabeth took this opportunity to flee silently to her room.

I believe I shall be ill now.

Chapter 4

The Gentlemen Arrive

A stately carriage made its way across the early spring English countryside, conveying two gentlemen of varying incomes and deportment. One was sandy haired and jolly, dressed in the proper costume one would expect of the younger son of an earl. The other was as dark as his companion was fair, as serious as his friend was not, and as rich as the day was long.

Fitzwilliam Darcy, for five years the master of Pemberley in Derbyshire, wore his habitual dour expression, designed to keep the world at bay. Unfortunately, one of the few humans on the planet that would not be put off by his demeanor was sharing his coach. Colonel the Hon. Richard Fitzwilliam, of His Majesty's ——th Horse, was his cousin, childhood friend, and the one man who truly understood the paragon that was Darcy. Most people acquainted with such an important personage would show the gentleman the proper deference. Colonel Fitzwilliam was not one of them.

"I say, Darcy," the officer exclaimed, "did you eat a lemon at the public house at the station?"

"Lemon?" Darcy was confused. "No, I had the mutton, just as you did. It was barely tolerable, I must say."

"I shall certainly agree as to the meal, Cuz. That sheep was probably older than Georgiana. No, I was referring to the decidedly sour expression on your kisser."

"On my kisser? Where did that term come from? More wisdom from your campfires?"

Fitzwilliam slapped his cousin's knee. "Ha! One can learn much from honest soldiers—more than from the drawing rooms of London!"

"True enough," said Darcy gravely. "Then you know why I keep my thoughts to myself."

"So you put on a disguise, which I thought you abhorred above all else."

"Disguise that misleads is what I abhor, Fitz. This is more a part, like an actor in a play."

The colonel raised his hands like an orator. "Out, out, brief candle! Life's but a walking shadow, a poor player that struts and frets his hour upon the stage, and then is heard no more. It is a tale told by an idiot, full of sound and fury, signifying nothing."

Darcy smirked, something he did rarely in company other than Richard's. "This is new—you quoting Shakespeare."

"Is that where it comes from? I thought it was from the Old Goat. Zounds, but I must have learned something at school after all!"

Darcy gave out a short snort of laughter. "The only thing you learned at Cambridge was how to sleep with your eyes open."

Fitzwilliam waved him off. "Do not scoff, sir. That is a useful talent in my profession."

"You may spend much more time in your tent in the future, should my uncle hear you again refer to him as a barnyard animal."

"Too true, which is why he never shall," Fitzwilliam laughed, and then grew serious. "Come, what is troubling you? You have not been yourself for weeks. Has anything untoward occurred?"

"No, no. I stayed with Bingley at his leased estate in Hertfordshire for a few weeks and returned. There is nothing amiss."

"Bingley—there is another one who has been out of sorts lately. I believe I shall avoid Hertfordshire in the future. There is something decidedly strange about a place that can have such an effect upon a fellow."

You have no idea, Fitz, Darcy thought to himself. Aloud he protested, "Do not be so harsh upon Hertfordshire. Bingley's ailment comes from a different source entirely."

"Ah! Then he has another broken heart."

"Yes. I have saved him from a most imprudent marriage."

"Have you, now? Was it a scarlet woman? A scullery maid?"

Darcy rolled his eyes. "No! Let us just say there were some objections to the lady and leave it at that."

Fitzwilliam shook his head. "And so you rode to his rescue *again*. What would Bingley do without you?"

Darcy shivered. "He finds a great reliance on my judgment to be a comfort. He is my friend. Should I just let him flounder?"

Fitzwilliam raised an eyebrow. "Perhaps you should, Cuz. One of these days your tendency to rush in and save your friends and family will come back to haunt you."

"Unlikely."

"Well, it certainly wears on you."

Darcy said ungraciously, "What do you mean?"

"You cannot say you are happy." His companion grunted. "We shall just have to get you married!"

Darcy started. "I beg your pardon?"

"Well, if you are going to be miserable, you might as well have the oldest reason in the world for it!"

Darcy grimaced. It was tiresome to be always the butt of Fitz's jokes. "Perhaps you are right. I am sure my aunt has some ideas on that score."

As expected, the bolt stuck home, and Richard lost all good humor. "Yes, what are you waiting for? All the family expects a union between Pemberley and Rosings." He turned to the window.

Darcy shook his head. He could not say what was more amusing—Richard's predictable reaction or his inability to know his own mind. Darcy knew his cousin was attached to Anne de Bourgh. It was *Fitz* who did not know it. "Yes, that would please Lady Catherine no end, I should think. It is well that Anne and I are of one mind about this. We shall never marry."

Fitzwilliam was not appeased. "So you say, yet the family expects it. Do not think they cannot change your mind."

Darcy frowned. "Do you speak for the earl?"

Fitzwilliam shook his head. "No, but the family grows inpatient with you. They say if you will not trouble yourself to find some lady agreeable to you, then you should marry Anne."

"And if I am disagreeable to Anne?"

"Yes, there is that, but my Aunt Catherine can be…persuasive."

"If we can hold out this long, we can hold out forever."

"Good." A curious expression crossed Richard's face before he turned to the window again.

Darcy glanced at the colonel. *It would be so easy to give Fitz a push in the right direction, but no! I should not play matchmaker. My talents lie in quite another direction.*

He recalled with pain his conversation with Charles Bingley, in concert with his sisters, about Jane Bennet's indifference. Never had he seen a man so defeated, so dejected. Bingley truly loved the woman, he saw. It was a tragedy.

Darcy rejoiced in his success at saving his friend from a *most improper and loveless* marriage. It had to be both to rouse Darcy to interference; proper and unloving was expected in their class. He could never involve himself in preventing a loving and improper union. After all, he could not completely dismiss a similar proposition for himself.

"When shall we arrive at Rosings?" asked Richard.

"In less than two hours, Fitz."

MRS. COLLINS ESCORTED HER TWO sisters to the grand house of Rosings, but to the puzzlement of her companions, Mary did not enter the building from the front door. Instead, she began to walk around the house. She would answer her sisters' questions with only a secret smile and kept moving. Finally, the group approached a door to the rear of one of the wings of the estate. Mary paused just as she reached for the knob.

"I must beg your promise not to reveal what occurs behind this door to anyone without first speaking to me. Forgive me, but I must insist on this."

The two were shocked, but Jane was able to utter, "It shall be as you wish, Mary."

Mary nodded in satisfaction and opened the door. Moving down a corridor, the ladies soon found themselves in a modest-sized sitting room. It was filled with furniture in good repair that had come from a distant age. Against one wall was a pianoforte. It was not of the highest quality, but it was not far from it. It was certainly finer than the one at Longbourn.

"This is Mrs. Parks's rooms," Mary explained, "our *sanctum sanctorum*."

"'Holy of holies?'" Jane frowned. "Mary, that is not funny."

"Oh, Jane, please!" said Elizabeth. "This is a lovely instrument." She slid her fingers over the wood and was about to reach for the keys when her eye fell to the music on the stand. "My heavens!" With trembling hands, Elizabeth took hold of the sheets of paper before her. "I cannot believe it." She flipped through the sheets before turning to her sister. "Mary, this music! It is the most recent available. I did not know that half of these pieces were published!"

"Does it meet with your approval?" came a voice from behind them. The ladies turned to see Anne de Bourgh close the door to the room behind her.

"Miss de Bourgh, of course it does!" cried Elizabeth. "I dreamed of playing some of these pieces, but the prices are so dear."

"How did you come by such a treasure?" asked Jane.

The girl's smile was broad. "I have my sources, Miss Bennet. I am glad you like our surprise. Mary was sure you would be delighted."

"Who would not be?" mumbled Elizabeth as she turned her attention back to the pages. "I feel unworthy even to touch them."

The girl laughed. "That is unfortunate as they are a gift for both of you."

"Miss de Bourgh, you cannot…it is too much!" sputtered Jane.

"Why not?" Anne responded with a twinkle in her eye. "I have copies for Mary, and I am but a beginner. It will be some time before I can dream of attempting what you hold in your hands."

Elizabeth could only shake her head as Jane said, "You are too kind. How can we ever repay you?"

"There is a condition, Miss Bennet. While you are here, you may only play those pieces in this room. That way I might have my own private recitals and the joy of your company uninterrupted."

Elizabeth was pleased yet baffled. She could not reconcile her opinion of the lady to the ever-changing nature of Miss de Bourgh. *First, she greets us most charmingly; then she ignores us before her mother. Now she gives us a most wonderful and expensive gift!* She recalled Mr. Wickham's description of the lady. It was not quite accurate, yet she could not dismiss what he said out of hand. *Poor girl! Does she feel she has to buy her friends?*

"Come, Mary, I wish to hear you play," requested the heiress.

"Surely, our guests should go first."

"In all propriety, you are correct, but I long to hear how you have mastered *Für Elise*, and I can wait no longer. I think your sisters will forgive me if you indulge this whim."

Jane smiled. "It shall be as you wish, Miss de Bourgh. I too would love to hear how Mary has improved."

Reluctantly, Mrs. Collins took her seat and began to play. Her sisters were pleasantly surprised to hear that Mary had indeed developed her talent. She was definitely no master, but her fingering and tempo were less forced. Without the need to compete for attention as she did at Longbourn, Mary had begun to allow the music to take prominence, rather than the performer. She listened now to the music, and that made a great difference.

It was then Elizabeth's turn. She was not as technically proficient as her sister, but she played with true emotion and feeling. Mary's music was a joy to the ear; Elizabeth's struck at the heart.

Anne had no complaints on how she spent the next hour and thought of ways to thank her benefactor, a gentleman with the initials *FD*, for the music.

The ladies were returning to Hunsford Parsonage, and had just turned the corner around the house, when they came upon two gentlemen descending from a beautiful coach in the driveway. "My goodness," whispered Jane, "Lizzy, it is Mr. Darcy!"

The group came to a halt behind Elizabeth, who was frozen in place. She could not believe that hateful man was at Rosings!

Jane leaned over and asked, "Should we greet him? I do not know what would be proper."

Before Elizabeth could formulate an answer, she saw Mr. Darcy start as his eyes glanced in their direction. He seemed to stand stock-still. Then with a comment to his companion, he began moving towards the ladies.

Heaven give me strength!

Mr. Darcy was all that was cool and correct as he did his duty. "Mrs. Collins, Miss Bennet, Miss Elizabeth. It is a pleasure to see you here at Rosings. Mrs. Collins, allow me to wish you and Mr. Collins joy."

Mary nodded. "You are very kind, Mr. Darcy."

A soft cough at Darcy's elbow reminded him to say, "Please allow me to introduce my companion. This is my cousin, Colonel Fitzwilliam. Colonel, may I introduce Mrs. Collins and her sisters, Miss Bennet and Miss Elizabeth Bennet."

"A great pleasure, ladies!" Colonel Fitzwilliam poured on the charm. "I am happy indeed that such lovely additions have graced Hunsford this spring. How long are you to visit, Miss Bennet?"

Jane appeared slightly discomposed by the colonel's attention. "We are to visit my sister and brother until the end of May, sir."

"Six weeks! That is excellent! I am sure we shall be in company often in the time to come. Miss Elizabeth, how does Kent suit you?"

Elizabeth could not help but notice that Mr. Darcy had returned to his usual taciturn self. "As we are just arrived ourselves, it would be premature to make a judgment, Colonel, but so far, I can offer no complaints." *It may become far less agreeable now;* her eyes flashed.

The colonel grinned. "I shall see to it that your opinion does not suffer, Miss Elizabeth, and my cousin joins me. Do you not, Darcy?"

"I would be happy to be of service." Elizabeth thought the proud man might have been talking to a servant. "If you ladies will excuse us."

Darcy bowed again and took a step back to allow Richard to take his leave of the Bennet sisters. A moment later, the gentlemen left and the ladies continued to the parsonage.

"What the devil were you about, Darcy?" demanded Fitzwilliam as soon as the ladies were safely out of hearing.

Darcy walked to the front door of Rosings as he answered. "I have no idea what you mean."

The colonel followed behind him. "Oh, you are not getting yourself out of this! You only act this rudely when you are provoked! When did you meet those ladies?"

"Last autumn in Hertfordshire."

"Ah, Hertfordshire! I may change my mind about the place. Zounds, what a beauty Miss Bennet is! In fact, all of them are quite lovely. I am going to enjoy myself this year!"

Darcy turned on his cousin. "You will behave yourself, Fitz, so help me!"

"Peace, Cuz! You know me better than that! I am no Wickham!"

"Must you mention his name?"

Fitzwilliam gave him a fierce glare. "I would not have to mention him if you would have given me leave to do what I wished after Ramsgate!"

"Quiet, Richard! Do you want Aunt Catherine to find out?"

Abashed, the colonel lowered his voice. "So, which one do you fancy? The elegant blonde or the brunette with the flashing eyes?"

Darcy growled. "I am not going to discuss the Bennet ladies with you."

The colonel raised his hands in mock surrender. "Very well—for now. I will find out, you know."

Darcy was afraid of just that.

Colonel Fitzwilliam's manners were very much admired at the parsonage, and the ladies all felt that he added considerably to the pleasure of their engagements at Rosings. It was some days, however, before they received any invitation. It was not until Easter-day, almost a week after the gentlemen's arrival that they were honored by such an attention, and then they were merely asked on leaving church to come in the evening. For the last week they had seen very little of either Lady Catherine or her daughter. Colonel Fitzwilliam had called at the parsonage more than once during that time, but Mr. Darcy they had only seen at church.

The invitation was accepted, of course, and at a proper hour they joined the party in Lady Catherine's drawing room. Her ladyship received them civilly, but it was plain that their company was acceptable only because there was no one else available. The lady, in fact, was engrossed by her nephews, speaking to them, especially to Darcy, much more than to any other person in the room.

Colonel Fitzwilliam seemed genuinely glad to see the party, and Mrs. Collins's pretty sisters had caught his fancy very much. He seated himself by them and talked so agreeably of Kent and Hertfordshire, of traveling and staying at home, of new books and music, that Elizabeth had never been half so well entertained in that room before. They conversed with so much spirit and flow, as to draw the attention of Lady Catherine as well as Miss de Bourgh and Mr. Darcy.

Lady Catherine called out, "What is that you are saying, Fitzwilliam? What is it you are talking of? What are you telling the ladies? Let me hear what it is."

"We are speaking of music, madam," said he.

"Of music! Then pray speak aloud. It is of all subjects my delight. I must have my share in the conversation if you are speaking of music. There are few people in England, I suppose, who have more true enjoyment of music than myself, or a better natural taste. If I had ever learnt, I should have been a great proficient. And so would Anne, if her health had allowed her to apply. I am confident that she would have performed delightfully."

At this, Elizabeth glanced at Miss de Bourgh, who showed no reaction to her mother's comment.

The grand dame continued. "How does Georgiana get on, Darcy?" Mr. Darcy spoke with affectionate praise of his sister's proficiency. "I am very glad to hear such a good account of her," said Lady Catherine, "and pray tell her from me, that she cannot expect to excel if she does not practice a great deal."

"I assure you, madam," he replied coldly, "that she does not need such advice. She practices very constantly."

"So much the better. It cannot be done too much, and when I next write to her, I shall charge her not to neglect it on any account. I often tell young ladies that no excellence in music is to be acquired without constant practice. I have told Mrs. Collins's sister several times that she will never play well unless she practices more. And though Mrs. Collins has no instrument, they are very welcome, as I have often told them, to come to Rosings every day and play on the pianoforte in Mrs. Parks's room. They would be in nobody's way, you know, in that part of the house."

Mr. Darcy looked a little ashamed of his aunt's ill breeding and made no answer. Jane noted it, but Elizabeth saw nothing.

When coffee was over, Colonel Fitzwilliam reminded Elizabeth of her promise to play for him, and she sat down directly to the instrument. He drew a chair near her. Elizabeth glanced at the music before her and gasped. It was one of the pieces Miss de Bourgh had acquired for them!

She turned and looked at Miss de Bourgh, but the young lady wore an inscrutable expression. Elizabeth then returned her attention to the instrument and began to play, and she made her way through the piece to general approval. Colonel Fitzwilliam was quite boisterous in his praise, which displeased Lady Catherine. It was decided by all that she should play again, and Elizabeth chose another selection of the secret gifts. Lady Catherine listened to half the song, and then began to talk as before to her other nephew until Mr. Darcy walked away from her and, moving with his usual deliberation towards the pianoforte, stationed himself so as to command a full view of the fair performer's countenance. Jane joined them.

Elizabeth saw what Mr. Darcy was doing and, at the first convenient pause, turned to him with an arch smile and said, "You mean to frighten me, Mr. Darcy, by coming in all this state to hear me? But I will not be alarmed, though your sister does play so well. There is a stubbornness about me that never can bear to be frightened at the will of others. My courage always rises with every attempt to intimidate me."

"Lizzy!" hissed Jane.

"I shall not say that you are mistaken," Darcy replied, "because you could not really believe me to entertain any design of alarming you. I have had the pleasure of your acquaintance long enough to know that you find great enjoyment in occasionally professing opinions which, in fact, are not your own."

Elizabeth laughed heartily at this picture of herself and said to Colonel Fitzwilliam, "Your cousin will give you a very pretty notion of me and teach you not to believe a word I say. I am particularly unlucky in meeting with a person so well able to expose my real character in a part of the world where I had hoped to pass myself off with some degree of credit. Indeed, Mr. Darcy, it is very ungenerous in you to mention all that you knew to my disadvantage in Hertfordshire and, give me leave to say, very impolitic too, for it is provoking me to retaliate, and such things may come out as will shock your relations to hear."

"I am not afraid of you," said he smiling.

"Pray, let me hear what you have to accuse him of," cried Colonel Fitzwilliam. "I should like to know how he behaves among strangers."

"You shall hear then, but prepare yourself for something very dreadful. The first time of my ever seeing him in Hertfordshire was at a ball. And at this ball, what do you think he did? He danced only four dances! I am sorry to pain you, but so it was. He danced only four dances, though gentlemen were scarce, and to my certain knowledge, more than one young lady was sitting down in want of a partner. Mr. Darcy, you cannot deny the fact."

"I had not, at that time, the honor of knowing any lady in the assembly beyond my own party."

"True, and nobody can ever be introduced in a ball room," Elizabeth responded carelessly. "Well, Colonel Fitzwilliam, what do I play next? My fingers await your orders."

"Perhaps," continued Darcy, "I should have judged better had I sought an introduction, but I am ill qualified to recommend myself to strangers."

"Shall we ask your cousin the reason of this?" said Elizabeth, still addressing Colonel Fitzwilliam. "Shall we ask him why a man of sense and education, and who has lived in the world, is ill qualified to recommend himself to strangers?"

"I can answer your question," said Fitzwilliam, "without applying to him. It is because he will not give himself the trouble."

"I certainly have not the talent which some people possess," said Darcy, slightly offended, "of conversing easily with those I have never seen before. I cannot catch their tone of conversation or appear interested in their concerns, as I often see done."

"My fingers," said Elizabeth, "do not move over this instrument in the masterly manner which I see so many women's do. They have not the same force or rapidity and do not produce the same expression. But then, I have always supposed it to be my own fault—because I would not take the trouble of practicing. It is not that I do not believe my fingers as capable as any other woman's of superior execution."

Darcy smiled and said, "You are perfectly right. You have employed your time much better. No one admitted to the privilege of hearing you can think anything wanting. We neither of us perform to strangers."

Here they were interrupted by Lady Catherine, who called to learn of the conversation. Elizabeth immediately began playing again. Lady Catherine approached and, after listening for a few minutes, said to Darcy, "She is not the sister, unfortunately. Miss Elizabeth would not play at all amiss if she practiced more and could have the advantage of a London master. She has a very good notion of fingering, though her talent is not equal to Mrs. Collins or her taste equal to Anne's. Anne would have been a delightful performer had her health allowed her to learn."

Elizabeth looked at Darcy to see how cordially he assented to his cousin's praise, but neither at that moment nor at any other could she discern any symptom of love for her.

Meanwhile, Colonel Fitzwilliam moved over to stand next to Miss Bennet, and they entered into a conversation over embroidery.

Lady Catherine continued her remarks on Elizabeth's performance, mixing with them many instructions on execution and taste. Elizabeth received them with all the forbearance of civility and, at the request of the gentlemen, remained at the instrument and took turns performing with Mary till her ladyship's carriage was ready to take them all home.

"ENJOYING YOURSELVES, COUSINS?"

Richard was startled, as he was about to strike the cue ball. "Anne! I did not hear you enter. Forgive me."

Anne walked around the table. "An interesting game, billiards. I have often wondered if I should like to learn it."

Darcy darkened. "It is not an activity for ladies, Anne."

"At one time, neither was riding, Darcy," she responded.

"Ha! She has you there, Darcy!" Richard thought for a moment. "Why not learn, Anne?"

"What?" cried Darcy. "Fitz—"

"Oh, come, man! The girl needs some entertainment."

"Thank you, Richard," Anne said. She picked up a cue stick and tried to hold it as Richard did, but she was having difficulty.

"That is wrong, Anne."

Anne sighed. "Perhaps you can demonstrate the correct manner, Richard?" He did so and sent the cue ball obediently towards its target.

Anne bent over the table and attempted to duplicate her cousin's shot. She missed the cue ball entirely.

"Fiddlesticks!" she cried. "Richard, help me. I am holding the stick at the wrong angle, I think. I need assistance." Richard attempted to demonstrate again, but Anne would not have it. "Richard, I have tried to copy you, but it does not serve. Show me."

"Very well." Richard put down his own stick and walked behind his cousin. "Anne—forgive me." He reached around her and set her hands in the proper manner.

"I see," she said. "But I need help in aiming."

Together they took a position behind the cue ball. With Richard's help, Anne successfully struck another ball with the cue ball.

"There!" he said as he released her. "You…er…you can do it." His face was very red.

"I may need more assistance," she said as she eyed the table. "The cue ball is quite a distance away."

"Umm, yes, but I just remembered I owe a letter to my mother. Please excuse me." With that, the colonel quickly quit the room.

Anne scowled, reached over, and executed a perfect bank shot to send a ball into a side pocket.

Darcy looked on with a raised eyebrow. "You are playing quite the game, Anne."

"Oh, do not lecture me, Darcy! What else can I do? Richard is as blind as a bat, and—"

"And the Bennet ladies are lovely."

Anne looked at Darcy with pain filling her eyes.

"Do not fear, Anne. Richard is a second son, and the Bennets are poor."

She hung her head. "It was un-Christian of me, I know, but I was jealous. And Mrs. Collins has been such a friend to me. She is the best friend I have besides you and Richard."

"I noticed the choice of music today. I wondered why you had me acquire it. Now I realize it was to share this gift with Mrs. Collins's sisters."

"Yes. They have been kind to me as well."

Darcy did not seem surprised.

Anne was still displeased. "If one of the Bennet girls does not capture Richard's affections, some other lady will certainly do so, one with fortune. What can I do?"

"He has resisted marriage this long, Anne. It must have been for a reason." He paused. "I would be willing to speak to him—"

"No! I want Richard's love, not his pity."

ELIZABETH SAT BY HERSELF THE next morning and wrote to her sisters while Mrs. Collins and Jane were gone on business into the village. She was startled by a knock at the door, signaling the arrival of a visitor. As she had heard no carriage, she thought it not unlikely to be Miss de Bourgh, and under that impression, she was putting away her half-finished letter when the door opened, and to her very great surprise, Mr. Darcy, and Mr. Darcy only, entered the room.

He seemed astonished on finding her alone, apologized for his intrusion, and informed her that he had understood all the ladies to be within. They then sat down, and after her enquiries about the health of those at Rosings had been made, the pair seemed in danger of sinking into total silence.

It was absolutely necessary, therefore, to think of something, and recollecting when she had seen him last in Hertfordshire and feeling curious to know what he would say on the subject of their hasty departure, Elizabeth observed, "How very suddenly you all quit Netherfield last November, Mr. Darcy. It must have been a most agreeable surprise to Mr. Bingley to see you all after him so soon, for, if I recollect correctly, he went but the day before. He and his sisters were well, I hope, when you left London."

"Perfectly so, I thank you."

Elizabeth found that she was to receive no other answer, and after a short pause, added, "I think I have understood that Mr. Bingley has not much idea of ever returning to Netherfield again."

"I have never heard him say so, but it is probable that he may spend very little of his time there in future. He has many friends, and he is at a time of life when friends and engagements are continually increasing."

"If he means to be but little at Netherfield, it would be better for the neighborhood that he should give up the place entirely, for then we might possibly get a settled family there. But, perhaps, Mr. Bingley did not take the house so much for the convenience of the neighborhood as for his own, and we must expect him to keep or quit it on the same principle."

"I should not be surprised," said Darcy, "if he were to give it up as soon as any eligible purchase offers."

Elizabeth made no answer. She was afraid of talking longer of his friend, and having nothing else to say, was determined to leave the trouble of finding a subject to him.

Mr. Darcy took the hint. "This seems a very comfortable house. Lady Catherine, I believe, did a great deal to it when Mr. Collins first came to Hunsford."

"I believe she did, and I am sure she could not have bestowed her kindness on a more grateful object."

"Mr. Collins appears very fortunate in his choice of a wife."

"Yes, indeed. His friends may well rejoice in his having met with one of the very few sensible women who would have accepted him, or would have made him happy if they had. My sister has an excellent understanding, though I am not certain that I consider her marriage to Mr. Collins as the wisest thing she ever did. She seems perfectly happy, however, and in a prudential light, it is certainly a very good match for her." A flash of remembrance of an overheard conversation and the echo of the words "*my Mary-kins*" turned Elizabeth's face beet-red.

Mr. Darcy appeared unconscious of it. "It must be very agreeable to her to be settled within so easy a distance of her own family and friends."

"An easy distance, do you call it?" Elizabeth shook her head at his nonsense. "It is nearly fifty miles!"

"And what is fifty miles of good road? Little more than a half-day's journey. Yes, I call it a very easy distance."

"I should never have considered the distance as one of the advantages of the match," cried Elizabeth. "I should never have said Mrs. Collins was settled near her family."

"It is a proof of your own attachment to Hertfordshire. Anything beyond the very neighborhood of Longbourn, I suppose, would appear far."

As he spoke, there was a sort of smile that Elizabeth fancied she understood. He must be supposing her to be thinking of Jane and Netherfield.

"I do not mean to say that a woman may *not* be settled too near her family. The far and the near must be relative and depend on many varying circumstances. Where there is fortune to make the expense of traveling unimportant, distance becomes no evil. But that is not the case here. Mr. and Mrs. Collins have a comfortable income, but not one as will allow frequent journeys, and I am persuaded my sister would not call herself near her family under less than half the present distance."

Mr. Darcy drew his chair a little towards her. "You cannot have a right to such very strong local attachment. You cannot have been always at Longbourn."

Elizabeth looked surprised. The gentleman must have experienced some change of feeling, for he drew back his chair, took a newspaper from the table and, glancing over it, said in a colder voice, "Are you pleased with Kent?"

A short dialogue on the subject of the country ensued, on either side calm and concise, and soon put an end to by the entrance of her sisters, just returned from their walk.

The *tête-à-tête* appeared to surprise them. Mr. Darcy related the mistake that had occasioned his intrusion on Miss Bennet, and after sitting a few minutes longer without saying much to anybody, he went away.

"What can be the meaning of this?" said Mary, as soon as he was gone. "Lizzy, Mr. Darcy must be fond of you, or he would never have called on us in this familiar way."

"Indeed, there must be some partiality towards you," agreed Jane.

Elizabeth then told them of his silence, and they agreed it did not seem very likely that he had any real attachment to her, contrary to Jane's wishes. After various conjectures, it was decided that his visit proceeded from the difficulty of finding anything to do, which was the more probable.

ALL FIELD SPORTS WERE OVER at that time of year, so within doors there was only Lady Catherine, books, and a billiard table for amusement. The nearness of the parsonage, the pleasantness of the walk to it, and the people who lived in it, tempted the two cousins to walk there almost every day. They called at various times of the morning—sometimes separately, sometimes together—and now and then were accompanied by Miss de Bourgh.

It was plain to all the ladies that Colonel Fitzwilliam came because he had pleasure in their society, a persuasion that, of course, recommended him still more. Elizabeth was reminded by her own satisfaction in being with him, as well as by his evident admiration for her and her sister, of her former favorite, George Wickham. Though in comparing the two men, Elizabeth saw a less captivating softness in Colonel Fitzwilliam's manners, but she believed he might have the best informed mind.

Why Mr. Darcy came so often to the parsonage was more difficult to understand. It could not be for society, as he frequently sat many minutes without opening his lips. And when he did speak, it seemed out of necessity, rather than by choice—a sacrifice to propriety, not a pleasure to himself. He seldom appeared to take lively interest in the conversation.

Mrs. Collins knew not what to make of him. She would have liked to believe Mr. Darcy's quiet demeanor the result of nervousness in the face of overwhelming love, and the object of that love her sister Elizabeth, but unsure, she set herself seriously to the task of finding the true nature of the man.

She watched Mr. Darcy whenever they were at Rosings and whenever he came to Hunsford but without much success. He certainly looked at Elizabeth a great deal, but the interpretation of that look was disputable. It was an earnest, steadfast gaze, but she often doubted whether there was much admiration in it.

She had once or twice suggested to Elizabeth the possibility of his being partial to her, but Elizabeth always laughed at the idea. Mrs. Collins did not think it right to press the subject, as there was a danger of raising expectations that might only end in disappointment. In her opinion, it did not admit a doubt that Elizabeth's dislike of the man would vanish if she could suppose Mr. Darcy to be in her power.

Chapter 5

A Walk in the Woods

As the weeks passed, the Bennet women were often in the company of the gentlemen from Derbyshire. Elizabeth grew perturbed that she could not walk the groves of Rosings Park without encountering either Mr. Darcy or Colonel Fitzwilliam—usually both. Jane was more sanguine; she had no objection to conversing with two well-informed men. At least she *thought* Mr. Darcy well-informed. He was at most times silent and reserved, almost to a painful extent.

Mary observed these actions with a close eye. She was concerned over Colonel Fitzwilliam and his attentions to her sisters, particularly Jane. She was aware of Miss de Bough's partiality to that gentleman, and as much as she wished that Jane would find her joy, Mary's heart hurt for the ailing heiress.

Mr. Darcy was the chief mystery. Had Elizabeth not made her decided dislike of the gentleman clear to her, Mary might have thought that her sister could become mistress of Pemberley. Anne had shared much with her friend from the parsonage, and Mary knew that, no matter what Lady Catherine proclaimed, her daughter had no intention of marrying her cousin—at least, not *that* cousin.

But Mr. Darcy's unusual behavior puzzled Mary. His actions were those of a besotted man, but his words—or rather, lack of them—put the lie to that supposition. To discuss him with her sisters was useless; Jane saw only the good in everyone, and Elizabeth dismissed the gentleman out of hand. There was only one person she could talk to about this, and it was not her husband.

ANNE DE BOURGH FROWNED AS Jane sighed over her needlework. "You certainly sound melancholy, Miss Bennet," she observed with concern. "Are you well?"

Jane started at the comment. "Oh, no, I am perfectly happy, Miss de Bourgh. Who could not be with your uncommon kindness?"

The heiress accepted Jane's explanation with a slight narrowing of her eyes and held her tongue.

Elizabeth spoke up. "It is such a lovely day. Shall we go for a walk, Jane?"

Jane looked at her sister. "It shall be as you wish. Please excuse us, Miss de Bourgh, Mary."

As the door closed behind the pair, leaving Anne and Mary alone in Mrs. Parks's room, Anne spoke to her friend. "What is troubling Jane?"

Mary considered what to say. Her intelligence was betwixt the Bennet sisters, but Anne had grown so much in her heart that she saw her as another sister. "Jane is unhappy for the oldest reason in the world."

"Impossible! Jane Bennet disappointed in love? What cad could break such a lovely and tender heart?"

Mary bit her lip. "I should not say, but I know you will keep my confidence. Last autumn a most eligible and agreeable gentleman took possession of a manor near Longbourn. Mr. Bingley impressed us all with his open manners, and his attentions to Jane seemed very marked to many in the neighborhood. It was a common expectation that Jane would be mistress of Netherfield Park before Easter. Yet within a week of a most wonderful ball held by Mr. Bingley, his whole party departed to London with hardly a word."

"Bingley? Are you speaking of Mr. Charles Bingley?"

"Yes. He is a great friend of your cousin. We made his acquaintance while Mr. Darcy was Mr. Bingley's guest."

"I have heard of the gentleman, although I have not met him. Darcy has spoken of him, and Richard, too." Anne frowned. "This is strange. From what I have been told, Mr. Bingley would be the last man I would expect to trifle with and disappoint a young lady, especially one such as Miss Bennet."

"That was our belief, but the letters Jane has received from Mr. Bingley's sisters have not given any hope of a future meeting."

"Hmmm…Richard has told me of Mr. Bingley's sisters: grasping social climbers, the both of them. I would not put much book into any sincerity from *that* corner." Anne took Mary's hands in hers. "Oh, Mary, I am so sorry. Does Jane suffer much?"

"It is hard to tell, as it is against Jane's character to wear her feelings openly. But it is my opinion that she feels his loss deeply."

Anne's emotions battled: Her joy that Jane's heart was quite attached away from Richard was tempered by her true concern for the sister of her dearest friend. Ultimately, she felt disgusted with herself, and she decided to change the subject.

"It is my hope that all will be well and that Jane will be reunited with her young man." *And leave Richard for me!* "Shall we practice, Mary?"

"Of course." Mary began playing. "Mr. Bingley is fortunate in his friendship with Mr. Darcy."

"Yes," answered Anne. "Bingley is his particular friend."

"That is well. Everyone should have such a close friend." The smile she gave the heiress gave no doubt of *her* closest friend. "But their difference in temperament—it is astonishing."

"Indeed?"

"Yes. While in Hertfordshire, Mr. Bingley charmed us all with his open countenance and happy, polite manner. While Mr. Darcy—well, he did not make the same impression."

Anne frowned. "Darcy is uncomfortable among those he does not know."

Mary shook her head sadly. "That is unfortunate. Mr. Bingley is an open book; all can see what a fine gentleman he is. But Mr. Darcy's demeanor serves him ill. He appears cold and aloof. No one knows what he is thinking."

"Mary, pray do not play innocent with me." Mary saw that Anne was giving her a most penetrating look. "Leave that for your husband. Do you have a question about my cousin?"

Mary gulped. "Forgive me. I…I did not know how to ask."

"If we are truly friends, then come right out and ask." Anne smiled kindly.

Mary paused. "Does Mr. Darcy admire my sister Elizabeth?"

A JUNIOR GROUNDSKEEPER ENTERED THE kitchen of Rosings for a bite to eat. The cook was a bit sweet on him and served the man some of the roast beef intended for her ladyship's dinner table.

"Thankee, Maggie. This is fine, indeed."

"Oh, go on with you!" she teased. "What have you been up to today, Mickey?"

He looked around. Seeing Mrs. Parks nowhere in sight, he answered, "I think the two young men who are visitin' have gone mad."

"Really?" she breathed. Gossip was her favorite sport.

"Aye. Did I not see them with me own eyes strikin' a wee rock, or ball, or somethin' with a strange bent stick?"

"You don't say!"

"And that's not all. They gave them sticks names—Driver, Cleek, Mashie, Niblick. They're walkin' all over the east pasture, pretty as you please, hittin' and chasin' those little…featheries, as they called 'em."

"Names for sticks? Featheries? Ooh, but that don't sound good. Why on earth would they be doing something like that?"

Mickey lowered his voice. "You can never tell about the upper classes, lass. It's my firm belief that half of 'em is touched in the head."

The cook giggled. Working at Rosings Park had certainly taught her *that*.

"HERE YOU ARE, GENTLEMEN," SAID the footman as he handed Darcy and Richard their featheries. At four shillings apiece, the handmade golf balls cost almost as much as a golf club, so they were certainly not left behind.

"Thank you, my man," responded Richard.

"Shall I take your clubs in now, sirs?" the footman asked.

"Yes, we are finished for today," said Darcy.

"Very good, sir." The footman picked up the golf bags and followed the two gentlemen in.

"Have you played St. Andrews yet, Richard?"

"No. I do have an army career, you know. But Father and the viscount are wild about it."

"They say it is the birthplace of golf. I cannot say whether that is true, but it is a magnificent place."

"Even the seventeenth hole?"

"Well, perhaps not *that* hole."

THE MEN CONTINUED TO WALK to the manor when they intercepted the two Miss Bennets, returned from a walk in the woods. Richard was his usual charming self while Darcy could hardly think of anything to say other than to blurt out his admiration for Elizabeth Bennet. As that certainly would not do, he resumed a guarded expression and remained silent.

ANNE OBSERVED THEIR MEETING FROM a window in her private apartments. Mary had left for the parsonage some time before, and Anne had time to consider Mary's question. She had noticed no marked attentions paid to Miss Elizabeth by Darcy, she had assured her friend. But now, as she thought more upon it, she had noticed that Darcy always seemed aware of Miss Elizabeth and took pains to converse with her.

She was relieved at the apparent friendly indifference by which Jane greeted the gentlemen, but Elizabeth was not as welcoming. She enjoyed Richard's company, that was obvious, but she seemed to spend much of the time regarding Darcy, whether from approbation or aggravation, Anne could not say.

She also watched Darcy. Knowing him as well as she knew herself, Anne felt a thrill course through her. Perhaps Mary was right. If so, her salvation was in the offing!

She would have to speak privately to Richard as soon as could be.

Colonel Fitzwilliam could not believe his ears. "You are serious, Anne?"

"Yes, Richard," said his cousin, "Darcy is in love."

"With one of the Miss Bennets?"

"With Miss *Elizabeth* Bennet, to be exact."

Colonel Fitzwilliam paced about the room. This information promised to be a foundation for diversion, something he always looked for during his visits to Rosings. "And how do you know this? What is the source of your information?"

She laughed. "Just behold the man himself, Richard! He is more serious than ever. You know how he is when he is affected. It is as if a fireplace poker has been inserted up his—"

"Anne!"

"Bah! You have said the same about him many a time."

"Yes, but I am a crude soldier. You must not repeat the campfire terms I use. You are a lady, highborn and beautiful."

"Stop it, Richard. Do not tease me."

"I do not tease you, Annie. One day you will bewitch some young gentleman who will take you away from all this—"

"Humph."

"—and you will make his life miserable." He ducked the thrown pillow.

"Richard, I am full earnest! What shall we do?"

"We?"

"Yes. You know Darcy will never approach the lady on his own. We must help him along."

Fitzwilliam looked thoughtfully at his cousin. "Does the lady feel the same?"

"Well, she certainly is not *indifferent* to our cousin, but she may harbor some misgivings about him."

"Misgivings? About Darcy's integrity?" The colonel snorted. "The man lives like a monk. He should be declared a saint!"

Anne giggled. "He is not as bad as all that. But if Miss Elizabeth was apprised of his true character, she might see him in a more favorable light. All Darcy needs is a bit of encouragement."

Fitzwilliam seemed to consider that. "It is important to you to see Darcy happy?"

"You know only Darcy's marriage to someone else will end Mother's schemes."

The colonel began pacing about again, his eyes everywhere except on Anne. "I still do not see why you two are so stubborn about the whole thing. Why not marry? You like each other. Many have married with less regard."

He did not know how his words pained his favorite cousin. "Darcy and I…we would not suit each other. We both know this. We agreed long ago. Our characters are too similar. We would not be happy, believe me, Richard." *Only one man could make me happy, and he is blind!* "But Mother—we have tried to tell her, but it is useless."

"I can image." He thought for a moment. "So, Darcy marrying Miss Elizabeth would make you happy?"

"It would make *Darcy* happy, and that pleases me."

Fitzwilliam smiled. "Very well, my girl. Leave it to me. I know some things that should help change the lady's mind. I will take the first opportunity to fill her head with Darcy's goodness, though I may need a stiff drink afterwards."

"Brandy or sherry?" She opened a cabinet near her desk.

The colonel was astonished. "Annie, you naughty girl! How long have you had your own personal stock?"

Anne giggled again. "Mrs. Jenkinson likes a nip in the evenings now and again. I personally prefer the port."

"Ah! A girl after my own heart!"

Anne looked at her cousin from under her lashes as she handed him his glass. *Yes, I am indeed after your heart, Colonel Fitzwilliam.*

A WEEK LATER, ELIZABETH FOUND herself alone in the cottage, for Jane was accompanying Mary on her rounds in the village. She asked to be excused, claiming to be behind in her correspondence.

Elizabeth tried to write a letter to Kitty, but her mind was unsettled. A bit of fresh air was what she needed, she thought. So donning her bonnet, she walked out into the fine Kent spring day.

Almost immediately, Elizabeth espied her cousin working diligently in his garden. The day was not warm, but a sheen of perspiration sat upon his brow as the tall man bent to his weeding. It was not Elizabeth's intention to spend her time in conversation with Mr. Collins, and she tried to walk away as quietly as she could, but the evil gravel underfoot gave her away.

"Elizabeth! Good day to you, my dear sister!" Mr. Collins cried.

Trapped, Elizabeth returned the greeting and walked towards him. "Your garden is looking very fine, sir." It was no idle compliment. The garden was an explosion of flowers and greenery, and the roses were as lovely as any Elizabeth had ever seen. She must own that her cousin was the excellent and diligent gardener.

The vain clergyman's pride was agreeably gratified. "It is most kind of you to say so, Eliza. Before you are the results of many hours of honest labor. Of course, my little bit of greenery is nothing compared to the incredible delights of Rosings Park—at least, that should be the case, but the master gardener has taken ill, I understand."

Elizabeth had to acknowledge that the gardens of Rosings were not what they should be.

Collins frowned. "Indeed! It is my belief that the under-gardener does not know his business. Oh, it is not to say that the vegetable gardens are anything but delightful. Such bounty! If only I could grow such melons! And the peas! Have you ever had anything as wonderful as a Rosings' pea?"

Elizabeth had to say she had not.

"*That* is what a pea should taste like! But being the expert vegetable gardener does not guarantee success in the flower garden."

"You certainly have a way with flowers, sir. Your roses are exquisite."

Elizabeth's honest observation was poorly repaid as Mr. Collins launched into a full discussion of methods and techniques. A full quarter-hour was spent on the proper usage of manure. Elizabeth bore it with tolerable humor, and soon the subject was exhausted.

"My sister is fortunate that she is the recipient of your diligence and expertise, sir."

"Indeed, Mrs. Collins is very happy with her lot in life. I know not,

Miss Elizabeth, whether she has yet expressed her sense of gratitude for your kindness in coming to us, but I am very certain you will not leave the house without receiving her thanks for it. The favor of your company and that of your sister has been much felt, I assure you. We know how little there is to tempt anyone to our humble abode. Our plain manner of living, our small rooms, and the little we see of the world must make Hunsford extremely dull to young ladies like yourselves. I hope both of you will believe us grateful, for we have done everything in our power to prevent your spending the time here unpleasantly."

Elizabeth was eager with her thanks and assurances of her happiness. She had spent four weeks with great enjoyment being with Mary, and the kind attentions she received gave her pleasure.

Mr. Collins was gratified, and with a more smiling solemnity replied, "Our situation with regard to Lady Catherine's family is indeed one of extraordinary advantage and blessing of which few can boast. You see on what a footing we are. You see how continually we are engaged there. In truth, I must acknowledge that, with all the disadvantages of this humble parsonage, I should not think anyone abiding in it an object of compassion while they are sharers of our intimacy at Rosings."

Words were insufficient for the elevation of his feelings, and he was obliged to walk about the garden while Elizabeth tried to unite civility and truth in a few short sentences.

"You may, in fact, carry a very favorable report of us into Hertfordshire, my dear sister. You have been a daily witness of Lady Catherine's great attentions to Mrs. Collins—and Miss de Bough's, too. Let me assure you, my dear Miss Elizabeth, that I can from my heart most cordially wish you equal felicity in marriage. My dear Mary and I have but one mind and one way of thinking. There is in everything a most remarkable resemblance of character and ideas between us." He paused and, in the same voice she had overheard in a more intimate setting, said, "We seem to have been designed for each other."

This was a thought that could not give any reassurance to Elizabeth.

I believe I shall be ill now.

"It gives me the greatest pleasure to hear that you and dear Jane have passed your time not disagreeably. We have certainly done our best to introduce you to very superior society, and I think we may flatter ourselves that your Hunsford visit cannot have been entirely irksome."

"It has been all delightful," she managed to utter.

"Perhaps," he thought aloud—a mighty undertaking, "perhaps Lady Catherine might be persuaded to introduce you to some worthy young men—of your own station, naturally."

"Naturally."

"A barrister or a—" he considered for a moment and said, "an officer. Colonel Fitzwilliam knows many good men of the lower gentry, I have no doubt." Elizabeth was appalled. "Now, now, Sister. We must be frank. It would not do to look too high. We must not disrupt the social order!"

"I…I have no intention to committing such a crime, Mr. Collins," Elizabeth finally managed to say. "I thank you for the consideration, but for my part, I do not like your way of getting husbands."

"Excuse me?"

"What I meant to say was that such arrangements are best left to one's own family. I do not wish to inconvenience either Lady Catherine or Colonel Fitzwilliam."

The clergyman was mollified. "Hmm, you are right, but it is a pity. You are not getting any younger, you know."

"What is this? I am not one and twenty!" Elizabeth exclaimed.

Mr. Collins shook his head. "A ripe age. But every flower that blooms eventfully wilts, my dear sister. Do not wait too long."

It would be several days before Fitzwilliam could put his plan to work. It seemed he could not escape the fellowship of his cousin. Darcy insisted on accompanying the colonel every time he even thought about visiting the parsonage. As much as he valued his friend and cousin, for once in his life, he would have been happy if Darcy had broken his leg—or at least sprained it.

Thus, ten days passed before an opportunity to meet with the ladies presented itself. Darcy was to ride the plantation with the steward, and Colonel Fitzwilliam waited patiently for him to leave, begging off the inescapable joy of riding through croplands and discussing drainage, before hurrying to the parsonage. There he found that the ladies had already left to walk the woods of Rosings. Undeterred, he left as soon as good manners would allow and went in search of the Miss Bennets. It took time to come upon them. Who knew what great walkers those girls were?

"Why, look, there is the colonel, Jane!"

The officer waved, and soon his long legs caught them up.

Jane smiled and said, "I did not know that you ever walked this way."

"I have been making the tour of the park," he replied, "as I generally do every year, and intended to close it with a call at the parsonage. Are you going much farther?"

"No, we should have turned in a moment. Shall we, Lizzy?"

"It shall be as you wish."

Jane gave Elizabeth a look of consternation, and Elizabeth failed to keep a small smile off her lips.

Accordingly, they walked towards the parsonage together. Richard was pleased that he had found the Bennet sisters alone, but he was at a loss to know how to begin his mission of extolling the virtues of Fitzwilliam Darcy. While he was engaged in devising a strategy, the ladies took it upon themselves to carry on the discourse.

"Do you certainly leave Kent on Saturday?" asked Jane.

"Yes, if Darcy does not postpone it again. But I am at his disposal. He arranges the business just as he pleases."

"And if not able to please himself in the arrangement, he has at least great pleasure in the power of choice," replied Elizabeth. "I do not know anybody who seems to enjoy the power of doing what he likes more than Mr. Darcy."

"He likes to have his own way very well," replied Colonel Fitzwilliam carefully. "But so we all do. It is only that he has better means of having it than many others because he is rich. I speak feelingly. A younger son, you know, must be inured to self-denial and dependence."

Elizabeth laughed. "The younger son of an earl? What have you ever known of self-denial and dependence? When have you been prevented by want of money from going wherever you chose or procuring anything you fancied?"

"Younger sons cannot marry where they like." *And Darcy can. Do you not see?*

"Unless where they like women of fortune, which I think they very often do."

"There are not many in my rank of life who can afford to marry without some attention to money."

Elizabeth said in a lively tone, "And pray, what is the usual price of an earl's younger son? Unless the elder brother is very sickly, I suppose you would not ask above fifty thousand pounds."

Jane colored at the idea, and Elizabeth changed the subject. "I imagine your cousin brought you down with him chiefly for the sake of having somebody at his disposal," Elizabeth said next. "I wonder he does not marry to secure a lasting convenience of that kind. But perhaps his sister does as well for the present, and as she is under his sole care, he may do what he likes with her."

"No, that is an advantage which he must divide with me. I am joined with him in the guardianship of Miss Darcy."

"Are you, indeed? And pray what sort of guardians do you make? Does your charge give you much trouble? Young ladies of her age are sometimes a little difficult to manage, and if she has the true Darcy spirit, she may like to have her own way as well."

As she spoke, Richard looked at her earnestly and immediately asked her why she supposed Miss Darcy likely to give them any uneasiness.

Jane saw that the colonel was uncomfortable and said, "You need not be frightened. My sister and I have never heard any ill of her, and I dare say she is one of the most tractable creatures in the world."

"Yes," agreed Elizabeth. "She is a very great favorite with the Bingley family."

"I know them a little. Their brother is a pleasant gentleman, and a great friend of Darcy's."

"Oh, yes," said Elizabeth dryly, "Mr. Darcy is uncommonly kind to Mr. Bingley and takes prodigious care of him."

Fitzwilliam smiled, glad that she had raised the subject. Finally, there was a time to enlighten the ladies as to Darcy's merit! "Yes, I truly believe Darcy does take care of him in those points where he most wants care. From something that he told me during our journey here, I have reason to think Bingley very much indebted to him."

"What is it you mean?" asked Jane.

"What he told me was merely this: He congratulated himself on having lately saved a friend from the inconveniences of a most imprudent marriage."

Elizabeth darkened. "Did Mr. Darcy give you his reasons for this interference?"

"I understood that there were some very strong objections against the lady." Jane looked stunned. "Miss Bennet! Are you unwell?"

"No, I am—it is only a headache. I am well, I assure you."

"And what arts did he use to separate them?" snapped Elizabeth.

"You are rather disposed to call Darcy's interference officious?" replied Richard, keeping one eye on a very pale Jane.

Elizabeth answered bitterly. "I do not see what right Mr. Darcy had to decide on the propriety of his friend's inclination, or why, upon his judgment alone, he should determine in what manner his friend was to be happy. But," she continued, quieting and turning to Jane, "as we know none of the particulars, it is not fair to condemn him. It is not to be supposed that there was much affection in the case."

"That is not an unnatural surmise," said Fitzwilliam in jest, "but it is lessening the honor of my cousin's triumph very sadly. If there is a man on earth who can spot a fortune hunter at a hundred paces, it is Darcy. Oh, the stories I could tell you of those London ladies and their matchmaking mamás!"

"Please," asked Jane, "can we talk of something else?"

Elizabeth looked at her sister. "Of course, Jane. Surely you wish to return to the parsonage to rest."

"Yes, please."

Jane remained silent while Elizabeth and Richard talked on

indifferent matters until the party reached the parsonage.

"There, I return you safe to your relations," said the colonel. "I hope that you will feel better later, Miss Bennet. You must not miss tea at Rosings, you know!"

The colonel's weak jest fell on indifferent ears, and to the ladies relief, he soon went away.

Once the door was closed, Jane's tears finally burst forth. Elizabeth tried to offer words of sympathy, but Jane would not listen and fled to their bedroom. Elizabeth gave her the privacy she desired and went into the sitting room. There she could think without interruption of all she had heard.

That Mr. Darcy had been concerned in the measures taken to separate Mr. Bingley and Jane, Elizabeth had never doubted, but she had always attributed to Miss Bingley the principal design and arrangement of them. Now it seemed that Mr. Darcy was the cause—his pride and caprice were the cause—of all that Jane had suffered and still continued to suffer. He had ruined every hope of happiness for the most affectionate, generous heart in the world, and no one could say how lasting an evil he might have inflicted.

"I understood that there were some very strong objections against the lady," were Colonel Fitzwilliam's words.

Oh, yes, objections indeed! thought Elizabeth. *Objections to her having one uncle a country attorney and another in trade in London, I am sure! For no one could say anything untoward about Jane! All loveliness and goodness as she is! She does not give two straws about Mr. Bingley's money, no matter what Colonel Fitzwilliam says!*

Neither could anything be urged against my father who, though with some peculiarities, has abilities which Mr. Darcy need not disdain and respectability which he will probably never reach.

When Elizabeth thought of her mother, her confidence gave way a little. A matchmaker she was, but there was not a wicked bone in her body. Of course, Mrs. Bennet wanted her daughters well married! It was their only protection in this world. Anyone could see that—even Mr. Darcy.

Elizabeth was quite decided at last that Mr. Darcy had been partly governed by the worst kind of pride and partly by the wish of retaining Mr. Bingley for his sister.

And for Colonel Fitzwilliam to report it so cavalierly, clearly he was sent to deliver a message, a message Mr. Darcy was too cowardly to deliver himself! How could there be such a man?

Chapter 6

A Proposal at Hunsford

Darcy moved quietly through the house, careful not to alert his aunt to his purpose. He succeeded in his aim, and he was soon ensconced within Mrs. Parks's rooms, listening to his cousin play the pianoforte—that is, if one could count performing scales as playing.

As Darcy moved over to a chair, his movements caught Anne's eye. "Zounds! I am discovered!"

Darcy shook his head as he sat. "*Zounds* indeed! It is confirmed: you have been spending too much time in Richard's company."

She sighed. "I suppose Richard told you about my little secret."

"He did. I am proud of you."

"Thank you, Fitzwilliam. Where is Richard, by the way?"

"Outside. I believe he was walking about the gardens with the Miss Bennets earlier."

"And you did not join him?"

"I could not, Anne. I was with the steward for hours. We have, in fact, just completed our ride. The ladies will return for tea with the Collinses, I understand."

Anne brightened. "Mrs. Collins is very fortunate in her sisters. Do you not think so?"

Darcy became uncomfortable with this conversation. As he did so often when uneasy, he rose and walked to the window.

"The Miss Bennets are in every way very lovely and agreeable ladies," he replied as he scanned the grounds of Rosings. "It is well that they have secured your friendship. Their connections are such that they have few opportunities to meet with superior people."

"Fie on you, Fitzwilliam Darcy! You sound as proud as my mother!"

Darcy turned open-mouthed to his cousin. "That was uncalled for, Anne! I do not sound—I mean, your mother—Oh, drat!"

Anne smirked. "You cannot say anything against her, can you? Even outside of her hearing?"

Darcy returned to his perusal of the grounds. "We both know how your mother is. There is no reason to disparage her. It is unseemly."

"Bah! She does not deserve you or your deference." The gentleman said nothing. "But I know of one deserving lady, my dear cousin."

Darcy turned his head slightly. "Of whom are you speaking?"

Anne returned to her scales. "Jane Bennet is all sweetness and light. Never have I met with a more agreeable person. Her face and features—exquisite! And her conversation is what it ought to be—not too much or too little, and never an unkind word." She paused as she finished the scale. "And such a lady as your wife would bore you to death!"

Darcy's face was one of puzzlement during the majority of this declaration. At the denouncement, he flushed and turned away to hide the laugh he strained to contain.

"She would be one whose heart would be difficult to secure, but she is a very admirable lady."

"To be sure, but her feelings are committed elsewhere."

The uneasy feeling that had been hovering about Darcy for the last fortnight returned. "Indeed? It is a fortunate man that wins Miss Bennet."

"If the man is worthy of her. She is disappointed in love, Fitzwilliam."

Darcy started. "What! Do you know this for certain?"

"I cannot say more, but trust me. I know of what I speak."

Darcy reached for a chair and settled himself. *Good Lord! Is she speaking of Bingley? But there was nothing! No strong attachment. I observed her most closely!*

Anne looked at her cousin with alarm. "Fitzwilliam, are you well?"

He looked back at her, hiding his confusion. "Never better. I hope Miss Bennet finds solace soon."

She returned to the pianoforte. "And Miss Elizabeth Bennet? Do you have the same wish for her?"

"Of...of course."

Anne gave him a satisfied smiled. "Now *there* is a rare treasure—brightness of mind and wit, and a pleasant face." Darcy nodded unconsciously. "Not every man would appreciate her. They would be jealous or intimidated. But to a man worthy of her and her mind—such a man would be very happy, I should think."

Darcy shuddered as he thought of anyone else securing Elizabeth Bennet's affections.

Anne stopped and turned to face Darcy. "Are you blind, Fitzwilliam? It is my opinion that Miss Elizabeth is not indifferent to you. No, not at all."

"What do you mean you shall not go to tea?"

Elizabeth asked Mr. Collins to lower his voice. "Jane is ill, and I must attend her. Please give Lady Catherine our regrets."

"Ill? Jane is ill?" cried Mary. "What is the matter?"

"A headache, but a painful one."

"I cannot leave! Husband, we shall all stay!"

Mr. Collins's heart beat wildly. "No! That will not be necessary! Eliza said herself that Jane has only the headache. Our servant can stay with her. It is not necessary for us to disappoint Lady Catherine de Bourgh so completely over so trifling a malady!"

Mary's eyes narrowed. "A servant watch over *my* sister? Mr. Collins, of what can you be thinking?"

I am thinking I shall spend very little time in your rooms in the near future, thought the clergyman morosely.

Elizabeth interjected. "No, no. This is unnecessary. I shall stay with Jane. You attend to Lady Catherine and Miss de Bourgh. All will be well, but should there be any hint of something serious, I shall send word directly."

"I do not like this, Lizzy," Mary stated in a stubborn voice reminiscent of Lydia's.

"Eliza is being quite reasonable, my dear. She shall take care of poor Jane, and we shall do our duty to our noble patroness."

Mary gave her husband a look that said she wished to recommend his *noble patroness* to the Devil, but said, "Very well, Lizzy. We shall go without you. But I am most seriously displeased!"

DARCY WALKED ANNE TO THE sitting room in full expectation of enjoying the vision of Elizabeth Bennet's lovely face. Instead, he found only his other cousin, his aunt, his aunt's clergyman, and the clergyman's wife.

"But what is this?" he blurted out. "Where are the Miss Bennets?"

"A thousand pardons, my dear Mr. Darcy," began Collins. "My sister Jane is indisposed, and Miss Elizabeth waits upon her. I tried to convince my younger sister to entrust Miss Bennet to our most attentive housekeeper, but she would not hear of it. Miss Elizabeth is…rather strong-minded for one so young."

"Mr. Collins!" cried his wife. "Had not Lizzy insisted I attend today, I assure you I would be with her at the parsonage this instant!"

"Of course, my dear wife. You are most attentive to others' needs."

Lady Catherine weighed in. "You are very right, Mrs. Collins. Hired help cannot always be counted upon to be attentive when one is ill. Miss Elizabeth's choice is right and proper. I hope that Miss Bennet shall recover quickly. She should stay out of the sun. She spends far too much time in it for it to be healthful for her. We shall all miss your sisters, Mrs. Collins, but we shall endeavor to carry on, I dare say. You are looking very well, Anne, especially on Darcy's arm. Does she not look well, Richard?"

"She is all loveliness, Aunt." The colonel said automatically.

Anne blushed.

For his part, Darcy heard hardly a word. "Aunt Catherine, forgive me, but I have just recalled some business that must be attended to this instant. I shall join you at supper." He rose and headed for the door.

Lady Catherine was astonished. "Nephew, where are you going?"

"Yes, Darce," chimed in Fitzwilliam. "Surely your business can wait until after tea."

"No! I must not tarry a moment longer!" He fled the room.

Anne simply smiled to herself. *Elizabeth, you are going to be a very happy woman!*

WHEN MARY AND MR. COLLINS were gone, Elizabeth, as if intending to prejudice herself as much as possible against Mr. Darcy, chose to examine all the comments and actions Jane had made or done since being in Kent. They contained no actual complaint, but there was a decided want of that cheerfulness which had always been part of her character. Jane was kindly disposed towards everyone; however, Mr. Darcy's shameful boast of what misery he had been able to inflict gave Elizabeth a keener sense of her sister's sufferings. And now that all was revealed, Jane's misery was complete.

It was some consolation for Elizabeth to think that Darcy's visit to Rosings would end on the day after next and a still greater one that, in less than a fortnight, she and Jane would quit this hateful county. Their departure for Hertfordshire would contribute to the recovery of their spirits, she was certain.

Elizabeth could not think of Darcy's leaving Kent without remembering that his cousin was to go with him, but agreeable as Colonel Fitzwilliam was, he had been Mr. Darcy's messenger, and therefore, she did not mean to be unhappy at his farewell.

While settling this point, she was suddenly roused by the sound of a knock on the door, and to her utter amazement, Elizabeth saw Mr. Darcy walk into the room. In a hurried manner, he immediately began his enquiry.

"I understand that your sister has taken ill."

Barely containing her composure, Elizabeth answered, "I thank you, sir; it is but a headache. I assure you she is in good health."

"You did not come to tea today, and they said Miss Bennet was ill." This statement was more to himself than anyone. He sat down for a few moments, and then getting up, walked about the room.

Elizabeth was surprised but said not a word. After a silence of several minutes, he came towards her in an agitated manner.

"In vain have I have struggled! It will not do. My feelings will not be repressed. You must allow me to tell you how ardently I admire and love you!" With that, he took a knee at her feet. "In spite of all my endeavors, I have found it impossible to conquer the strength of my feelings. The inferiority of your family, the miserable connections, the denigration, the lack of judgment I display, the harshness that I will be rightly judged by my family—all this is as *nothing* against my attachment to you! I have struggled greatly, and I hope I shall be rewarded. Miss Bennet, will you accept my hand in marriage?"

Elizabeth's astonishment was beyond expression. She could easily see that the gentleman had no doubt of a favorable answer. He spoke of apprehension and anxiety, but his countenance expressed a profound self-assuredness. Such an expression only exasperated Elizabeth further, and when he ceased, the color rose into her cheeks.

"In such cases as this, it is, I believe, the established mode to express a sense of obligation for the sentiments avowed, however unequally they may be returned. It is natural that obligation should be felt, and if I could feel gratitude, I would now thank you. But I cannot.

"I have *never* desired your good opinion, and you have certainly bestowed it most unwillingly. I am sorry to have occasioned pain to anyone. It has been most unconsciously done, however, and I hope will be of short duration. "

Mr. Darcy, still on one knee, his eyes fixed on her face, seemed to understand her words with no less resentment than surprise. His complexion became pale with anger, and the disturbance of his mind was visible in his every feature. He was struggling for the appearance of composure, and he would not open his lips until he had attained it. The pause was, to Elizabeth's feelings, dreadful.

At length, after gaining his feet and crossing to the mantle, Darcy turned, and in a voice of forced calmness, he demanded, "And *this* is all the reply which I am to have the honor of expecting! I might, perhaps, wish to be informed why, with so little endeavor at civility,

I am thus rejected. But it is of small importance."

"I might as well enquire," replied she, "why, with so evident a design of offending and insulting me, you chose to tell me that you liked me against your will, against your reason, and even against your character? Was not this some excuse for incivility, if I was uncivil? But I have other provocations. You *know* I have. Had not my own feelings decided against you, had they been indifferent, or had they even been favorable, do you think that any consideration would tempt me to accept the man who has been the means of ruining, perhaps forever, the happiness of a most beloved sister?"

As she pronounced these words, Mr. Darcy appeared more grave than angry. He listened without attempting to interrupt her while she continued.

"I have every reason in the world to think ill of you. No motive can excuse the unjust and ungenerous part you acted there! You dare not—you cannot—deny that you have been the principal, if not the only, means of dividing them from each other, of exposing one to the censure of the world for caprice and instability, the other to its derision for disappointed hopes, and involving them both in misery of the acutest kind! Can you deny that you have done it?"

"I...I do not deny that I did everything in my power to separate my friend from your sister, for I had good reason to do so at the time. I have recently been given over to other thoughts on that matter."

"Other thoughts? Sir, my sister lies inconsolable upstairs due to your interference! She is no fortune-hunter, no matter what you think!" Darcy turned his back to her. "Oh, yes turn away! Are you afraid to see the fruits of your labors? But you must be. Why else would you send your cousin to inform us of your triumph? Wicked man!"

Darcy faced her. "My cousin?"

"But it is not merely this affair on which my dislike of you is founded!" Elizabeth continued, talking over the question Darcy was trying to form. "Long before it had taken place, my opinion of you was decided. Your character was unfolded in the recital which I received many months ago from Mr. Wickham."

His eyes flashed in anger, and color had returned to his cheeks.

"You take an eager interest in *that* gentleman's concerns!"

"How can I not, knowing what his misfortunes have been?"

"His misfortunes!" repeated Darcy contemptuously. "Yes, *his* misfortunes have been great indeed."

His unfeeling tone aroused Elizabeth's fury like never before. "You have reduced him to his present state of poverty. You have withheld the advantages designed for him! He was your childhood friend, yet you have done all this! How can you treat the mention of his misfortunes with contempt and ridicule?"

"And this," cried Darcy, as he walked with quick steps across the room, "is your opinion of me! This is the estimation in which you hold me! My faults, according to this calculation, are heavy indeed!" He moved to her. "But perhaps, these offences, real or otherwise—"

"Otherwise?"

"—might have been overlooked, had not your pride been hurt by my honest confession of the scruples that had long prevented my forming any serious design. These bitter accusations might have been suppressed had I, with greater policy, concealed my struggles. But disguise of every sort is my abhorrence. I am not ashamed of the feelings I related; they were natural and just. Could you expect me to rejoice in the inferiority of your connections? To congratulate myself on the hope of relations whose condition in life is so decidedly beneath my own?"

Elizabeth felt herself growing angrier every moment, yet she kept her tone icy cold. "You are mistaken, Mr. Darcy, if you suppose that the mode of your declaration affected me in any other way than to spare me the concern which I might have felt in refusing you, had you behaved in a more gentleman-like manner."

She saw him start at this, but she continued. "You could not have made me the offer of your hand in *any possible way* that would have tempted me to accept it! From the very beginning, from the first moment of my acquaintance with you, your manners, impressing me with the fullest belief of your arrogance, your conceit, and your selfish disdain of the feelings of others, were such as to form that groundwork of disapprobation on which succeeding events have built so immoveable a dislike. I had not known you a month before I felt that you were the last man in the world whom I could ever be prevailed on to marry!"

Darcy held up his hand, and he spoke in a very subdued manner. "You have said quite enough, madam. I perfectly comprehend your feelings, and have now only to be ashamed of what my own have been. Forgive me for having taken up so much of your time, and accept my best wishes for your health and happiness."

With these words, he hastily left the room, and in the next moment, Elizabeth heard him open the front door and quit the house. She herself could not stir for the world, frozen as she was to her chair.

She looked up at the sound of her sister's voice. Jane had opened the door and moved to her. "Whatever is the matter? I heard loud voices."

"Oh, Jane!"

Elizabeth threw herself into her sister's arms.

Fitzwilliam Darcy strode along the road connecting the parsonage and Rosings, his anguish increasing with every step. His mind was in turmoil, and he was occupied in making some sense of it.

Something must have happened recently! Anne was so confident! How could they have known about Bingley? Why did I ever get involved with that? Miss Bennet upset? Fitz said nothing about her being—

Fitz! Oh, God, Richard, what have you done? What did you tell them? You could not have been that stupid!

He did not notice Mr. and Mrs. Collins walking from Rosings nearby.

"My dear, Mr. Darcy looks quite upset. We should go and offer him comfort."

"No, Mr. Collins, I do not believe he is in any mood right now. We should not beard the lion in his own den. Come along; we must see to Jane."

Minutes later, Darcy raced up the stars of Rosings, the sound of his aunt's unanswered command that he explain his absence from tea ringing along the halls.

Colonel Fitzwilliam was changing after tea when the door to his room flew open. "Darcy! There you are! Where the devil have you—"

He could say no more. Darcy's fist had connected with his jaw.

THERE WAS A PAINFUL TUMULT in Elizabeth's mind, and from overwhelming weakness, she sat down and cried, Jane her silent witness. As she reflected on what had passed, Elizabeth's astonishment was increased by every review.

That she should receive an offer of marriage from Mr. Darcy was incomprehensible! That he should have been in love with her for so many months was equally unfathomable! That he was so much in love as to wish to marry her in spite of all the objections that made him prevent his friend's marrying her sister was most incredible!

While it was somewhat gratifying to have inspired, however unconsciously, so strong an affection, Mr. Darcy's pride, his abominable pride, his shameless avowal of what he had done with respect to Jane, and the unfeeling manner in which he had mentioned his cruelty towards Mr. Wickham soon overcame the pity which the consideration of his attachment had for a moment excited.

Once she had gathered control of her emotions, Elizabeth explained to her sister all that had befallen her. For a short time, Jane forgot her own sorrow, so great was her amazement.

"Mr. Darcy proposed! You cannot be serious!"

"He did, Jane, just now."

"He was in love with you all this time? It is astonishing!"

"I have refused him, of course!"

"Of course. But…poor Mr. Darcy!"

"You have not forgotten what he did to you, Jane?" Elizabeth instantly regretted her words as Jane began to cry, and that brought Elizabeth to tears once more.

It was the sight of the Bennet sisters weeping in each other's arms that greeted the returning Collinses. After a few aborted attempts to mollify the young ladies, the tall clergyman admitted defeat and retreated to his study. It was only then that all was explained to Mary.

The ladies were deep in discussion well into the night. Mr. Collins, a loyal believer in Mr. Franklin's *"Early to bed, and early to rise"* axiom, had already retired, and so the ladies were under no fear of discovery.

"I knew it!" Mary declared. "I knew there was some admiration on his part towards you, Lizzy."

"Be that as it may, Mary, how could he, in good conscience, expect me to accept him? Mr. Darcy, the destroyer of all of dear Jane's hopes!"

"Elizabeth, please. If you truly liked him—"

"I do not, Jane, especially after his cruel treatment of Mr. Wickham! You should have heard him. He almost boasted of it!"

Mary frowned. "As I have said before, I do not have the high opinion of that man that you do, Lizzy. From what Miss de Bough tells me—"

Elizabeth harshly interrupted her sister. "They are all alike! Do you truly expect Miss de Bourgh to go against her family?"

Mary grew very still. In a cold voice she said, "I trust my friend, Elizabeth, and I would ask you not to speak of her in such a manner."

Elizabeth saw how upset Mary had become, and she was ashamed. "I had no right to talk ill of Miss de Bourgh. I am sorry. Please forgive me."

"If you knew how very much she liked you, you would never say such a thing." Elizabeth nodded. "And I will tell you now that I am quite vexed with Mr. Darcy's interference with Mr. Bingley."

Jane said nothing. A few minutes later, she excused herself to bed. The other ladies soon followed.

Chapter 7

Two Letters

Jane and Elizabeth walked the groves of Rosings early the next morning, discussing Mr. Darcy's shocking proposal.

"Poor Mr. Darcy!" said Jane for perhaps the fourth time. "I cannot blame you for refusing him, Elizabeth. I know how much you dislike the man, but to have loved you for so long—since Meryton! He must have been bitterly disappointed by your refusal."

Elizabeth was rather annoyed by her sister's view. "Have you forgotten how he influenced Mr. Bingley? I will certainly never forgive him for it!"

"No, I have not forgotten." Jane sighed and looked out over the plantation.

They walked on in silence for a while. Elizabeth did not know what thoughts Jane meditated upon; her own reflections were disturbing enough. To her discomfort, Elizabeth found her feelings were intensely conflicted. She had to own that there was a twinge of regret for her intemperate words in declining Mr. Darcy's suit, for Elizabeth was not an unkind person. She wished pain on no one, especially on a gentleman who declared an affectionate attachment to her.

But other thoughts overcame the pity she had felt for a moment. She had been and remained offended over Mr. Darcy's overbearing behavior in Hertfordshire, irate over his cruel treatment of Mr. Wickham, and incensed by his interference in Jane's affairs. No, it was impossible that she should even for a moment consider the disappointment he must have suffered, when Jane suffered so much more.

She would not think of his handsome face and fit figure, of his sharp mind and piercing eyes—eyes that had *not* looked upon her in disfavor but signified intense passion! No, she would not think about that at all!

Elizabeth was roused from her ruminations by Jane's gentle, hesitant voice. "I have been thinking about Mr. Bingley—"

Whatever Jane meant to say was lost, for a certain tall, proud gentleman suddenly appeared before them.

"Miss Bennet, Miss Elizabeth, I have been walking the grove sometime in the hope of meeting you." Mr. Darcy removed two letters from his pocket. "Would you ladies do me the honor of reading these letters?"

Elizabeth was too shocked to say a word as she took her letter, but Jane spoke to Darcy with composure.

"To what do these letters portend, Mr. Darcy?"

The gentleman colored. "I am a poor orator, Miss Bennet, as I have learned to my regret. These letters are an explanation of my actions and, in your case, offer several heartfelt apologies. I must to London to set right what I have done. Please excuse me."

Elizabeth finally got a good look at Mr. Darcy's face. "You are injured, Mr. Darcy! What has befallen you?"

Darcy touched his blackened eye. "Nothing I did not deserve. I bid you good day, ladies."

He turned to walk towards Rosings, but Jane's voice detained him.

"Mr. Darcy, I cannot accept any letter from you." She allowed the unopened message to fall to the ground. "If you have anything you wish to tell me, I am at leisure to hear it."

Darcy was flustered. "Miss Bennet, I—"

"Jane!" hissed her sister, but the lady was unmoved. Elizabeth then looked up at the gentleman. Never had she seen him so uncomfortable. Some dark part of her heart cheered at the sight.

Mr. Darcy began pacing back and forth before the ladies, apparently involved in some inner struggle. A decision made, he turned to the Bennet women.

"Does Miss Bennet know of our *interview* last evening?" he asked Elizabeth. Confirmed in his suspicion, he said, "I will tell you all, but I must ask that you permit me to speak at length without interruption. After I have said my piece, I will answer any questions you may have. Is this agreeable to you?" The ladies nodded their agreement, and after finding a fallen log upon which they could sit, he began.

"Three offences of a very different nature were laid to my charge by you, Miss Elizabeth." He counted them out on his fingers. "The first mentioned was that, regardless of the sentiments of either, I had detached Mr. Bingley from you, Miss Bennet. The second was that, with malice beforehand, I dispatched Colonel Fitzwilliam to inform you of my success in that enterprise. The third was that I had, in defiance of honor, ruined the immediate prosperity and blasted the prospects of Mr. Wickham. My character requires that I answer these accusations. You ladies must pardon, therefore, the freedom with which I demand your attention. Your feelings, I know, will bestow it unwillingly, but I demand it of your justice."

Elizabeth could not believe that he could justify his actions and raised one scornful eyebrow. This did not go unnoticed by Mr. Darcy.

"Be not alarmed, Miss Elizabeth," he continued coldly, "that there will be any repetition of those sentiments or renewal of those offers, which were last night so...disgusting to you. Those wishes cannot be too soon forgotten, and the sooner this interview is done, the better."

Stung, Elizabeth turned away.

Mr. Darcy spoke as he paced. "I cannot deny the justice of the first charge. Indeed, until recently, I congratulated myself on being of use to my friend." He paused and dropped his head. "It is only within the last two days that I have learned that the foundations of my actions were false. My letter to you, Miss Bennet, was an explanation of my actions." Mr. Darcy turned to fully face Jane, his bearing like a man giving testimony to a judge weighing his fate. "I absolutely deny that I suspected you sought my friend's fortune, that I told Colonel Fitzwilliam that I thought that, or that I sent him on such a mission as has been alleged. Enclosed within your letter is his written apology for the pain and mortification he has undoubtedly caused you."

"But then why would the colonel do such a thing?" cried Elizabeth.

Mr. Darcy's mouth twisted. "A mistake on his part, nothing more. He did not know Miss Bennet was the lady involved in the affair."

"Come, come—this is not good enough!"

Darcy closed his eyes and then said in a low voice, "He thought of impressing you, Miss Elizabeth, with examples of my goodness. Apparently, he was matchmaking."

Elizabeth could only stare, stupefied.

He offered a painful grin. "Yes, a poor choice of tales, was it not? I have...*discussed* this with him. He has seen the error of his ways."

"Thus your eye, Mr. Darcy?" asked Jane.

"Just so," he responded with a nod. "Please allow me to tell you of Charles Bingley. Bingley has been my particular friend since our days at Cambridge. His fortune came from his father's business in trade, but he meant to live like a gentleman. I have few friends, but those I do have are like family to me. We are not related, but to all intents and purposes, Bingley is my brother. He asked me to accompany him to the estate in Hertfordshire he was looking to acquire—"

"Netherfield Park," Elizabeth could not help blurting out.

"Yes, Miss Elizabeth. I had not been long in Hertfordshire, before I saw that Bingley preferred Miss Bennet to any other young woman in the country. But it was not until the evening of the dance at Netherfield that I had any awareness of his feeling a serious attachment to you." His voice grew more earnest. "You must understand that I had often seen Bingley in love before; it had never been serious. At that ball, while I had the honor of dancing with your sister," he nodded to Elizabeth, "I could perceive that his partiality was beyond what I had ever witnessed in him."

His intense eyes now were focused on Jane. "I also watched you. Here I must give you pain. Please forgive me, Miss Bennet, but while I found your looks and manners open, cheerful, and engaging—you received his attentions with pleasure—I could not see any indication of peculiar regard for my friend."

A small gasp escaped Jane's lips, and Mr. Darcy's face filled with regret. "I am now of the opinion that your true feelings were quite the opposite. If it was so, if I was misled by such an error to inflict pain on you, your resentment is not unreasonable. But I did not believe you to be indifferent because I wished it. I believed it on impartial conviction."

"And this was the only reason, sir?" Elizabeth cried, once again breaking her agreement and ignoring Jane's unspoken request to remain silent. "I assure you that my sister's affections were quite attached to Mr. Bingley! Are you saying that having one uncle a country lawyer and another in trade had nothing to do with your interference?"

"I could have set that aside, as I did for myself!" he shot back with some passion.

Elizabeth colored as she remembered.

Mr. Darcy gathered his features into his usual stony expression and continued. "I must admit that my objections to the marriage were not merely those which I have related before. The situation of your mother's family, though objectionable, is nothing in comparison of that total want of propriety so frequently, so almost uniformly, betrayed by your mother, by your two younger sisters, and occasionally even by your father."

"My father!" cried Elizabeth.

Darcy's chin rose. "Pardon me. It pains me to offend you. Let it give you consolation to consider that no one can condemn the manner by which you ladies conduct yourselves. Mrs. Collins joins you in my estimation." The two ladies could not speak for the world.

Turning back to Jane, Darcy said in a far kinder voice, "I will only say further that my motivation stemmed from a desire to preserve my friend from what I esteemed a most unhappy connection for *both parties* involved."

In a low voice, Jane asked, "And did Mr. Bingley's sisters share your misgivings?"

"His sisters' uneasiness had been equal to my own, but I will not scruple to guess their true motivations. Bingley left Netherfield for London on the day following with the design of soon returning, but once there, we readily engaged in pointing out to my friend the certain evils of an unequal marriage. Unequal in *affection*, I point out."

Darcy struggled at this point. "Bingley believed you returned his affection with sincere, if not equal, regard. But my friend has great natural modesty and a stronger dependence on my judgment than on his own. I cannot blame myself for having acted thus, except that it was done on faulty intelligence.

"That I have wounded your feelings is certain, Miss Bennet, but it was unknowingly done. He is my friend, and I could do no less for him. Now I must ask you to confirm what I have recently learned. Miss Bennet, were your feelings sincerely attached to Mr. Bingley?"

Jane could only nod.

Darcy appeared anguished. "Then I have done a great injustice to you and to him! I must set right that which I have damaged. I will go to London directly to confess my superior knowledge of your feelings to my friend. I do not doubt the reception I will receive—a break between us is not inconceivable—but as unpleasant as it is likely to be, I shall not waver from my purpose. However, I offer no hopes other than my confession. The rest must lie with the gentleman."

Jane would not lift her eyes to the man. "You truly believed I was indifferent to Mr. Bingley?"

"I did, yes."

"Then I forgive you."

"Jane?" Elizabeth was all astonishment.

Darcy's voice was choked with emotion. "You are too kind, Miss Bennet. I deserve no such consideration."

"In any case you have my forgiveness."

"Thank you, madam, but it will be no little time before I can forgive myself! I shall do right by you, I swear. I shall speak to Bingley in London as soon as may be done."

In a strained voice Jane said, "You should do as you must."

Before Elizabeth could react to her sister's statement, Darcy began to address her. "The third offence laid at my door was that I had, in defiance of honor, ruined the prosperity and blasted the prospects of Mr. Wickham, the companion of my youth, the acknowledged favorite of my father, and a young man who had scarcely any other dependence than on our patronage. I can certainly understand your outrage; indeed, I should never be in the company of anyone who had done such a thing without good reason."

"You claim *good reasons* for doing something so dastardly?" cried Elizabeth.

Mr. Darcy was undaunted by her accusation. "I do. It seems that my word as a gentleman is not good enough, and I can only refute it by laying before you the whole of his connection with my family.

"Mr. Wickham is the son of a very respectable man who had for many years the management of all the Pemberley estates. He was godson to my father, who supported him at school and afterwards at Cambridge. My father was not only fond of this young man, he also had the highest opinion of him, hoping the church would be his profession." Darcy frowned. "As for myself, it is many, many years since I first began to think of Wickham in a very different manner. His vicious propensities and his want of principle could not escape my close observation. I cannot blame my father; he had no opportunity to see Wickham in unguarded moments.

"My excellent father died about five years ago. His attachment to Mr. Wickham was to the last so steady that in his will he recommended that if Wickham took orders, he desired that a valuable family living might be his as soon as it became vacant, as well as a legacy of one thousand pounds. His own father did not long survive mine, and within half a year from these events, Mr. Wickham wrote to inform me that, having finally resolved against taking orders, he hoped I should not think it unreasonable for him to expect some more *immediate* pecuniary advantage. He had some intention, he claimed, of studying the law and pointed out that the interest of one thousand pounds would be insufficient to support him. I rather wished than believed him to be sincere. I knew that he ought not to be a clergyman, and the business was soon settled. He accepted three thousand pounds. All connection between us seemed dissolved."

Four thousand pounds! Can it be believed? thought Elizabeth.

"For about three years, I heard little of him, but upon learning of the death of the incumbent of the living which had been designed for him, Wickham applied to me again by letter. His circumstances, he assured me, were exceedingly bad. *This* I had no difficulty in believing, recalling his behavior at school. Wickham had found the law a most unprofitable study and now wished for the living that had been proposed for him. You will hardly blame me for refusing to comply with this entreaty or for resisting every repetition of it. His resentment was in proportion to the distress of his circumstances, and he was doubtless violent in his abuse of me to others. After this, every appearance of acquaintance was dropped. How he lived I know not."

Darcy paused and looked closely at his audience. "But last summer he again most painfully obtruded on my notice. I must now mention a circumstance which I would wish to forget myself. Having said this much, though, I feel no doubt of your secrecy."

Secrecy? though Elizabeth. His choice of words was mysterious and heavy, exacerbated by a most stern expression. Elizabeth felt a sense of doom.

In a tone slow, heavy, and painful, he said, "My sister, who is more than ten years my junior, was left to the guardianship of Colonel Fitzwilliam and myself after the death of my parents. About a year ago, she was taken from school and thence to Ramsgate with her companion, a Mrs. Younge, in whose character we were most unhappily deceived. Mr. Wickham also went to that place by design, following a plan he hatched, I learned later, in concert with Mrs. Younge. He recommended himself to Georgiana's affectionate heart, and she was persuaded to believe herself in love and consented to an elopement. She was then but fifteen."

There was a pair of gasps.

"Fortunately, I joined them unexpectedly a day or two before the intended elopement. Georgiana, unable to hide anything from me, acknowledged the whole plan. You may imagine what I felt and how I acted! Mr. Wickham left the place immediately, and Mrs. Younge was, of course, removed from her charge. Mr. Wickham's chief object was unquestionably my sister's fortune of thirty thousand pounds, but I cannot help supposing that the hope of revenging himself on me was a strong inducement. Had he succeeded, his revenge would have been complete indeed.

"This, ladies, is a faithful narrative of every event in which Mr. Wickham and I have been concerned together," said Mr. Darcy finally. "I suppose you have no reason to believe me. Therefore, I can offer the services of Colonel Fitzwilliam for the truth of everything related, acquainted as he is with every particular of these transactions."

DARCY STOOD ROCK STILL. HE knew not how he could, when every part of him trembled with powerful emotion, but he could do no less. He awaited the final moments of his acquaintance with Elizabeth Bennet as a Darcy should—proud, unfearing, and accepting of his fate.

Jane glanced at Elizabeth, who looked too overcome to speak, so it was she who responded.

"Mr. Darcy, I thank you for this information. I understand how painful it was to relate, and speaking for my sister, we are honored by your candor and trust. We, of course, shall keep what you have shared with us in confidence. Your sister shall have no fear of exposure from us." She bent and picked up her letter.

Darcy bowed, but his eyes remained on Elizabeth. "I expected no less from you. Thank you."

Suddenly Elizabeth blurted out, "But your sister—how horrible! Tell us not that she still suffers from— She is quite recovered, is she not?"

Darcy grimaced. "She is well in body but not, I fear, in spirit. She is not as happy as she once was. I would give all I have to have Georgiana back as she was."

Elizabeth turned away, but Darcy saw the tears in her eyes.

Jane was far calmer. "Mr. Darcy, you have said much that we have to consider. Would you care for these letters back?" She held hers out.

"No, I wrote them for you. Do with them what you wish."

Darcy knew he was being dismissed. He did not know what he was to expect when he began his confession. Jane's quick forgiveness was surprising. He did not know what was in Elizabeth's mind. Her concern for Georgiana told him that she at least believed him about Wickham. Other than that, he had no idea.

He hesitated, for he knew that he would never see Elizabeth again. Finally, with one last earnest glance at her, Darcy took his leave.

"I thank you for your time, ladies. God bless you both."

With that, he bowed, turned, and strode back to Rosings.

The sisters sat in stunned silence. Then, as one, they opened their letters and read. After the ladies finished their own letters, by unspoken agreement, they exchanged messages.

If Elizabeth, when Mr. Darcy came upon them, did not expect a renewal of his offers, she had formed no expectation at all of the contents of the letters. But such as they were, it may be well supposed how eagerly she heard what he had to say and what opposing emotions they excited.

Her feelings as she listened were scarcely to be defined. With amazement did she first understand that he believed any apology to be in his power, and steadfastly was she persuaded that he could have no explanation to give. With a strong prejudice against everything he might say, Elizabeth heard his account of what had happened at Netherfield. His belief of her sister's insensibility, she instantly resolved to be false, and his account of the real objections to the match made her too angry to have any wish of doing him justice. He expressed nothing for what he had done which satisfied *her,* though it apparently was enough for Jane. His style was not penitent but haughty. It was all pride and insolence!

How Jane could so quickly forgive him was a mystery to Lizzy.

But when that subject was succeeded by his account of Mr. Wickham and Elizabeth reread with a somewhat clearer attention to his message, astonishment, apprehension, and even horror, oppressed her. She wished to discredit it entirely, repeatedly thinking, *"This must be false! This cannot be! This must be the grossest falsehood!"*

When she had gone through the whole letter, though scarcely knowing anything of the last page or two, Elizabeth put it hastily away, protesting that she would not regard it, that she would never look in it again.

"Lizzy," said her sister, "I wish to return to the parsonage. Shall you come?"

Elizabeth could barely look at her sister. "I beg leave to stay in the woods, Jane. My mind is all bewilderment. A walk is what I need."

"Very well, I understand. Do not be too long."

She assured Jane that she would not tarry, and she was alone within a short time. Elizabeth walked the woods and glens of Rosings in a perturbed state of mind with thoughts that could rest on nothing. Before long, her letter was unfolded again and, collecting herself as well as she could, Elizabeth began the mortifying perusal of all that related to Wickham.

The account of Wickham's connection with the Pemberley family was exactly what he had related himself, and the kindness of the late Mr. Darcy, as recounted by his son, agreed equally well with Wickham's own words. So far, each recital confirmed the other, but when it came to the will, the difference was great.

Four thousand pounds was an immense amount! It was twice what Longbourn produced in a year. Invested prudently, the amount could have allowed Wickham to live, while not lavishly, at least comfortably if he practiced economy. He would never be without a bed or a meal. The Darcys, father and son, had been exceptionally generous.

The extravagance and general profligacy that Mr. Darcy laid to Mr. Wickham's charge exceedingly shocked her, the more so as she could bring no proof of its injustice. She had never heard of Wickham before his entrance into the ——shire Militia. Of his former way of life, nothing had been known in Hertfordshire but what he told himself. As to his real character, had information been in her power, Elizabeth had never felt a wish of enquiring. His countenance, voice, and manner had established him at once in the possession of every virtue. She tried to recollect some instance of goodness, some distinguished trait of integrity or benevolence that might rescue him from the attacks of Mr. Darcy, but no such recollection befriended her.

She could see Wickham instantly before her, in every charm of air and address. But she could remember no more substantial good than the general approbation of the neighborhood and the regard which his social powers had gained him in the mess.

Elizabeth returned to her letter. The story that followed, of Wickham's designs on Miss Darcy, received some confirmation from what Colonel Fitzwilliam had said only the morning before. She had no reason to question Colonel Fitzwilliam's character. His written apology to Jane, which Jane had shared, was heartfelt. For a moment, Elizabeth almost resolved on applying to him for confirmation, but the idea was checked by the awkwardness of the application and by the fact that he was attempting to forward his cousin as a possible companion of her future life! At length, her impulse was banished by concluding the exercise was unnecessary. Mr. Darcy never would have hazarded recommending his cousin for verification if he had not been well assured of that gentleman's corroboration.

She perfectly remembered everything that had passed in conversation between Wickham and herself in their first evening at Mr. Philips's. She was now struck by the impropriety of such communications to a stranger, and she wondered how it had escaped her notice before. She saw the indelicacy of putting himself forward as he had done and the inconsistency of his professions with his conduct. She remembered that he had boasted of having no fear of seeing Mr. Darcy—that Mr. Darcy might leave the country, but he should stand his ground. Yet Wickham had avoided the Netherfield ball the very next week. She remembered also that, until the Netherfield family had quit the country, he told his story to no one but herself, but after their removal, it had been everywhere discussed. Mr. Wickham had then no reserves or scruples in sinking Mr. Darcy's character, though he had assured her that respect for the father would always prevent him from exposing the son.

How differently did everything now appear in which Mr. Wickham was concerned! His attentions to Miss King were now the consequence of views solely and hatefully mercenary. The mediocrity of her fortune proved no longer the moderation of his wishes, but his eagerness to grasp at anything. His behavior to herself could now have had no tolerable motive. He either had been deceived with regard to her fortune or had been gratifying his vanity by encouraging the preference that Elizabeth believed she had most incautiously shown.

Every lingering struggle in Mr. Wickham's favor grew fainter and fainter and furthered the justification of Mr. Darcy. Mr. Bingley, when questioned by Jane, had long ago asserted his friend's blamelessness in the affair. That, proud and repulsive as were Darcy's manners, Elizabeth had never, in the whole course of their acquaintance, seen anything that betrayed him to be unprincipled or unjust or anything that spoke him of irreligious or immoral habits.

Among his own connections, he was esteemed and valued. Even Wickham had allowed him merit as a brother, and Elizabeth had often heard him speak so affectionately of his sister, which proved him capable of some amiable feeling. Had his actions been as Wickham represented them, so gross a violation of everything right, they could hardly have been concealed from the world. And a friendship between a person capable of such shameful acts as Wickham claimed and such an amiable man as Mr. Bingley was incomprehensible.

Elizabeth grew absolutely ashamed of herself. Of neither Darcy nor Wickham could she think without feeling that she had been blind, partial, prejudiced, and absurd.

How despicably have I acted! I, who have prided myself on my discernment! I, who have valued myself on my abilities! How humiliating is this discovery! Yet, how just a humiliation! Had I been in love, I could not have been more wretchedly blind.

But vanity, not love, has been my folly. Pleased with the preference of one and offended by the neglect of the other on the very beginning of our acquaintance, I have courted prepossession and ignorance, and driven reason away where either was concerned.

Till this moment, I never knew myself.

From herself to Jane, from Jane to Bingley, her thoughts were in a line that soon brought to her recollection that Mr. Darcy's explanation there had appeared very insufficient, and she read Jane's letter again. Widely different was the effect of a second perusal.

How could Elizabeth deny that credit to Mr. Darcy's assertions in one instance that she had been obliged to give in the other? He declared himself to have been completely unaware of her sister's attachment, and she could not help remembering Charlotte's opinion.

"If a woman conceals her affection with the same skill from the object of it, she may lose the opportunity of fixing him, and it will then be but poor consolation to believe the world equally in the dark. There is so much of gratitude or vanity in almost every attachment that it is not safe to leave any to itself. We can all begin freely—a slight preference is natural enough—but there are very few of us who have heart enough to be really in love without encouragement. In nine cases out of ten, a woman had better show more affection than she feels. Bingley likes your sister undoubtedly, but he may never do more than like her if she does not help him on."

Elizabeth felt that Jane's feelings, though fervent, were little displayed and that there was a constant complacency in her air and manner not often united with great sensibility. Apparently, Jane recognized that, and that must have been the reason she forgave Mr. Darcy so readily.

When Elizabeth came to that part of the letters in which her family was mentioned in terms of such mortifying yet merited reproach, her sense of shame was severe. The justice of the charges struck her too forcibly for denial, and the circumstances to which Mr. Darcy particularly alluded, as having passed at the Netherfield ball and as confirming all his first disapprobation, could not have made a stronger impression on his mind than on hers. His compliment to herself and her sisters was not unfelt. It soothed, but it could not console her for the contempt that had been self-attracted by the rest of her family, and as she considered that Jane's disappointment had in fact been the work of her nearest relations, she felt depressed beyond anything she had ever known before.

After wandering along the lane for two hours, giving way to every variety of thought, reconsidering events, determining probabilities, and reconciling herself as well as she could, to a change so sudden and so important, fatigue and a recollection of her long absence made Elizabeth at length return home.

ELIZABETH ENTERED THE HOUSE WITH the wish to appear cheerful and the resolution to repress the thought that would make her unfit for conversation. She was immediately told that the two gentlemen from Rosings had each called during her absence. Mr. Darcy, remained only for a few minutes before taking his leave, but Colonel Fitzwilliam had remained with them at least an hour, hoping for her return.

"They asked about Jane, of course," Mary said, "but she remained upstairs, indisposed. Both gentlemen seemed quite concerned."

"Even Mr. Darcy?"

"Yes, even so." Mary gave her sister a most pitying look.

"You...you did not berate them, I hope."

"It was not necessary."

LATER THAT DAY, THE TWO men rode in the carriage in silence until finally Darcy could stand no more.

"How is your jaw?"

"About the same as your eye, I should think."

Darcy paused. "I am sorry, Fitz."

"As am I. Once again, my big mouth has gotten me into trouble. How was I to know that Miss Bennet was Bingley's *undesirable lady?*"

"What possessed you to say such a thing?"

"Believe it or not, Darcy, I was trying to help you! I thought by showing what a caring, conscientious friend you are to Bingley, it would ease your way with Miss Elizabeth." At his cousin's look of incredulity, he continued. "You have been rather obvious, Cuz. Anne and I discussed it."

"Oh, wonderful! Who else knows my business?"

"Aunt Catherine is oblivious."

"At least that is something."

"Why in the world did you warn Bingley off Miss Bennet? She is an angel!"

"Because I am an idiot!"

"Too right, there." The colonel thought for a moment. "So what do you do now?"

"I must repair the damage I have caused." *And learn to live without Elizabeth Bennet.*

"Need any help?"

"If I do, I know where to turn. Thank you, Fitz."

"Do not mention it, idiot."

Chapter 8

Return to Longbourn

Mary and Elizabeth were practicing in Mrs. Parks's room when Anne de Bourgh entered.

"Mary, might I speak with Miss Elizabeth for a few moments?"

Mary gave her sister a knowing look. "I shall take a stroll about the rose garden, shall I?"

Mrs. Collins stepped from the room, leaving the two women alone. Elizabeth was at the pianoforte, looking uncomfortable. Anne saw her uneasiness but began directly.

"I understand that you have refused my cousin. May I ask why?"

Elizabeth was beyond shocked. "Miss de Bourgh," she was able to utter after a few moments, "I do not know where you could have heard such a thing."

"From a very reliable source." Richard told her of the event as soon as he was able, after seeking aid for his injured jaw. "It is within your rights not to confirm this information, but I had hoped that our friendship would have given us some level of intimacy."

Elizabeth would not look at the girl. "You may rest assured that I am not engaged to Mr. Darcy."

Anne frowned. "That is unfortunate, for I thought you well-suited to one another." At Elizabeth's astonished look, she continued. "You must not give much consideration to my mother's schemes. Darcy is very dear to me as my friend and cousin, and while Mother may wish for a union between Rosings and Pemberley, neither Darcy nor I want a closer relationship. We are too similar for us to achieve the happiness we desire in marriage with each other. Taciturn, shy, and serious, we need partners who will lighten our moods, not sober it. I am only interested in his happiness." *And mine—if I can get Darcy married, Mother may look elsewhere for a union. And where better to look than Matlock?* "I know you admired him. Why have you refused him?"

"Miss de Bourgh, that must remain between Mr. Darcy and me."

Anne was deeply affronted at the abrupt dismissal. She was not used to such treatment, and it was not in her character to stand for it. It did not matter that Elizabeth Bennet's personal affairs were none of her business; she would be satisfied here and now.

Nostrils flaring, the heiress shot back in true *de Bourgh* fashion, "Headstrong, obstinate girl! Can you not see that I am trying to help you? You have surely discussed this with your sisters! Will you not confide in someone who can tell you the particulars of Darcy's character? Are you so in love with your opinions that you cannot have them challenged? Perhaps it is for the best! Perhaps you are not good enough for him!" Miss de Bourgh was furious. She turned to walk out the door.

Elizabeth, stunned at Anne's attack, could not stop herself from crying, "So you think him perfect, do you?"

The lady stopped and then slowly turned back with a smile on her face. "So he insulted you, did he? I should have known. How did he do it?"

Elizabeth, caught out, looked down into her hands. Miss de Bourgh joined her on the bench. "Come, my friend. Tell me what the lovable fool did."

Sighing, Elizabeth told her of Darcy's interference with Jane and Bingley.

Anne's reaction was volatile. "Oh, Darcy! Will you never learn that you cannot solve every problem?" She gave Elizabeth a sad smile.

"Miss Bennet, my unfortunate cousin is unswerving in his devotion to his family and friends. There is nothing he would not do to protect them, even from themselves. If one is among those he loves, he will be their champion forever! Unfortunately, Darcy is also aware of his excellent brain and abilities. He is constantly trying to make better what needs repair, whether the recipient wants his aid or not. Richard and I have warned him of his tendency to involve himself in matters that are better left alone, and he means well, but…" She shrugged. "Perhaps he has finally learned his lesson. Did he not say he would correct his mistake?"

Elizabeth nodded.

"Then you can be as sure of his actions as you are that the sun will rise tomorrow. I hope that gives your sister some relief. But surely, that is not all."

She then told her of Wickham's allegations. "I know them now to be untrue, and I am heartily sorry for taking his side. You had warned Mary. I should have believed her."

Miss de Bourgh looked at her strangely. "How much did Darcy tell you?"

Elizabeth explained that he had told her of Wickham's history at Pemberley.

Anne, suspicious, raised an eyebrow. *Surely, he did not tell her of Georgiana!* "Is that all?"

"No, but I must decline saying anything further."

Miss de Bourgh gasped. "He told you about *Ramsgate*?"

Elizabeth paled. "You know about that?"

Richard had told her months ago. "Yes, but you must say nothing about this to Mother! She has always questioned Darcy's ability to raise Georgiana. Should she become aware of this, she would stop at nothing to take her away." Anne shook her head. "Darcy must trust you, indeed! How could he make such a mess if it?"

Elizabeth looked down. "He was not kind in speaking about my family."

Miss de Bourgh took her hand with a pitying look. "I can image what he said. Poor, poor fool. He was trying to impress you with his struggles—with what he was giving up, I suppose. I can just hear him. Oh, Darcy, you are your own worst enemy!"

Elizabeth bit her lip. "Not everything he said was untrue, though it was uttered with little grace."

"Mary has told me of your family—of your mother and younger sisters. I cannot judge with a mother such as mine." She paused. "How long had you known of Darcy's actions with regards to your sister?"

"Only a few hours. Colonel Fitzwilliam mentioned it in passing while we were walking the grounds."

Anne spurted, "What? In passing? Was—was Miss Bennet in attendance?"

Elizabeth nodded.

"He said that in front of Jane? Good Lord! What on earth for?"

"He believed it was a story worth repeating. He thought it reflected well on Mr. Darcy."

This was Richard's idea of praising Darcy? "Oh! I will wring his blasted, beautiful neck when next we meet!"

"Miss de Bourgh!"

Anne saw she had said too much. Partly to comfort Elizabeth and partly to distract her from her outburst, Anne took the lady's hands in hers. "I am afraid that this is partially my fault, Miss Elizabeth."

"Yours?"

"I asked the colonel to— We wanted to impress— Oh, this is mortifying!" She looked away in humiliation.

Elizabeth looked upon the heiress in wonder. "You have been trying to match me with Mr. Darcy?"

"I am afraid so," Anne admitted. "But I knew nothing of Darcy's advice to Mr. Bingley! I am sorry, Miss Elizabeth."

Elizabeth sighed. "I am sure you meant well."

Anne continued, trying to convince her friend. "We meant everything good, I assure you." She looked up. "Darcy did say he would explain everything to Bingley. Everything will soon be right." She squeezed Elizabeth's hands and grew serious. "Miss Elizabeth, Darcy is his own man. If he decided to offer you marriage, you can be sure that he valued you above all else. That he told you of Ramsgate shows that he trusts you, and Darcy trusts hardly anyone! This alone must show the depth of his feelings. Will you not give him another chance?"

Elizabeth looked away. "My abuses of him must preclude any renewal of his addresses."

Anne knew she was not wholly successful. With regret she said, "I am sure he deserved it. What a muddle. Oh, what fools we mortals be!"

"I assure you, I feel it exceedingly," declared Lady Catherine. "I believe nobody feels the loss of friends so much as I do. But I am particularly attached to these young men and know them to be so much attached to me! They were excessively sorry to go! But so they always are. The dear colonel rallied his spirits tolerably until just at last, but Darcy seemed to feel it most acutely—more, I think, than last year. His attachment to Rosings certainly increases." She leered in Anne's general direction, which caused distress in four ladies' hearts.

"However, I must see to the doorknobs. Darcy had the most unfortunate accident."

"Is that so, Lady Catherine?" asked Mary.

"Indeed! He came down to breakfast the day he and the colonel departed with the most shocking damage to his eye! He said he had slipped and struck his face against the knob of his bedroom door on his way to the floor. Most singular! I must replace the knobs at once!"

"Of course, Lady Catherine!" cried her parson. "A person of your standing cannot have inferior hardware polluting the shades of Rosings!"

"Umm, my dear Lady Catherine," observed Mary, "might it be more economical to see to the rug beside his door? Surely, that was the cause of his mishap."

"Perhaps, perhaps—the rug shall definitely be examined—but I cannot have decorations that injure my guests! The knobs shall certainly be replaced!" Her tone signaled that the discussion was over.

Lady Catherine observed, after dinner, that the Miss Bennets seemed out of spirits. Immediately accounting for it herself by supposing that they did not wish to go home again so soon, she demanded, "You must write to your mother to beg that you may stay a little longer. Mrs. Collins will be very glad of your company, I am sure."

The ladies shared a look. "I am much obliged to your ladyship for your kind invitation," replied Jane, "but it is not in our power to accept it. We must be home Saturday next."

The grand dame was a bit put out. "Why, at that rate, you will have been here only six weeks. I expected you to stay two months. I told Mrs. Collins so before you came. There can be no occasion for your going so soon. Mrs. Bennet could certainly spare you both for another fortnight."

Elizabeth spoke up. "But our father cannot. He wrote last week to hurry our return."

"Oh! Your father, of course, may spare you if your mother can. Daughters are never of so much consequence to a father." She dismissed the idea with a wave of her fan. In a voice that declared she was giving the greatest of gifts, Lady Catherine proclaimed, "And if you will stay another month complete, it will be in my power to take one of you as far as London, for I am going there for a week early in June. There will be very good room for one of you—and indeed, if the weather should happen to be cool, I should not object to taking you both, as you are neither of you large."

Anne blushed at her mother's remark, but Jane responded, "You are all kindness, madam, but I believe we must abide by our original plan."

Lady Catherine surrendered and turned to Mary. "Mrs. Collins, you must send a servant with them. You know I always speak my mind, and I cannot bear the idea of two young women traveling post by themselves. It is highly improper. You must contrive to send somebody. I have the greatest dislike in the world to that sort of thing. Young women should always be properly guarded and attended, according to their situation in life. I am excessively attentive to all those things."

"My father is to send a servant for us," Elizabeth pointed out.

"Oh! He keeps a man, does he?" Elizabeth bit her lip. "I am very glad you have somebody who thinks of those things. Where shall you change horses? Bromley, of course. If you mention my name at The Bell, they will be very attentive to you."

REFLECTION MUST BE RESERVED FOR solitary hours. Whenever Elizabeth was alone, she gave way to it as the greatest relief, and not a day went by without a solitary walk in which she might indulge in all the delight of unpleasant recollections.

So it was that she was in a fair way of soon knowing Mr. Darcy's letter by heart. She studied every sentence, and her feelings towards its writer were at times widely different. When she remembered the style of his address, she was still full of indignation. But when she considered how unjustly she had condemned and upbraided him, her anger was turned against herself, and his disappointed feelings became the object of compassion. His attachment excited gratitude, his general character respect, but she could not for a moment repent her refusal, no matter how Miss de Bourgh sang Mr. Darcy's praises.

Her own past behavior was a constant source of vexation and regret, and the unhappy defects of her family were a source of yet heavier chagrin. They were hopeless. Her father, contented with laughing at them, would never exert himself to restrain the wild giddiness of his youngest daughters. Her mother, with manners so far from propriety herself, was entirely insensible of the evil. Elizabeth had frequently united with Jane in an endeavor to check the imprudent behavior of Kitty and Lydia, but while they were supported by their mother's indulgence, what chance could there be of improvement? Kitty, weak-spirited, irritable, and completely under Lydia's guidance, had been always affronted by their advice. Lydia, self-willed and careless, would scarcely give them a hearing. They were ignorant, idle, and vain. While there was an officer in Meryton, they would flirt with him, and while Meryton was within a walk of Longbourn, they would be going there forever.

Anxiety on Jane's behalf was another prevailing concern for Elizabeth. Mr. Darcy's explanation, by restoring Bingley to her former good opinion, heightened Elizabeth's sense of what Jane had lost. His affection was proved to have been sincere, and his conduct was cleared of all blame, unless any could be attached to his reliance on his friend's opinion. How grievous, then, was the thought that Jane had been deprived of a situation so desirable in every respect, so replete with advantage, so promising for happiness, by the folly and indecorum of her own family!

When to these recollections was added the development of Wickham's character, the happy spirits which had seldom been depressed before, were now so much affected as to make it almost impossible for Elizabeth to appear tolerably cheerful.

The day for leaving was upon them, and to the ladies' surprise, a representative from Rosings was in attendance to see them off.

"Farewell, Miss Bennet, Miss Elizabeth," said Anne de Bourgh. "I hope to see you soon again at Rosings Park. I beg leave to write to you."

The Bennet sisters assured the heiress that they would be happy to correspond with her.

Mr. Collins was beside himself. "Such an honor! I hope, my sisters, you appreciate what condescension has been offered to you by the generous heart of the daughter of my most noble patroness, Lady Catherine de Bourgh!"

"I am sure they do, Mr. Collins," said his wife. "Please see to the coachman. I believe he is in need of your supervision." With her husband so occupied, Mary was able to speak freely with her sisters. "Thank you for your visit. It is said that absence makes the heart grow fonder. If that is so, I fear that my heart will break for missing my sisters! Please write to me as often as you can." She kissed them both, and none was without tears. "Courage, my loves; all will be right soon. Trust in the goodness of our Lord. Goodbye, goodbye!" The party waved as the coach rolled away.

The two sat in some silence as they considered the events of the last six weeks. Finally, Elizabeth broke the stillness.

"Mr. Darcy said he was to speak to Mr. Bingley. Surely, he will be coming back to Netherfield. I am persuaded he will come to see you."

"Perhaps," said Jane quietly. "And you—what do you think of Mr. Darcy now after your conversation with Miss de Bourgh?"

Elizabeth could not say, for she did not know. *Do I want him to renew his addresses, now that I know my opinion of his character and intentions were in error? I should not; my feelings are not what they ought.*

She turned and looked out the window of the carriage. "What I think of Mr. Darcy is of no consequence. Our interview must forever quash whatever tender feeling he may have held for me at one time. I am content. I do not bear him any grudges, Jane, truly. I only hope that he may find his happiness." Elizabeth turned to her sister. "There is one point on which I want your advice before we reach home. I want to be told whether you think we ought to make our acquaintances understand Wickham's character."

Janet paused a little and then replied. "Surely, there can be no occasion for exposing him so dreadfully. What is your own opinion?"

"I believe it ought not to be attempted. Mr. Darcy has not authorized us to make his statements public. Miss de Bourgh seemed shocked that I knew of them and begged me to keep it from her mother. Every particular relative to Mr. Darcy's sister was intended for ourselves alone, and if we endeavor to inform people as to the rest of Mr. Wickham's conduct, who will believe us? Wickham will soon be gone, and there is an end to it and him! At present, I will say nothing about it."

"You are quite right," Jane agreed. "To have his errors made public might ruin him forever. He might now regret what he has done and could be anxious to reestablish a good character. We must not make Mr. Wickham desperate."

THE USUAL CHAOS AWAITED THE sisters at home. Lydia and Kitty met the carriage at Bromley, waving from the windows of the inn. They had brought money to buy a meal, but had spent it all on bonnets and ribbons. Once packed into the carriage, the two girls squealed and argued the entire way home. The only news they brought was that Miss King had gone. Her uncle in Liverpool had recalled her there, and Mr. Wickham was again free as a bird.

"I am sure that Wickham never cared three straws about her," claimed Lydia. "Who could about such a nasty little freckled thing?"

Lydia's joy was tempered by the fact that the militia was removing to Brighton and Mr. Bennet had not seen fit to accompany them there.

"Lizzy, pray speak to Papa about letting us all go to Brighton! He is being so disagreeable about it! But he listens to you. We must go to Brighton!"

The thought of Wickham being far away from Hertfordshire was agreeable to the two eldest occupants in the carriage. "Lydia, do not beg me to go to Father, for if I do, I shall certainly advise him that we *not* go to Brighton."

The next five miles were very unpleasant, but the party arrived at Longbourn without further incident.

They were greeted emotionally by their mother with shrieks of, "Oh, you are both home again, yet unmarried! Oh my nerves!"

And reunited with their father who whispered, "I am glad you are come back, Lizzy, and you, Jane. Very glad indeed."

It was two days before Elizabeth learned of a scheme by which Lydia would remove to Brighton with the militia in the company of Colonel Forster's very young wife, and she decided to speak to her father.

She represented to him all the improprieties of Lydia's general behavior, the little advantage she could derive from the friendship of such a woman as Mrs. Forster, and the probability of her being yet more imprudent with such a companion at Brighton, where the temptations must be greater than at home.

Mr. Bennet heard Elizabeth attentively, and then said, "Lydia will never be easy until she has exposed herself in some public place or other, and we can never expect her to do it with so little expense or inconvenience to her family as under the present circumstances."

"If you were aware," said Elizabeth, "of the very great disadvantage to us all which must arise from the public notice of Lydia's unguarded and imprudent manner—nay, which has already arisen from it—I am sure you would judge differently."

"Already arisen!" repeated Mr. Bennet, chuckling. "What, has she frightened away some of your admirers? Such squeamish youths as cannot bear to be connected with a little absurdity are not worth a regret, Lizzy. Come, let me see the list of the pitiful fellows who have been kept aloof by Lydia's folly."

Elizabeth blushed. "Indeed you are mistaken. I have no such injuries to resent. It is not of particular but of general evils of which I am complaining. Our importance and our respectability in the world must be affected by the wild volatility, the disdain of all restraint which marks Lydia's character. If you, my dear father, will not take the trouble of checking her exuberant spirits and teaching her that her present pursuits are not to be the business of her life, she will soon be beyond the reach of improvement. Lydia's character will be fixed, and she will, at sixteen, be the most determined flirt that ever made herself and her family ridiculous! In this danger Kitty is also involved. She will follow wherever Lydia leads in the pursuit of all that is vain, ignorant, idle, and absolutely uncontrolled! Oh, my dear father, can you suppose it possible that they will not be censured and despised wherever they are known?"

Mr. Bennet saw that Elizabeth's whole heart was in the subject, and affectionately taking her hand, said in reply, "Do not make yourself uneasy, my love. Wherever you and Jane are known, you must be respected and valued. You will not appear to less advantage for having two—or I may say, three—very silly sisters."

Elizabeth flushed at her father's cruel judgment of Mary. She was uncertain of the root of her improved opinion of her sister; she did not know whether it was due to her becoming Mrs. Collins or was a result of spending more time with her. Whatever the cause, Elizabeth now would never call Mary silly.

Her father continued. "We shall have no peace at Longbourn if Lydia does not go to Brighton. Colonel Forster is a sensible man and will keep her out of any real mischief, and she is luckily too poor to be an object of prey to anybody. The officers will find women better worth their notice, mark my words. Let us hope, therefore, that her being there may teach her of own insignificance. At any rate, Lydia cannot grow many degrees worse without authorizing us to lock her up for the rest of her life!" He chuckled at his own jest.

With this answer, Elizabeth was forced to be content, and she left him disappointed and sorry.

IT MIGHT WELL BE IMAGED that, with her quiet demeanor and sanguine disposition, Jane Bennet was not a young lady who felt deeply.

Of course, the reverse was the truth.

She was deeply shocked that Mr. Darcy had convinced Mr. Bingley of her supposed indifference, shocked enough to be angry as well as broken-hearted. Mr. Darcy's unexpected letter and apology had done away with her anger for that gentleman, but the contents of her letter as well as Elizabeth's had affected Jane far more than anyone might have imagined.

Mr. Darcy's observations of her family's conduct had unearthed feelings Jane had not known she possessed. She saw the justice in his charges. Her mother and younger sisters could be mortifying, and as she was not her father's favorite, Jane readily accepted that his caustic wit could be found to be offensive to others, as it had been to herself countless times.

All her life, Jane submerged her occasional unpleasant feelings for her family's actions, telling herself that love must be unconditional, but with the light of truth shining strongly on those emotions, she saw that she had been ill served by this inclination. Hiding undesirable emotions led to masking positive ones, too, when they grew too strong. No wonder an observant man like Mr. Darcy would misconstrue her attachment to Mr. Bingley.

A resolution was made: No longer would she hide her true feelings. Thus liberated, Jane was able to consider her family in an unbiased light. What she saw gave her little comfort. Her father's refusal to heed Lizzy's warnings about Lydia and Brighton only proved his unsuitability as a parent. Someone had to be a responsible person, and since her mother was hopeless, that someone had to be the family's eldest child.

Jane frowned as she recalled her relationship with Mary. They had never been close before Mary's marriage to Mr. Collins. For all the love Jane had for her family, she had reserved the largest portion of her affection for Elizabeth. In Kent, as Jane grew to know Mary better, the more she rose significantly in her esteem. There was a lesson there.

Kitty had long been under the influence of Lydia, and *she* was her mother's daughter. Pretty, frivolous, silly, unfeeling for anyone but herself, Lydia was a dangerous example for someone as easily led as

Kitty. If neither her mother nor her father would be a parent to Kitty, Jane would take the girl in hand. It was her duty as the eldest.

Jane sat alone with her thoughts in the garden a fortnight after her return from Kent, as was her occupation of late, when approaching steps caught her attention. She was only slightly surprised at the sight of Mr. Bingley walking with purpose towards her. She rose as he greeted her.

"Miss Bennet! I am happy—very happy to find you unoccupied today."

Jane, true to her character, submerged her turbulent feelings but remained fully aware of them. "I am happy to see you again. Mr. Bingley. It has been some time."

"Yes." The man was in a state of agitation. "Yes, we have not met since the ball at Netherfield on the twenty-sixth of November. It has been above five months, at least!"

"I believe you are correct." Jane was surprised that he remembered the exact date, a date she knew by heart. "Shall we go inside? My mother would be very pleased to have your company."

"Of course...but may I have a private moment with you first?" At Jane's startled expression, he added, "I must explain my absence from Hertfordshire."

Jane nodded, but she could not speak for the world.

"Miss Bennet, I must tell you that when I was last in Hertfordshire I found your company to be most enjoyable. Indeed, I may safely say that the weeks I spent here were the happiest days of my life. After the ball November last, my family and I removed to our town house in London, as we were to spend Christmas there. In London, people that are very close to me—people whose judgment I have trusted in the past—came to me with their concerns for my happiness. I was led to believe that they had it on good authority I was misinformed as to the depth of our acquaintance and that they were convinced of your indifference to me. This was distressing news, indeed! As I had no reason at the time to doubt the sincerity of their concerns, I gave their opinions far more weight than I ought. But do not think that my thoughts were of a resentful nature! Oh, no! I stayed away from

Netherfield for *your* sake, so that I would no longer injure you with my attentions. Through my disappointment, I believed I thought of nothing but you.

"It is only within the last few days that I have learned I was misinformed. You cannot imagine my happiness to be made aware that my friends were mistaken, and you should know that I felt most severely for the mortification you must have endured. You believed that I had abandoned you, I am sure. How could you feel otherwise? I am ashamed. I resolved to come to Longbourn as soon as may be to offer to you this explanation and apology. Dear Miss Bennet, please forgive this trusting fool. I shall never fail you again."

Jane could not look at Mr. Bingley during this declaration. She fought with her doubts, but at the end of his speech, she forced herself to raise her head. The earnest, eager expression on Mr. Bingley's face settled everything in her mind.

"Mr. Bingley, I thank you for your apology. It is accepted. I am not unaware of the facts you have related. Mr. Darcy, whom I met in Kent, confessed his role in this matter." As Bingley started to speak, she held up her hand. "Have no fear on his part. He apologized for his actions, an apology I would be happy to accept if I felt that he had any reason to offer it. He was only being watchful for the best interest of his particular friend and acted with your happiness in mind. In a like situation, I should not have done differently. He also promised to correct his mistake. Your being here is evidence that he has kept his word. Mr. Darcy remains my friend."

Bingley smiled slightly. "I am glad to hear it."

"So, Mr. Bingley, I do forgive you. Was there anything else you wished to discuss, or shall we now go inside?"

Bingley frowned, but he pressed on. "Miss Bennet, I believe you misunderstand me. I am glad you bear Darcy no animosity, though *I* remain disappointed in him, at least I shall for a little while. However, as he had already a blackened eye, I saw no reason to complete the pair." His jest fell on deaf ears. "I hope I have eased what hurt you have suffered and that we shall be as we were."

Jane could bear no more. "Sir, I must ask. What are your intentions?"

"Miss Bennet, you must know that my intentions are entirely honorable. Miss Bennet...my dear Miss Bennet, please allow me to ask that I may pay court to you. Let me prove my regard. I know my heart now. Will you let me demonstrate the affection I hold for you?"

Jane closed her eyes as Bingley took her hand. Her mind was in a whirl. She reached for the control she utilized when she was embarrassed by her mother's thoughtlessness, her father's neglect, her sisters' silliness and, occasionally, Lizzy's impertinence.

"Mr. Bingley, you may call upon me if you wish. I have no objection to your company. But I beg that you do not speak to my father about a courtship. I feel I must tell you that I doubt you will be successful in your suit."

Bingley was so undone he forgot himself. "What? Do you say he will refuse me?"

Jane knew she would have to be explicit, although she could not look at him. "Mr. Bingley, I enjoy your company. However, I require more than easy manners and an open countenance in the companion of my future life. That person must be a reliable and useful man, one whom my progeny and I may rely upon. I do not wish for my security to be dependent upon the will and opinions of others." She closed her eyes. She would have to be brutal. "I will marry one man, not two."

Bingley blinked. "You...you do not love me?"

Jane turned to him, tears running down her beautiful face. "I said nothing of love, Mr. Bingley, but...but one cannot live on love!" With that, the lady leapt to her feet and ran into the house.

Bingley watched helplessly as Jane fled. His mind could take in nothing except the despair that filled his breast. His Jane—his angel—had rejected him. He could do nothing but mount his horse and ride slowly back to Netherfield, observed by no one except a distraught Elizabeth Bennet from her bedroom window.

JANE EXPECTED THE KNOCK ON her door. "Come in, Lizzy."

Elizabeth peeked around the door. "Are you well?" She moved over to her sister and took her outstretched hand. "I could not help but see your interview with Mr. Bingley. I am so sorry."

Jane nodded. "I assumed you did. You seem to know everything that happens about Longbourn, Sister."

Elizabeth flushed. "I assure you I was not spying on you, Jane!"

No, you were spying on Mr. Bingley. "I believe you, Lizzy. And I am glad you are here."

Elizabeth sat on the bed. "Do you wish to speak of it?"

Jane sighed as she looked away. "I suppose so. Mr. Bingley came to apologize and to ask to court me. I accepted the first and declined the second."

Elizabeth was intently confused. "You forgave him yet rejected him?" Jane nodded. "Oh, Jane, why? Do not his actions speak of his attachment to you?"

Jane began to weep. "Yes, they do. I believe he loves me."

"I do not understand!"

"There is more to this than our feelings! A marriage may be sweet words and caresses in the night, but it is also about providing for a roof over our heads and food on our table. And...a gentleman with an estate has many responsibilities. Do not use our father as a guide. You know what we do for him. If we did not help him, I fear to know what condition Longbourn would have fallen into."

Elizabeth looked into her lap. It was painful to be reminded again of her father's failings. "But Jane, you do not think Mr. Bingley is of the same temperament as Father."

"I do not know! All I know is that he does nothing without Mr. Darcy's guidance!" At Elizabeth's look she added, "Please, I do not blame Mr. Darcy for this. I believe he means to be helpful to his friend, but he cannot—should not—do that forever. Mr. Bingley must know his own mind and be his own master." Her tears redoubled. "Or he is no husband for me!"

She fell into Elizabeth's lap, inconsolable, and Elizabeth could do nothing except hold her, her own thoughts in disarray.

Chapter 9

A Trip to the Peaks

Charles Bingley sat in the study of Netherfield, holding a glass of whiskey, staring into the evening fire. He had eaten nothing since his return from Longbourn, and his only words to the staff were to be left alone. He had much to think on— principally, the words thrown at him like daggers from Jane Bennet.

"I feel I must tell you that I doubt you will be successful in your suit."

"I require more than easy manners and an open countenance in the companion of my future life."

"I will marry one man, not two."

"Deuce take it!" he cried out loud. "This is Darcy's fault!" His thrown glass shattered in the fireplace.

That was crystal. Bingley shook his head at his own stupidity. *You are a damn fool, Charles! This is not Darcy's fault any more than breaking that glass is Darcy's fault. This is my fault—my blasted wariness. Perhaps Father was right. I will never live up to the kind of gentleman he wanted.*

His mind flowed back to his demanding father. He pushed and prodded his children. *They* would never live like tradesmen. No, they would take their place in society, and Charles would be the master of a great estate. He had been given the best schools, the best clothes, the best connections.

But how do you run *an estate, Father?* Charles wondered. That had not been a part of his upbringing.

Louisa and Caroline succeeded in becoming the superficial people who were his father's idea of landed gentry. Charles never seemed to meet his demanding expectations. Where his father was hard, Charles was soft. Where his father was suspicious, Charles was trusting. Where his father was frugal, Charles was generous.

Am I really such a failure, Father?

The only way he could earn his father's grudging respect was to be always correct—to have the best grades, to make no mistakes. That was part of the reason Charles had made such a friend as Fitzwilliam Darcy in school. Darcy was brilliant. He knew everything, and what he didn't know, he knew where to go to find the answer. Until Jane, Darcy had never steered him wrong.

Charles had felt such resentment and then amazement at Darcy's confession not two days earlier. It was but a moment's work to heartily forgive his friend and make arrangements to return to Netherfield. Minimal staff attended to him now; it was all he could arrange at short notice. He thought to open the rest of the house after his interview with Jane, assuming Darcy approved.

"I do not wish for my security to be dependent upon the will and opinions of others," she had said.

Bingley brooded as he stared into the dying fire. He had tried so hard not to make a mistake, and now that turned out to be the biggest mistake of his life. Jane was right. He had relied too much on others. It was time to be his own man. But lord, how was he to do that?

"Mr. Bingley, you may call upon me if you wish. I have no objection to your company."

Did he have a chance? Could he prove himself to her? Did he have a choice?

"I enjoy your company. However, I require more than easy manners and an open countenance in the companion of my future life. That person must be a reliable and useful man, one whom my progeny and I may rely upon. I do not wish for my security to be dependent upon the will and opinions of others. I will marry one man, not two."

"You do not love me?" He had asked her.

"I said nothing of love, Mr. Bingley, but…but one cannot live on love!"

Bingley never felt so wretched in his life. *I have no choice. I must learn how to live without Darcy because I cannot live without Jane.*

·

ELIZABETH WAS NOW TO SEE Mr. Wickham for the last time. On the final day of the regiment's remaining in Meryton, he dined with others of the officers at Longbourn. So little was Elizabeth disposed to part from him in good humor that on his making some enquiry as to the manner in which her time had passed at Hunsford, she mentioned Colonel Fitzwilliam and Mr. Darcy's having spent three weeks at Rosings and asked him if he were acquainted with the colonel.

Wickham looked surprised and displeased, but with a moment's recollection and a returning smile, he replied that he had formerly seen him often. After observing that Colonel Fitzwilliam was a very gentlemanlike man, he asked Elizabeth how she had liked him. She answered warmly in the colonel's favor.

With an air of indifference, Mr. Wickham soon afterwards added, "How long did you say that he was at Rosings?"

"Nearly three weeks."

"And you saw him frequently?"

"Yes, and my sister, too, almost every day."

"His manners are very different from his cousin's."

"Yes, very different. But I think Mr. Darcy improves on acquaintance."

"Indeed!" cried Wickham with a stern look that did not escape her. He added in a gayer tone, "Is it in address that he improves? Has Mr. Darcy deigned to add ought of civility to his ordinary style? For I dare not hope that he is improved in essentials."

"Oh, no!" said Elizabeth with sly smile. "In essentials, I believe, he is very much what he ever was. When I said that he improved on acquaintance, I did not mean that either his mind or manners were in a state of improvement, but that from knowing him better, his disposition was better understood."

Wickham's alarm now appeared in his heightened complexion

and agitated look, and Elizabeth rejoiced at nettling him. For a few minutes, he was silent until, shaking off his embarrassment, he turned to her again and said in the gentlest voice, "You, who so well know my feelings towards Mr. Darcy, will readily comprehend how sincerely I must rejoice that he is wise enough to assume even the appearance of what is right. I imagine this is merely adopted on his visits to his aunt, of whose good opinion and judgment he stands much in awe, and towards forwarding the match with Miss de Bourgh."

Elizabeth could not repress a smile at this, but she answered only by a slight inclination of the head. She saw that he wanted to engage her on the old subject of his grievances, and she was in no humor to indulge him. The rest of the evening passed with the appearance of usual cheerfulness on his side, but with no further attempt to converse with Elizabeth, and they parted with mutual civility and a mutual desire of never meeting again.

Yes, go away, you villain. May I never see you again!

LYDIA SET OUT EARLY THE next morning for Brighton. The separation between her and her family was rather more noisy than pathetic. Kitty was the only one who shed tears, but she wept from vexation and envy. Mrs. Bennet was diffuse in her good wishes for the felicity of her daughter and impressive in her injunctions that she should not miss the opportunity of enjoying herself as much as possible. It was advice that Lydia was sure to follow. In the clamorous happiness of Lydia's bidding farewell, the more gentle *adieus* of her sisters were uttered without being heard.

Had Elizabeth's opinion been drawn only from her family, she could not have formed a very pleasing picture of conjugal felicity or domestic comfort. Her father, captivated by youth and beauty, had married a woman whose weak understanding and illiberal mind had, very early in their marriage, put an end to any real affection for her. Respect, esteem, and confidence had vanished forever, and all Mr. Bennet's views of domestic happiness were overthrown.

Neither Jane nor Elizabeth had been blind to the impropriety of their father's behavior as a husband. They had always seen it with pain, but respecting his abilities and grateful for his affectionate treatment of them, they endeavored to forget what they could not overlook and to banish from their thoughts that continual breach of decorum that, in exposing his wife to the contempt of her own children, was so highly reprehensible.

The time fixed for the beginning of the Gardiner's northern tour was now fast approaching, and Jane was to go with them. A fortnight only was wanting of it, when a letter arrived from Mrs. Gardiner that at once delayed its commencement and curtailed its extent.

Mr. Gardiner was needed in London again within a month, and as that left too short a period for them to go so far and see so much as they had proposed, they were obliged to give up the Lakes and substitute a more contracted tour. They were to go no farther northward than Derbyshire.

Mrs. Gardiner had a peculiarly strong attraction to that county. The town where she had formerly passed some years of her life, and where they were now to spend a few days, was probably as great an object of her curiosity as all the celebrated beauties of Matlock, Chatsworth, Dovedale, or the Peaks.

Jane was sanguine, but Elizabeth was excessively disappointed. She had set her heart on seeing the Lakes and still thought there might have been time enough, but it was her business to be satisfied and certainly her temper to be happy, and all was soon right again.

With the mention of Derbyshire, there were many ideas connected. It was impossible for Jane to see the word without thinking of Pemberley and its owner, both of which she mentioned to her sister.

"But surely," responded Elizabeth, "Derbyshire is a rather large county. I may enter his county with impunity, I am sure." Her private anxieties she kept to herself.

Mr. and Mrs. Gardiner with their four children at length appeared at Longbourn. The children, two girls of six and eight years old and two younger boys, were to be left under the particular care of their cousin Kitty. While not the general favorite that Jane was and without her sister's steady sense and sweetness of temper, Kitty's exuberance for the task exactly adapted her for attending to them in many ways, such as playing with them and loving them.

In a private interview with Kitty, Jane advised her, "My dear sister, you are now responsible for our little cousins. It is a heavy burden, I know, but it is one you must bear, for there is no one else. Our mother is not of the temperament to diligently care for another's children, even if they are her nieces and nephews."

Kitty blinked at Jane's direct words. "Oh, Jane, I am frightened! It is such a responsibility! I do not know whether I am able to properly care for four children under the age of nine!"

"Trust in your heart! You know what is right. Mrs. Hill will be here, and she will help." Jane smiled. "I know you can do this. When in doubt, do as I would do."

Jane's confidence had the desired effect, and Kitty relaxed in the face of such trust in her abilities. It was a new experience for her, for no one had said such encouraging words to her before.

The Gardiners stayed only one night at Longbourn and set off the next morning with Jane and Elizabeth in pursuit of novelty and amusement.

"Mr. Bingley," intoned the butler, "Mr. Darcy to see you."

Bingley looked up from his paperwork in surprise. "Show him in."

Darcy walked in, showing only a hint of the nervousness he felt. His heart warmed at Bingley's address. "Darce! Come in, my dear fellow!"

Darcy gestured at Bingley's desk, overflowing with papers. "I hope I do not disturb you."

"This? These are reports from my steward at Netherfield as well as a few abstracts discussing the new methods of farming. Would you care to take a look?"

"I should be happy to." A few minutes perusal was all that was needed for Darcy to exclaim, "Allow me to say that I am impressed with the improvements to your fields. Your hard work has born good fruit."

"Coming from you, that is high praise indeed!" The two friends fell into a discussion over crop rotation. Once that subject had been thoroughly explored and a glass of wine consumed, Bingley asked, "Now, while I enjoy our discussions, am I right in supposing you had another reason to call on me today?"

"Indeed I did—to see you and offer an invitation. Georgiana and I are returning north and wondered whether you would like to accompany us."

"To Pemberley?" At Darcy's nod, Bingley frowned. "I...I do not know, Darce. I have much to do."

Darcy felt sick at Bingley's dark mood. He had known of Miss Bennet's rejection of his friend and felt not a little guilty. Had he only held his tongue, his friend would have been happily married by now!

"Come, Charles, you need a bit of diversion. It is obvious your new steward has things well in hand. The shooting will be at its peak in Derbyshire. I must have you use this new double-barreled gun I have just purchased."

"If you just bought it, would you not wish to use it yourself?"

"It is tempting, to be sure, but as you are such a bad shot, I will still get the lion's share of the coveys no matter what I shoot."

"Balderdash! I outshot you last time! Do you not remember?" Bingley caught the grin Darcy was trying to hide. "Oh, very well. But I cannot go alone."

Darcy blanched. "Caroline?"

"Yes. Sorry, old man, but I was to go to Scarborough with her and the Hursts."

"They are welcomed too, Charles."

Bingley laughed. "It is well to see there is something you cannot do, Darcy! You are the worst liar I have ever met! Come, we will go with you. It will give us something to do rather than think of...what could have been."

Darcy wore a rueful smile. He had confided to Bingley that Elizabeth Bennet had rejected his offer in Kent when he confessed his interference with Miss Bennet.

"Yes, let us make merry together in Derbyshire."

It was to the little town of Lambton, the scene of Mrs. Gardiner's former residence where she had lately learned that some acquaintances still remained, that the party from Hertfordshire arrived after having seen all the principal wonders of Derbyshire. The Bennet girls learned from their aunt that Pemberley was within five miles of Lambton. It was not in their direct road, but not more than a mile or two out of it. In talking over their route the evening before, Mrs. Gardiner expressed an inclination to see the place again. Mr. Gardiner declared his willingness, and Jane was applied to for her approbation.

She glanced at her sister. "I have no opinion on the matter. I leave it to Lizzy."

"My love, should not you like to see a place of which you have heard so much?" asked her aunt. "A place, too, with which so many of your acquaintance are connected. Mr. Wickham passed all his youth there, you know."

Elizabeth was distressed. She felt that she had no business at Pemberley and was obliged to assume a disinclination for seeing it. She said that she was tired of great houses; after going over so many, she really had no pleasure in fine carpets or satin curtains.

"If it were merely a fine house richly furnished," said Mrs. Gardiner, "I should not care about it myself, but the grounds are delightful. They have some of the finest woods in the country."

Elizabeth said no more, but her mind could not acquiesce. The possibility of meeting Mr. Darcy while viewing the place instantly occurred to her. It would be dreadful! She blushed at the very idea, but felt she could not further object without explaining herself to an embarrassing degree.

Jane was of like mind, for she knew of her sister's distress. Accordingly, when she retired at night, she asked the chambermaid if she knew whether the family was residing at Pemberley for the summer. A most welcome negative response followed the question, and Jane swiftly relayed the information to her sister.

Her alarm being now removed, Elizabeth was at leisure to feel a great deal of curiosity to see the house herself. When the subject was revived the next morning and she was again applied to, Elizabeth could readily answer with a proper air of indifference that she had no dislike to the scheme.

To Pemberley, therefore, they were to go.

THE BENNET GIRLS, AS THEY drove along, watched for the first appearance of Pemberley Woods with some uneasiness, and when at length they turned in at the lodge, their spirits were in a high flutter. The park was very large and contained great variety of ground. They entered it in one of its lowest points, and drove for some time through a beautiful wood, stretching over a wide extent.

Elizabeth's mind was too full for conversation, but she saw and admired every remarkable spot and point of view. They gradually ascended for a half-mile and then found themselves at the top of a considerable eminence where the wood ceased, and the eye was instantly caught by Pemberley House, situated on the opposite side of a valley.

It was a large, handsome, stone building, standing well on rising ground and backed by a ridge of high woody hills. In front, a stream swelled. Its banks were neither formal nor falsely adorned and without any artificial appearance. Elizabeth was delighted. She had never seen a place for which nature had done more, or where natural beauty had been so little counteracted by an awkward taste. They were all of them warm in their admiration, and at that moment, Elizabeth felt that to be mistress of Pemberley might be something!

The carriage descended the hill, crossed the bridge, and drove to the door. While examining the nearer aspect of the house, all of Elizabeth's apprehensions of meeting its owner returned. On applying to see the place, they were admitted into the hall, and Elizabeth, as they waited for the housekeeper, had leisure to wonder at her being where she was.

The housekeeper, Mrs. Reynolds, was a respectable-looking, elderly woman, much less fine and more civil than Elizabeth had any notion of finding her. They followed her into the dining-parlor.

No gold leaf here! Elizabeth thought impishly to herself.

It was a large, well-proportioned room, handsomely fitted. Elizabeth, after slightly surveying it, went to a window to enjoy its prospect.

The hill, crowned with wood, from which they had descended, was a beautiful object. Every disposition of the ground was good, and Elizabeth looked on the whole scene with delight—the river, the trees scattered on its banks, and the winding of the valley as far as she could trace it. As they passed into other rooms, from every window there were beauties to be seen. The rooms were lofty and handsome, and their furniture suitable to the fortune of their proprietor, but Elizabeth saw, with admiration of his taste, that it was neither gaudy nor uselessly fine, with less of splendor and more real elegance than the furniture of Rosings.

And of this place, I might have been mistress! With these rooms, I might now have been familiarly acquainted! Instead of viewing them as a stranger, I might have rejoiced in them as my own and welcomed to them as visitors my uncle and aunt.

But no, that could never be! My uncle and aunt would have been lost to me. I should not have been allowed to invite them.

"And your master is away?" asked Mr. Gardiner.

"Aye, that he is," Mrs. Reynolds replied, adding, "but we expect him tomorrow with a large party of friends."

Elizabeth's eyes sought her sister's. How happy they were that their own journey had not by any circumstance been delayed a day!

Her aunt now called her to look at a picture. Elizabeth approached and saw the likeness of Mr. Wickham suspended, amongst several other miniatures, over the mantelpiece. Her aunt smiled and asked her how she liked it.

The housekeeper came forward and sniffed. "*That* young gentleman is the son of my late master's steward and was brought up at the Darcy family's expense. He is now gone into the army, but I am afraid he has turned out very wild." Mrs. Gardiner looked at her niece with a smile, but Elizabeth could not return it.

"And that," said Mrs. Reynolds with a smile, pointing to another of the miniatures, "is my master—and very like him."

"I have heard much of your master's fine person," said Mrs. Gardiner, looking at the picture. "It is a handsome face, but, Lizzy, you can tell us whether it is his like or not."

Mrs. Reynolds seemed surprised at Elizabeth knowing her master. "Does that young lady know Mr. Darcy?"

"My sister and I know him a little."

"And do you ladies not think him a very handsome gentleman?"

Jane answered quietly, "Yes, very handsome."

"I am sure I know none so handsome." Mrs. Reynolds then directed their attention to one of Miss Darcy, drawn when she was only eight years old.

"And is Miss Darcy as handsome as her brother?" asked Mr. Gardiner.

"Oh, yes! The handsomest young lady that ever was seen and so accomplished! She plays and sings all day long. In the next room is a new instrument just came down for her—a present from my master. She comes here tomorrow with him."

"He is certainly a good brother," said Jane.

"And this is always the way with him. Whatever can give his sister any pleasure is sure to be done in a moment. There is nothing he would not do for her."

Mr. Gardiner continued the conversation. "Is your master much at Pemberley in the course of the year?"

"Not so much as I could wish, sir, but I dare say he may spend half his time here, and Miss Darcy is always down for the summer months."

"If your master would marry, you might see more of him."

"Yes, sir, but I do not know when that will be. I do not know who is good enough for him." At Mr. and Mrs. Gardiner's smile, Mrs. Reynolds continued. "I say no more than the truth and what every-body will say that knows him! I have never had a cross word from him in my life, and I have known him ever since he was four years old. I have always observed that they who are good-natured when children are good-natured when they grow up, and he was always the sweetest-tempered, most generous-hearted boy in the world.

"Some people call him proud, but I am sure I never saw anything of it. To my fancy, it is only because he does not rattle away like other young men."

"This fine account of him," whispered her aunt to Elizabeth as they walked, "is not quite consistent with his behavior to our poor friend."

Elizabeth was mortified. "Perhaps we might be deceived."

"That is not very likely; our authority was too good."

No, our authority was not good at all.

In the gallery there were many family portraits. Elizabeth walked on in quest of the only face whose features would be known to her. At last it arrested her, and she beheld a striking resemblance of Mr. Darcy, with such a smile over the face as she remembered to have sometimes seen when he looked at her. She felt a twisting sensation in her chest as she again realized the extent of her folly. She stood several minutes before the picture in earnest contemplation, feeling Jane's gaze on her, and returned to it again before they quitted the gallery. Mrs. Reynolds informed them that it had been taken in his father's lifetime.

At this moment in Elizabeth's mind, there was certainly the gentlest sensation towards Mr. Darcy that she had ever felt in the height of their acquaintance. The commendation bestowed on him by Mrs. Reynolds was of no trifling nature.

What praise is more valuable than the praise of an intelligent servant? As a brother, a landlord, a master, how many people's happiness is in your guardianship! How much pleasure or pain was in your power to bestow! How much good or evil must be done by you!

Every idea that had been brought forward by the housekeeper was favorable to Mr. Darcy's character, and as she stood before the canvas on which he was represented and fixed her eyes upon it, Elizabeth thought of his regard with a deeper sentiment of gratitude than had ever risen before. She remembered its warmth and softened its impropriety of expression.

When the entire house that was open to general inspection had been seen, the party returned downstairs and, taking leave of the housekeeper, were consigned over to the gardener, who met them at the hall door. As they walked across the lawn towards the river, Elizabeth turned back to look again. Her uncle, aunt and sister stopped also, and while conjecturing as to the date of the building—

The owner of it himself suddenly came forward from the road which led behind it to the stables.

The only sound was Jane's sudden intake of breath.

Elizabeth and Darcy were within twenty yards of each other, and so abrupt was his appearance, that it was impossible to avoid his sight. Their eyes instantly met, and the cheeks of each were overspread with the deepest blush. He absolutely started, and for a moment seemed immoveable from surprise, but shortly recovering himself, he advanced towards the party.

He spoke to Elizabeth, if not in terms of perfect composure, at least of perfect civility. "Miss Elizabeth! I hope I find you well."

"Mr. Darcy! I...I am well, thank you." She had instinctively turned away, but stopping on his approach, received his compliments with an embarrassment impossible to be overcome.

Jane immediately came to her sister's aid. "Mr. Darcy. Good day, sir. We had no idea that you were at home."

Had his first appearance, or his resemblance to the picture they had just been examining, been insufficient to assure the Gardiners that they now saw Mr. Darcy, the gardener's expression of surprise on beholding his master must immediately have told it. They stood a little distance away while he was talking to their nieces.

"Miss Bennet, I am happy to see you. Is your family well?" He spoke to Jane, but Elizabeth saw that his eyes were more frequently on her.

"They are in good health, sir."

"Are you visiting the neighborhood?"

"Yes, we are."

"Where are you staying?"

Elizabeth willed herself to speak. "At the Green Man, in Lambton."

Amazed at the alteration in his manner since they last parted, every sentence that he uttered was increasing her embarrassment, every idea of the impropriety of her being found there recurring to her mind, and the few minutes in which they continued together were some of the most uncomfortable of her life.

"Ah...yes, fine inn, that. Your family, are they well?"

Jane smiled. "They are well."

Darcy did not seem much more at ease. When he spoke, his accent had none of its usual sedateness, and he repeated his enquiries as to the time of her having left Longbourn and of her stay in Derbyshire so often and in so hurried a way, as plainly spoke the distraction of his thoughts. At length, every idea seemed to fail him, and after standing a few moments without saying a word, he suddenly recollected himself and took his leave.

The others then joined them and expressed their admiration of his figure, but Elizabeth heard not a word and, wholly engrossed by her own feelings, followed them in silence. She was overpowered by shame and vexation.

My coming here is the most unfortunate, the most ill-judged thing in the world! How strange must it appear to him! In what a disgraceful light I must appear! It must seem as if I have purposely thrown myself in his way again! Oh, why did I come?

His behavior is so strikingly altered; what could it mean? That he should even speak to me is amazing! But to speak with such civility, to enquire after my family!

Only Jane seemed aware of Elizabeth's inner struggle, but with her aunt and uncle remaining so close at hand, she could not act.

They had now entered a beautiful walk by the side of the water, and every step brought forward a nobler fall of ground or a finer reach of the woods, but it was some time before Elizabeth was sensible of any of it. Though she answered mechanically to the repeated appeals of her uncle and aunt and seemed to direct her eyes to such objects as they pointed out, she distinguished no part of the scene.

The others had walked enough ahead for Jane to attempt to talk to Elizabeth.

"My dear sister! How can you bear it?"

"Oh, Jane! What must he think of me?"

"He seemed to meet you with pleasure."

"With pain or pleasure, I cannot say. He certainly had not met me with composure!" *In defiance of everything, am I still dear to him? Oh, what is he thinking?*

They crossed by a simple bridge. It was a spot less adorned than any they had yet visited, and the valley, here contracted into a glen, allowed room only for the stream and a narrow walk amidst the rough coppice-wood that bordered it. Elizabeth longed to explore its windings, but when they had crossed the bridge and perceived their distance from the house, Mrs. Gardiner, who was not a great walker, could go no farther and thought only of returning to the carriage as quickly as possible.

Her nieces were, therefore, obliged to submit, and they took their way towards the house on the opposite side of the river, in the nearest direction. Their progress was slow, for Mr. Gardiner, though seldom able to indulge the taste, was very fond of fishing and was so much engaged in watching the occasional appearance of some trout in the water and talking to the gardener about them that he advanced but little.

Whilst wandering on in this slow manner, they were astonished by the sight of Mr. Darcy approaching them. The walk being less sheltered than on the other side allowed them to see him before they met. Elizabeth, however surprised, was at least more prepared for an interview than before and resolved to appear and to speak with calmness.

With a glance, Elizabeth saw that he had lost none of his recent civility, and to imitate his politeness, she began, "Mr. Darcy, I must say that your home is lovely, charming, and delightful. I am sorry to intrude upon you. Had we known you were to be here, we would not have troubled you."

Darcy's eyes were both warm and nervous. *Why, he is shy!* she realized with a start. *How is it I have never realized that before?*

"Ladies, I am truly happy to welcome you to Pemberley. Forgive my abrupt welcome. I was not properly prepared to greet guests." He indicated his change of clothes. "I am now armed to play the host to you." He indicated the others. "Will you do me the honor of introducing me to your friends?"

This was a gesture for which Elizabeth was quite unprepared, and she could hardly suppress a smile at his seeking the acquaintance of some of those very people against whom his pride had revolted in his offer to her.

Jane made the introductions, and Elizabeth could not but be pleased, could not but triumph at his more than cordial response. It was consoling that he should know she had *some* relations for whom there was no need to blush. She listened most attentively to all that passed between them and gloried in every expression, every sentence of her uncle that marked his intelligence, his taste, or his good manners.

The conversation soon turned to fishing, and she heard Mr. Darcy invite Mr. Gardiner to fish at Pemberley as often as he chose while in the neighborhood, offering at the same time to supply him with fishing tackle and pointing out those parts of the stream where there was usually the most sport.

Mrs. Gardiner, who was walking arm-in-arm with her two nieces, gave Elizabeth a look expressive of her wonder. Elizabeth said nothing, but it gratified her exceedingly. Her astonishment, however, was extreme.

Why is he so altered? From what can it proceed? It cannot be for me. It cannot be for my sake that his manners are thus softened. My reproofs at Hunsford could not work such a change as this. I should say that he still loves me if I did not know it to be impossible.

Soon Mrs. Gardiner grew fatigued by the exercise of the morning, and finding her nieces' arms inadequate to her support, joined her husband. Mr. Darcy took her place by her nieces, one on each arm, and they walked on together.

After a short silence, it was Elizabeth who first spoke. "Mr. Darcy, your housekeeper informed us that you would certainly not be here till tomorrow."

"True, but as I had business with my steward, I rode on ahead. My party will join me early tomorrow, and among them are some who will claim an acquaintance with you both." Here he glanced at Jane. "Mr. Bingley and his sisters."

Jane colored, but for Elizabeth's sake, she said, "How lovely! I hope they are in good health."

Darcy did not answer the lady, but to Elizabeth he said, "There is also one other person in the party who more particularly wishes to be known to you. Will you allow me, or do I ask too much, to introduce my sister to your acquaintance during your stay at Lambton?"

The surprise of such an application was great indeed. "Miss Darcy? I should be pleased—Jane?"

Jane smiled. "I would be delighted to meet her and to be reacquainted with the Bingleys."

They now walked on in silence, each of them deep in thought.

Neither Bennet girl was comfortable—that was impossible—but Elizabeth was flattered and pleased. Mr. Darcy's wish of introducing his sister to her was a compliment of the highest kind.

Soon the driveway was achieved, and after the ladies declined refreshments, Mr. Darcy handed them into the carriage. As it drove off, Elizabeth saw him walking slowly towards the house, watching their progress.

MR. GARDINER EXCLAIMED AS SOON as it was acceptable, "Mr. Darcy is perfectly well behaved, polite, and unassuming."

"There is something stately in him to be sure," replied his wife, "but it is confined to his air and is not unbecoming. I can now agree with the housekeeper that though some people may call him proud, I have seen nothing of it. To be sure, Lizzy, he is decidedly handsome! But how came you to tell us that he was so disagreeable?"

Elizabeth said that she had liked him better when they met in Kent than before, and that she had never seen him so pleasant as this morning.

"But perhaps he may be a little whimsical in his civilities," replied her uncle. "Your great men often are and, therefore, I shall not take him at his word about fishing, as he might change his mind another day and warn me off his grounds."

Jane now came to his defense. "Uncle, you have entirely mistaken Mr. Darcy's character. If he invited you to fish, I believe you may rely on it."

"From what we have seen of him," continued Mrs. Gardiner, "I really should not have thought that he could have behaved in so cruel a way by anybody as he has done by poor Wickham. He has not an ill-natured look. On the contrary, there is something pleasing about his mouth when he speaks. And there is something of dignity in his countenance that would not give one an unfavorable opinion of him. But to be sure, the good lady who showed us the house did give him a most flaming character! I could hardly help laughing aloud at times. But he is a liberal master, I suppose, and that, in the eye of a servant, demonstrates every virtue."

Elizabeth glanced at Jane. She felt compelled to say something in vindication of Mr. Darcy's behavior to Mr. Wickham and, therefore, gave them to understand, in as guarded a manner as she could, that by what she had heard from his relations in Kent, his actions and his character were by no means faulty, nor Wickham's so amiable, as they had been considered in Hertfordshire.

In confirmation of this, Jane related the particulars of all the pecuniary transactions in which they had been connected, without actually naming her authority, but stating it to be such as might be relied on.

Mrs. Gardiner was surprised and concerned. "But why have you told us nothing of this before?"

Again after exchanging glances with her sister, Elizabeth replied, "I did not wish to speak of something I was told but not certain of."

Speaking with love and kindness, her aunt returned, "Then this is a changed Elizabeth, indeed."

Chapter 10

Tea at Pemberley

The Bennet girls had determined that Mr. Darcy would bring his sister to visit two days hence. But their conclusion was false, for the very next morning, visitors came. The sisters had been walking about the place with some of their new friends and just returned to the inn when the sound of the parlor-maid knocking on the door announced visitors.

"Mr. and Miss Darcy to see you, sir."

Miss Darcy and her brother appeared, and the introductions were made. Elizabeth was astonished to see that her new acquaintance seemed just as embarrassed as they were. She had been told by Wickham that Miss Darcy was exceedingly proud, but the observation of a very few minutes convinced Elizabeth that she was only exceedingly shy. *Like her brother!*

Miss Darcy was taller than Elizabeth, and though little more than sixteen, her figure was well formed, her appearance womanly and graceful. Her countenance reflected sense and good humor, and her manners were perfectly unassuming and gentle. Elizabeth, who had expected to find in her as acute and unembarrassed an observer as Mr. Darcy, was much relieved by discerning different feelings.

Their conversation was interrupted by Mr. Darcy. He spoke to Mr.

Gardiner, but his eyes were on Jane. "My friend, Mr. Bingley, waits outside and wishes to visit. May I bring him in?"

Mr. Gardiner looked at his niece, and even though her color was high, he granted permission.

Elizabeth saw that Jane was in a quandary. Her sister had only just steeled herself for meeting Mr. Bingley at some undetermined point in the future, but now that time was at hand. How Elizabeth stopped from clutching Jane's hand in support she did not know. To her relief, when Bingley walked in a moment later, Jane was able to return his greeting with civility.

Bingley's features and manners were all that she remembered, but there seemed a reserve that was new to him. When he glanced at her, Elizabeth could see a ghost of pain that seemed to darken his blue eyes.

"I am very surprised to see you here, Miss Bennet," Bingley said, "but glad, too. Was your journey enjoyable?"

"It was, sir. I had not had much chance to see the world, and my uncle was very kind to take us. Derbyshire is lovely."

"It is a pretty country, but there are many lovely spots in Britain. I have found Hertfordshire much to my liking."

"Indeed, sir? I should not disagree with you, as I have lived there all my life. Do you plan to stay at Netherfield?"

"Yes, I do. The place suits me, I think. I have begun improvements to it, you know."

She did not, and confessed her ignorance.

"Oh, yes. The property is very good but has lacked serious management. Fortunately, the new steward and I are of like minds about what needs to be done. Take the pastureland..."

Elizabeth, conversing with the charmingly modest Georgiana, allowed herself to steal a glance at the others from time to time. She was relieved that Jane and Bingley could converse in an increasingly comfortable manner, and she was pleased beyond measure that Darcy had taken the opportunity to become better acquainted with the Gardiners. Never, even in the company of his dear friends at Netherfield or his dignified relations at Rosings, had she seen him so desirous to please, so free from self-consequence or unbending reserve as now.

As he knows them better, he is more relaxed. I am such a fool!

"Four sisters," Georgiana was saying. "Oh, I should love to have sisters."

Elizabeth could not help herself. "With such a brother, I do not understand why."

The girl blushed. "He is the best brother in the world. I do not deserve him." Elizabeth saw the distress on the girl's face, and her anger at the perpetrator of her anguish was rekindled. She impulsively reached for her hand.

"You are mistaken, I am sure. I believe you deserve every good thing in the world." She looked at Darcy. "Your brother thinks so, and we both know that Mr. Darcy is never wrong."

Their visitors stayed with them over a half-hour, and when they arose to depart, Mr. Darcy called on his sister to join him in expressing their wish of seeing Mr. and Mrs. Gardiner and the Miss Bennets to dinner at Pemberley before they left the country. It was clear to all that Miss Darcy was little in the habit of issuing invitations, but she readily obeyed. Mrs. Gardiner looked at her nieces and, satisfied that Jane was not opposed and Elizabeth was eager, accepted with gratitude.

The sisters wanted nothing but to retire to their shared room to discuss the morning's activities, but their desire was thwarted by their aunt.

"Girls, we have been making inquiries throughout Lambton, and I must say that Mr. Wickham is not held in much estimation. It is said he leaves debts wherever he goes." It was plain that her loyalties had switched from "poor Mr. Wickham" to "charming Mr. Darcy."

"Indeed," added their uncle, "and to our wonderment, it seems that Mr. Darcy has been known to settle his debts in full. A remarkable gentleman." His eye fell upon Elizabeth during this statement, but she refused to acknowledge it.

The group then settled that such a striking civility as Miss Darcy's coming to them on the very day of her arrival at Pemberley ought to be met by some exertion of politeness on their side. Consequently, they decided it would be civil to wait on her at Pemberley the following morning. Mr. Gardiner would also go there. The fishing scheme had been renewed and a positive engagement made of his meeting some of the gentlemen at Pemberley by noon.

THE CARRIAGE RIDE BACK TO Pemberley was quiet, as the three passengers were lost in thought. Georgiana was overjoyed at finally meeting the Miss Elizabeth Bennet she had heard about *ad nauseam*. She found her as lovely and kind as Fitzwilliam and Richard had described and far more refined than Caroline Bingley had suggested. Georgiana liked Miss Elizabeth very much and was perfectly prepared to love her and all of her relations. The girl's remark of wishing for a sister was no slip of the tongue. Might her brother have finally found his happiness? She hoped that future interactions with the Bennet sisters while they visited Derbyshire might give Fitzwilliam a chance to propose.

Charles Bingley fought the urge to leap out of the carriage and run back to the inn. Initially, Jane Bennet was very reserved during their *tête-à-tête*, but as Bingley talked about Netherfield and the passion he now had for his home, he could almost feel her esteem radiate from her. Bingley's pride in his estate was no play-acting, for he felt that he at last had found his place in the world. Should he prove himself to his angel— No, she was not *his* angel. Not now. But perhaps there was hope for his suit?

Fitzwilliam Darcy tried not to hope. He was thankful for this chance to prove that Elizabeth's criticisms finally had been taken to heart. He still had held some resentment for her refusal when he had returned to London. But it was during his humiliating confession with Bingley, when he had revealed all, including her refusal, that he admitted to himself that he had been totally in the wrong. He could not understand how he could have been so arrogant, so presumptuous, to a woman he claimed to adore. Many days and nights were spent in painful contemplation before Darcy came to the realization that, while he was master of a great estate and owner of a large fortune, in truth, Elizabeth Bennet was his superior in all ways that truly mattered.

He was uncomfortable with those he did not know, so he withdrew, suspicious of their motives. Elizabeth enjoyed people, no matter their station, and tried to place them at ease.

"Had you behaved in a more gentleman-like manner."

Darcy closed his eyes. How those words burned! Yes, he had lost his opportunity to claim her as his own, yet he would still do right by his lady-love.

Even if she did not love him in return.

"LIZZY, HE STILL LOVES YOU," Jane began once the sisters finally achieved the privacy they so desperately desired. "Do not look at me in that manner; I know of what I speak."

Elizabeth would not hear of it. "He cannot, not after what I said to him in Kent! You must be mistaken. Remember his letter!"

Jane bent to take her hands. "I do remember both of Mr. Darcy's letters. I must admit I would not wish to receive another like them, but you must look beyond his choice of words. Look to his actions. He kept his promise and spoke to Mr. Bingley. Can you imagine how mortifying that must have been?"

Elizabeth realized that, until that moment, she had not thought of it.

"And his manners are much changed. Surely, you have noticed that."

"I have, and know I have greatly wronged him, Jane. He is not proud, only shy with strangers."

"And how do you account for his manners towards our aunt and uncle? Does that not show he has taken your criticisms to heart?

Elizabeth was pained to be reminded of her words to Mr. Darcy. "If only I could take back what I said. My words were inexcusable! Jane, I cannot hope; it is useless!"

Jane gently made Elizabeth to look at her. "Do you love him, Lizzy? Would you accept him if he renewed his addresses?"

"I do not know if I love him; yet, I think I would accept him."

Jane smiled. "I think he is a good man and would make you happy."

Elizabeth smiled in return. "There was more than one good man in our sitting room this morning. What think you of Mr. Bingley now?"

Jane turned away and spoke in a low tone. "He is much the same as he was, Lizzy, yet different." She choked back a sob. "I have hurt him deeply. I can see it in his eyes." She sat on the bed, and Elizabeth tried to comfort her. "He…he spoke of Netherfield, of what he is doing there, of the improvements he is making."

"Oh, Jane, we had no idea!"

"It is not our fault. Our father shows little interest in the workings of the other estates, and our mother is only concerned over matters of society and gossip, so I can well understand their disinterest. Unless Mr. Bingley reestablished his residency, they cared not what happened to Netherfield."

"Perhaps he has listened to your words, as well!" *Like Mr. Darcy listened to me!* Lizzy admitted to herself.

"Perhaps. Oh, I am so confused! My heart says one thing, my mind another! Can I risk myself yet again?"

"Do *you* love him?"

Jane was silent for a few moments. "I have never stopped loving him. But I do not know if it is right to do so if I am unsure whether Mr. Bingley can be his own man."

Elizabeth hugged her sister. "We shall be in Lambton for a few more days. Perhaps we shall learn the truth of these matters." She then decided to lighten the mood. "Now—what are we to wear to Pemberley tomorrow?"

CONVINCED AS ELIZABETH NOW WAS that Miss Bingley's dislike of her had originated in jealousy, she could not help feeling how very unwelcome her appearance at Pemberley must be to her, and she was curious to know with what degree of civility Miss Bingley would renew their acquaintance. Her only real fear was that Miss Bingley would be unkind to Jane.

Jane showed no such concern. She seemed reconciled to the fact that Mr. Bingley's sisters disapproved of her. She cared not two straws about it, for she told Elizabeth that, if it was her destiny not to be united for life with Charles Bingley, what did it matter what two unpleasant persons thought of her?

On reaching the house, Elizabeth and Jane were shown through the hall into the salon, whose northern aspect rendered it delightful for summer. They were received by Miss Darcy, who was sitting there with Mrs. Hurst, Miss Bingley, and the lady with whom she lived in London, Mrs. Annesley. Georgiana's reception of them was cordial, but she seemed somewhat shy and fearful that she might do something wrong. That appearance might easily give those who felt themselves inferior the belief of her being proud and reserved. Her guests, however, felt compassion and pitied her.

By Mrs. Hurst and Miss Bingley, the sisters were noticed only by a curtsey; once they were seated, an awkward pause continued for a few moments. It was first broken by Mrs. Annesley, a genteel, agreeable looking woman, whose endeavor to introduce some kind of discourse proved her to be more truly well bred than either of the others. Between her and Mrs. Gardiner, with occasional help from Jane and Mrs. Hurst, a conversation was carried on. Miss Darcy looked as if she wished for courage enough to join in it, and sometimes did venture a short sentence when there was least danger of its being heard.

Elizabeth soon saw that she was being closely watched by Miss Bingley and that she could not speak a word, especially to Miss Darcy, without calling her attention. This observation would not prevent her from trying to talk to the shy girl, however.

"Have you the opportunity of using your present, Miss Darcy?"

It took a moment for the girl to understand the object of her question. "Oh, yes! The pianoforte is lovely. I have never played on a better one. But I am afraid that my talents do not do it justice."

"Not do it justice! Oh, my dear Miss Darcy!" Miss Bingley exclaimed. "Miss Elizabeth, I assure you I have heard no one play as well as Miss Darcy, and I have hopes she will favor us with a performance this morning."

Elizabeth could not help but notice the look of horror on their hostess's face. "While I would be delighted to hear her play and I doubt not her ability, I believe the shortness of our visit this morning would not do her justice, and selfishly, I would like to continue our discussion of composers we began yesterday, Miss Darcy."

Georgiana looked strangely at Elizabeth at first, but when she recognized the change of subject from performance, she seemed grateful for the way Elizabeth steered the conversation with ease.

"Oh, yes. I must say I prefer Mr. Beethoven to Mr. Mozart. What is your opinion?"

Miss Bingley jumped in. "Oh, yes! Beethoven is far superior!"

Elizabeth smiled. "I must disagree, as I enjoy Mozart very much. But my sister, Mary, is of your opinion. She explained it to me. Beethoven is for the music lover, while Mozart leads the listener to discover music and is the stepping-stone towards a more general appreciation of music. He acts as an initiator, a bridge towards the discovery and appreciation of other musicians. Mr. Beethoven's genius takes music to a new level, one that is only fully appreciated by those that have studied music intently. So it follows that you ladies, as accomplished as you are, should join Mary in showing the greater interest in Beethoven, while I, a mere enthusiast, should lean towards Mozart."

Georgiana could not help but smile at the enormous compliment Elizabeth had paid to her studies. Caroline appeared to be displeased by the offhand reference to Mrs. Collins's superiority.

The servants entered the room with cold meat, cake, and a variety of all the finest fruits in season. Mrs. Annesley gave a significant look and a smile to Miss Darcy to remind her of her post. With an embarrassed blush, Georgiana bent to her task, and the beautiful pyramids of grapes, nectarines, and peaches soon collected her guests around the table.

While the ladies were thus engaged, Mr. Darcy and Mr. Bingley entered the room. They had been some time with Mr. Gardiner who, with two or three other gentlemen from the house, was fishing by the river and had left him only on learning that the ladies of the family intended a visit to Georgiana that morning. Miss Darcy, on her brother's entrance, applied herself much more to talking, and Elizabeth saw that he was anxious that Georgiana and she should become acquainted and forwarded, as much as possible, every attempt at conversation on either side.

Miss Bingley saw all this likewise and took the first opportunity to express her displeasure by saying with sneering civility, "Pray, Miss Eliza, are not the ——shire militia removed from Meryton? They must be a great loss to *your* family."

In Darcy's presence, Miss Bingley dared not mention Wickham's name, but Elizabeth instantly comprehended that he was uppermost in her thoughts, and the various recollections connected with him gave her a moment's distress, but exerting herself vigorously to repel the ill-natured attack, Elizabeth answered the question in a tolerably disengaged tone. While she spoke, an involuntary glance towards the gentleman showed her Darcy earnestly looking at her with a heightened complexion, and his sister, overcome with confusion, was unable to lift up her eyes.

Miss Bingley had intended to discompose Elizabeth by mentioning a man whom she believed Elizabeth favored to make her betray a sensibility that might injure her in Darcy's opinion and perhaps to remind him of all the follies and absurdities of some members of her family.

Elizabeth's collected behavior, however, soon quieted Darcy's emotion. Georgiana also recovered in time, though not enough to be able to speak any more.

Darcy gazed at Elizabeth with undisguised admiration. His ardent look was not lost upon the lady, and their eyes seemed to speak to each other in silent conversation.

Thank you, Miss Elizabeth.

Mr. Darcy, I am so sorry.

It is I who must apologize for bringing such ill-mannered people into my house. Thank you for helping Georgiana.

Who could not? She is all loveliness and sweetness.

She is everything to me.

Bingley wished to lighten the mood. "I say, Miss Bennet, the weather is very fine! Would you not say so, Georgiana?"

"Yes, very fine," answered Georgiana.

"I believe it is the proper weather for a picnic. Do you not think so?"

Georgiana looked puzzled. "I am sure it is."

"I like nothing more than a picnic. And you, Miss Bennet? Do you enjoy a picnic?"

Jane smiled modestly, obviously taken by Bingley's boyish charm. "Yes, I enjoy them very much." "Miss Elizabeth, surely you join your sister in this sentiment?"

Elizabeth smiled broadly at her amusing friend. "We have enjoyed picnics very much at Longbourn, sir."

"That settles it! We shall have a picnic—tomorrow if the weather cooperates! What say you, Darcy? Where is the best picnicking spot at Pemberley?"

Darcy looked cautiously at his friend, as though he had gone mad. "I would say that the small pond would make a superior place for such an outing, Bingley."

"Will you ladies attend? Please say that you will," Georgiana pleaded.

The Gardiners begged off, but the Bennet girls gave their assurances of attending. The conversation continued into other matters until the time to leave was upon them.

WHILE MR. DARCY WAS ATTENDING the party to their carriage, Miss Bingley was venting her feelings in criticisms of Elizabeth's person, behavior, and dress. Her opinions of Jane she kept to herself. She knew her design of preventing a marriage between that lady and her brother would fail if she were overt. No such restriction was felt for Miss Elizabeth, however.

When Darcy returned to the salon, Miss Bingley could not help repeating to him some part of what she had been saying to his sister.

"How very ill Eliza Bennet looks this morning, Mr. Darcy," she cried. "I never in my life saw anyone so much altered as she is since the winter. She is grown so brown and coarse! Louisa and I were agreeing that we should not have known her."

However little Mr. Darcy might have liked such an address, he contented himself with coolly replying that he perceived no other alteration than her being rather tanned—a common consequence of traveling in the summer.

"For my own part," Miss Bingley rejoined, "I must confess that I never could see any beauty in her. Her face is too thin, her complexion has no brilliancy, and her features are not at all handsome. Her nose wants character; there is nothing marked in its lines. Her teeth are tolerable, but not out of the common way. And as for her eyes, which have sometimes been called so fine, I never could perceive anything extraordinary in them. They have a sharp, shrewish look, which I do not like at all. And in her air altogether, there is a self-sufficiency without fashion which is intolerable.

"I remember when we first knew her in Hertfordshire, how amazed we all were to find that she was a reputed beauty. And I particularly recollect your saying one night, after they had been dining at Netherfield, *'She a beauty! I should as soon call her mother a wit.'* But afterwards she seemed to improve on you, and I believe you thought her rather pretty at one time."

Georgiana's eyes flew to her brother.

"Yes," replied Darcy, who could contain himself no longer, "but that was only when I first knew her, for it is many months since I have considered her as one of the handsomest women of my acquaintance!"

Georgiana's cough sounded very much like a laugh.

Darcy went away with his sister, and Miss Bingley was left to all the satisfaction of having forced him to say what gave no one any pain but herself.

Mr. Bingley, who had witnessed all, now entered the fray with his newfound confidence.

"Caroline, I would have words with you— No, Louisa, stay. This concerns you as well. I repeat what I said before. I bear you no ill will for your advice regarding Miss Bennet. You were looking after my best interests, I dare say— No, Caroline, not a word! Let me make myself rightly understood. I intend to court Miss Bennet for the usual purpose. I know my own mind, and I shall not be swayed. You will treat my intended—*and all of her family*—with the respect that is due them as daughters of a gentleman. As head of the family, I know you will attend to my decision. If you feel this task is beyond you, you shall quit my company immediately. This is the last that I will have to say about this subject. The matter is now closed.

"On a new subject, will you attend tomorrow's picnic or not?"

Chapter 11

Letters from Longbourn

The day broke over the forests and glens of Pemberley to witness its owner striding across a field. Fitzwilliam Darcy was agitated—rest was impossible—and needed to conquer his highly emotional state. All his life Darcy had hidden his innermost feelings from a cold and uncaring world, a world that looked upon him and saw only his wealth, not the man. Was there one woman in England who would see him for *who* he was and not *what* he was? Just when he thought he might have to broaden his search to Scotland, he had found her in Hertfordshire—and lost her in Kent.

But now he had a second chance. Darcy had taken Miss Elizabeth's criticisms to heart. He had made amends. He had tried to repair things between Miss Bennet and Bingley. *And now* she *is here. What good fortune!* Darcy vowed to do everything in his power to show proofs of his improvements.

Yet, what could he expect? She had rejected him utterly. Was there any hope for him now? She did not seem unhappy to meet him again after the initial shock. And the way she and Georgiana got on was all and more than he had dreamed. The look they had shared the day before... Dare he hope again? He wrestled with the temptation to ride to Lambton immediately and propose a second time.

Darcy sat on an old wooden footbridge over a small stream and berated himself. No, he could not so inflict himself on her until he was more certain of her feelings. It had been his inability to truly gauge her thoughts that led to the humiliation at Hunsford. *What pride and arrogance!* He blushed at the memory.

He looked about his grand estate. *Here I am at home; here I can be myself. Father would be embarrassed to see what I have become—prideful and aloof. But school and Town were so different. The demands upon me—the lack of principles, of morals. Oh, Father, I wish I had been better prepared.*

He shook his head. *Look at me. I, who claim to abhor disguise of any sort, have been wearing a mask for years! Outside of Pemberley, only my family and a few close friends know who I really am. And not all of my family—I have been standoffish with Aunt Catherine for ages.*

He looked over at the pond he had suggested for today's picnic. *Yes, Bingley had a grand idea. Here, Miss Elizabeth will see the real Fitzwilliam Darcy. This will be the best picnic ever held in Derbyshire!*

A creaking of the boards drew his attention. *Hmm, must have this bridge repaired. I will have a word with the steward tomorrow about it.* Darcy stood and returned to the house for breakfast.

ELIZABETH CRIED AS SHE SAT up in bed.

"Lizzy, what is the matter?" asked her sister, who shared her bed.

Elizabeth looked about the room, reassuring herself that she was in Lambton. "A…a passing dream, Jane, nothing more."

"It must have been a mighty dream to awaken you in such a manner." Jane sat up. "Come, share this vision with me."

Elizabeth blushed. "Do not ask, I beg you."

"You have always shared your dreams with me before. Come, it will settle you. Now, was it a nightmare?"

Though embarrassed, Elizabeth was able to assure her that she did not have a nightmare.

"That is well. But you know that nightmares never come true. Your dream was a pleasant one?"

Oh Lord! "It was not *un*pleasant."

"Good. That is often a harbinger of the future."

That is what I fear.

"So, what was the dream about?"

"Jane, it was a silly nothing. I can hardly remember it. Are you able to see the clock?"

Jane was distracted by the question. "No, but I smell food from downstairs."

"Then let us prepare for breakfast." With that, Elizabeth threw off the covers and went into the dressing room to begin her toilette. She was glad of the escape, for how could she tell her most innocent sister of her dream: Elizabeth, in a bedroom at Pemberley, being very agreeably ravaged by Mr. Darcy?

"I DO NOT UNDERSTAND WHAT the fuss is all about!"

"Caroline, for the last time, I must ask you to be civil!"

"I mean nothing against sweet Jane, Charles, I assure you—but a picnic? How very *common*!"

Darcy strode into the breakfast room, adjusting his cravat. "What is common, Miss Bingley?"

Caroline looked up at Darcy and saw nothing that comforted her. His outburst from the evening before still rang in her ears: *"For it is many months since I have considered her as one of the handsomest women of my acquaintance."* She had hoped it was hyperbole, but as Caroline took in his dress with a practiced eye, she realized that he meant every word he said. Mr. Darcy, always fastidious in his dress, had used extra care today. In a fine green coat with bluff trousers, he cut an imposing figure. She knew in her heart that he had not dressed for her, but for Miss Bennet, curses upon that name! Caroline Bingley's slim hopes were fading fast. Only a miracle could save her now. Might it rain?

"How is the weather today, Brother?" asked Georgiana, terminating the unfortunate silence.

"A fine, sunny day. Perfect for a picnic," Darcy answered, turning to Miss Bingley.

I believe I shall be ill now, thought Caroline.

IT WAS GENERALLY ASSUMED THAT Jane Bennet was possessed of the most pacific temperament in the world, and it safely could be said that most people were correct on that score, at least given the evidence the lady in question chose to present. In actuality, Jane was as prone to fits of agitation as the next female. She simply kept her more passionate emotions to herself.

Jane's placid demeanor was in grave danger of cracking this day as she dressed for what she expected to be a momentous picnic at Pemberley, for it was obvious to her that Charles Bingley still held some admiration for her. This fact would have been pleasing to most unmarried ladies. Mr. Bingley was handsome, kind, deferential, amusing, thoughtful, and in possession of five thousand pounds a year. Jane was not immune to Mr. Bingley's charms, and her mother would never let her forget his fortune.

Last spring, Jane had made the choice of rejecting Mr. Bingley's suit, using the strongest words she had ever used in her life. Such words surely must have destroyed any tender feelings that had existed. She could only account for his present kindness as an essential of the gentleman's character. It could not be that Mr. Bingley felt any more for her than he felt for her sister Elizabeth. To wish for, to expect any more, would be ridiculous—impossible.

Jane sighed. It was obvious to her that Elizabeth was coming to an acceptance of Mr. Darcy's most marked regard. Should she desire it, Elizabeth could be mistress of Pemberley before Christmas. Elizabeth, who never went looking for her heart's desire, would soon achieve it: a marriage of love to a handsome, clever, and intelligent man. His improved manners were due to Elizabeth's reproofs, Jane was sure, and what could show true regard more than that? The man was violently in love with her sister.

And Mr. Bingley? He said he had begun improvements to his estate at Netherfield. Jane had no reason to doubt him. But had he truly changed? Was it his idea, or did his friend advise him to see to his farms? She did not know and could not ask.

Not that it was of any importance. Jane had killed any love Charles Bingley might have had for her. She *must* have, for no regard could withstand her most hateful words. It was a shame, really.

For Jane was still in love with him.

CHARLES BINGLEY WAS NERVOUS AS he checked his pocket watch for the third time in an hour. He was to see his sweet Jane again, and he did not want to ruin the opportunity.

He glanced at the newspaper in front of him, but it could not hold his attention. Georgiana had persuaded Caroline and Louisa to help with the preparations for the picnic, though Charles was not fooled by his sisters' compliance; he had made it clear the evening before that he would brook no foolishness from either of them.

He looked at his great friend. Yes, he had forgiven Darcy for his interference, but he had not forgotten it. What was more devastating was Jane's refusal: *One cannot live on love.* Charles had to credit the lady's insight; it was his duty to provide for his family, and he had done a poor job of it. It was time to be a man, and by heaven, Charles Bingley would be his own master!

He just hoped he was doing it right.

He longed to ask for Darcy's advice. Even Hurst had to admit that Pemberley was the best managed estate they had ever visited, and though there might be a finer place than Pemberley, they never heard of it. However, Charles could not ask. He had to learn the hard way to make mistakes, to take chances.

At least his steward seemed to know his business. The fields were in far better shape than Charles had hoped. New tenants were already applying for land. Netherfield Park was not a grand estate, but they would get the most from it. Should they prove successful, Bingley might consider a larger place in the future.

No, Charles Bingley's luck was changing. How fortunate that just as he was looking for a new steward, the very man knocked at his door in London! This was a sign! He would be the self-reliant man he was supposed to be! He would earn Miss Bennet's regard—he would!

It was not known whether Bingley's confidence would have survived had he known that his new steward came to his door by way of Pemberley and Matlock.

The sound of Darcy placing down his quill stirred Bingley out of his ruminations. "Are you done there, Darcy?"

"Yes, let me seal this letter, and I am at your disposal."

Within a quarter-hour, the two gentlemen were on their way to the stable and thence to Lambton.

THE BENNET GIRLS WERE NERVOUSLY preparing for the picnic planned by Miss Darcy. Mr. and Mrs. Gardiner looked upon them with open affection and amusement.

"My dear, I believe we are in the way."

"I must agree with you. What is your advice?"

"Perhaps we may step over to the church down the street. Did you not wish to speak to the rector?"

Mrs. Gardiner nodded. "Indeed I did. I wished to look up some old family records. Girls, we shall be back within the hour. We will be in good time for your outing, never fear." With that, the pair took their leave of their nieces.

The ladies had just completed their preparations when two letters from Kitty were delivered, both from Longbourn. One had been addressed poorly and had only arrived at its true destination in concert with the second. The one misdirected was the first to be attended to, as it had been written five days before.

Jane, anxious for any news, read aloud as Elizabeth attended. The beginning contained an account of all their little parties and engagements, with such news as the country afforded, but the latter half, which was dated a day later and written in evident agitation, gave more important intelligence.

Since writing the above, dearest sisters, something has occurred of a most unexpected nature. I am afraid of alarming you, but be assured that we are all well. What I have to say relates to Lydia. Just as we were all gone to bed, an express came at twelve last night from Colonel Forster to inform us that Lydia was gone off to Scotland with one of his officers—with Wickham!

I must own that I am not very much surprised. Lydia has written to me of her affection for that gentleman. Yet I am very, very sorry to learn of so imprudent an action on both sides! Why not gain my father's consent? We could have stood up with her at her wedding! I always wanted to be a bridesmaid—I think Lydia is being very selfish. But I am willing to hope the best.

Mama is sadly grieved, for she cannot plan the wedding. Papa bears it better and calls Lydia a silly girl. Lydia and Wickham were off Saturday night about twelve, it is conjectured, but were not missed until yesterday morning at eight. The express was sent off directly. My dear sisters, they must have passed within ten miles of us! Colonel Forster gives us reason to expect him here soon. Lydia left a few lines for his wife, informing her of their intention.

I must conclude, for I cannot be long from Mama. I am afraid you will not be able to make it out, for I hardly know what I have written.

Without allowing herself or Elizabeth time for consideration and scarcely knowing what she felt, Jane, on finishing this letter, instantly seized the other, and opening it with the utmost impatience, read what had been written a day later.

Dearest sisters, I hardly know what I would write, but I have bad news for you, and it cannot be delayed. Romantic as an elopement between Mr. Wickham and our Lydia would be, we are now anxious to be assured it has taken place at all, for there is but too much reason to fear they are not gone to Scotland!

Colonel Forster came yesterday, not many hours after the express, having left Brighton the day before. Though Lydia's short letter to Mrs. Forster gave them to understand that they were going to Gretna Green, Denny expressed his belief that Wickham never intended to go there, or to marry Lydia at all! Colonel Forster instantly took alarm and set off from Brighton, intending to trace their route. He did trace them easily to Clapham, but no farther, for on entering that place, Wickham and Lydia removed into a hackney-coach and dismissed the chaise that brought them from Epsom. All that is known after this is that they were seen to continue on the London road.

I know not what to think. I thought Wickham as the most agreeable gentleman!

After making every possible enquiry on that side London, Colonel Forster came into Hertfordshire, anxiously searching at all the turnpikes, and at the inns in Barnet and Hatfield, but without any success. He came to Longbourn and broke his apprehensions to us.

Our distress, my dear sisters, is very great. Papa and Mama believe the worst, but I cannot think so ill of him. Many circumstances might make it more eligible for them to be married privately in Town than to pursue their first plan. I grieve to find, however, that Colonel Forster is not disposed to depend upon their marriage. He shook his head when I expressed my hopes, and said he feared Wickham was not a man to be trusted. Mama is very ill and keeps her room, and as to Papa, I never in my life saw him so affected. He is so angry with me for having concealed their attachment! But it was a matter of confidence—what choice did I have? I am truly glad, Jane and Lizzy, that you have been spared something of these distressing scenes, but now, as the first shock is over, I own that I long for your return. Papa has been so mean. Adieu.

I take up my pen again to do what I have just told you I would not, but circumstances are such that I cannot help earnestly begging you to come here as soon as possible. I know my dear uncle and aunt so well that I am not afraid of requesting it, though I have still something more to ask of Uncle Gardiner.

Papa is going to London with Colonel Forster to try to discover Lydia. What he means to do, I am sure I know not, but his excessive distress might lead him to fight Wickham, and he would surely lose! Colonel

Forster is obliged to be at Brighton again tomorrow evening, so who will stop Papa? I think my uncle's advice and assistance would be everything in the world. He will immediately comprehend what I must feel, and I rely upon his goodness.

"Oh! Where, where is my uncle?" cried Elizabeth as Jane finished the letter, darting from her seat in eagerness to find him without losing a moment of precious time. As she reached the door, Jane close on her heels, it was opened by a servant, and Mr. Darcy and Mr. Bingley appeared, early for their appointment.

Elizabeth's pale face and impetuous manner made the gentlemen start, and before either could recover himself enough to speak, she exclaimed, "I beg your pardon, but I must leave you! I must find Mr. Gardiner this moment on business that cannot be delayed! I have not a moment to lose!"

"Good God! What is the matter?" cried Darcy with more feeling than politeness.

Bingley stepped forward. "We will not detain you a minute, but let me, or Darcy, or the servant find Mr. and Mrs. Gardiner! You are not well. You cannot go yourself—or you, Miss Bennet."

Elizabeth hesitated, but her knees trembled under her, and she felt how little would be gained by her attempting to pursue her aunt and uncle. Calling back the servant, therefore, she commissioned him, though in so breathless a manner as made her almost unintelligible, to fetch the couple home instantly.

When the servant had quit the room, Elizabeth sat down, unable to support herself and looking so miserably ill that it was impossible for Darcy to leave her.

In a tone of gentleness and commiseration, Darcy said, "Let me call your maid. Is there nothing you could take to give you present relief? A glass of wine—shall I get you one? You are very ill."

"No, I thank you," Elizabeth replied, endeavoring to recover herself. "There is nothing the matter with me. I am quite well. I am only distressed by some dreadful news which I have just received from Longbourn." She burst into tears as she alluded to it, and for a few minutes, could not speak another word. Darcy, in wretched suspense, could only observe her in compassionate silence.

Jane, too, was overcome with emotion, but it was she who recovered first, and spoke while a troubled Bingley attempted to comfort her.

"We have just had a letter from our sister, Kitty, with such dreadful news. It cannot be concealed from anyone. My youngest sister has left all her friends—has eloped—has thrown herself into the power of…of Mr. Wickham! They are gone off together from Brighton."

Elizabeth cried, "You know him too well to doubt the rest! She has no money, no connections, nothing that can tempt him to— She is lost forever."

Bingley was in open-mouthed in amazement, while Darcy was fixed in astonishment.

"When I consider," Elizabeth added, in a yet more agitated voice, "that I might have prevented it! I, who knew what he was! Had I but explained some part of it only—some part of what I learnt—to my own family! Had his character been known, this could not have happened! But it is all too late now."

"I am grieved, indeed," cried Darcy, "grieved—shocked. But is it certain, absolutely certain?"

"Oh yes! They left Brighton together on Sunday night and were traced almost to London, but not beyond. They are certainly not gone to Scotland."

"And what has been done? What has been attempted to recover her?" asked Bingley.

Jane looked up. "My father is gone to London, and Kitty has written to beg my uncle's immediate assistance. We shall be off, I hope, in a half-hour."

Elizabeth shook her head. "But nothing can be done. I *know* very well that nothing can be done! How is such a man to be worked on? How are they even to be discovered?" Her voice started to crack. "I…I have not the smallest hope. It is every way h-horrible!" Darcy shook his head in silent acquiescence. "When my eyes were opened to his real character. Oh, had I known what I ought, what I dared, to do! But I knew not—I was afraid of doing too much. Wretched,

wretched, mistake!"

"Elizabeth!" cried Jane. "It is not your fault alone! I, too, should have revealed him to our family and acquaintances. It is my fault as much as anyone's! But I never thought someone could be so evil." She broke down and left Bingley's side to move to her sister. Elizabeth, with tears in her own eyes, tried to console her.

Darcy made no answer. He seemed scarcely to hear her and walked up and down the room in earnest meditation, his brow contracted and his air gloomy.

Elizabeth observed and instantly understood it. Under such a proof of family weakness, such a deep disgrace, she should neither wonder at nor condemn his reaction. It was exactly calculated to make her understand her own wishes, and never had she so honestly felt that she could have loved him as now, when all love must be vain. Her heart was breaking.

"Damn and blast!" shouted Bingley, startling the room. "I will not have it! Miss Bennet, Miss Elizabeth—do not fret! Come, Darcy, we shall set this to rights!" With that, he dashed out of the room. Jane stood up in shock.

Darcy looked after his friend, grimaced, and turned to the ladies. "Dear ladies, please excuse my friend's outburst. I am afraid you have long desired our absence. We have nothing to plead in excuse of our stay but real concern. Would to heaven that anything could be said on my part that might offer consolation to such distress! But I will not torment you with vain wishes which may seem purposely to ask for your thanks. This unfortunate affair will, I fear, prevent my sister's having the pleasure of your company today."

"Oh, yes," replied Jane. "Be so kind as to apologize for us to Miss Darcy. Say that urgent business calls us home immediately. Conceal the unhappy truth as long as it is possible. I know it cannot be long."

He readily assured them both of his secrecy, again expressed his sorrow for her distress, wished it a happier conclusion than there was at present reason to hope and, leaving his compliments for her relations, with only one serious, earnest, look to Elizabeth, Darcy turned to go away.

Jane cried out after him, "Mr. Darcy, you are going after them, are you not? After Mr. Wickham and my sister?"

Darcy struggled to regain his voice, but he could not deceive her. "Yes. Yes, I am."

Elizabeth was shocked. "No! This is impossible! You would so debase yourself? You would deal with that…cad? After what he has done to you and yours? You cannot!" As if an invisible sting pulled her, she moved towards him.

Darcy turned to her. "This is *my* fault, Miss Elizabeth. Had not my abominable pride held my tongue, I should have let the world know of Wickham's true character. In my arrogance, I considered my family's comfort superior to the well-being of my neighbors, no matter how many yeomen's daughters were ruined. And now another innocent has fallen to the charms of that reprobate! I must make amends."

"This is not your doing, sir!"

"I think it is. I must try to help your sister."

Elizabeth looked at him in amazement, tears still running down her lovely face. "You will do this thing—this wonderful thing—for my family? After what I said to you in Kent?"

Darcy's face twisted in pain. "What did you say that I did not deserve? You cannot know how those words are burned into me. I have tried to learn from my mistakes, to do better, to be the man my parents taught me to be. You have properly humbled me, Miss Elizabeth, and this incident proves that I have failed in my responsibility to my fellow man.

"I would not give you false hopes, but I—Bingley and I—will do what we can. Please do not distress yourself. While my heart hurts for you and your family, which I respect so much, there is nothing untoward in my intended actions. I seek no reward or seek to make you feel in any way indebted to me. I look for nothing for myself. I do this because duty demands this of me."

Elizabeth's tear-stained eyes looked into Darcy's. "Find them and I am yours."

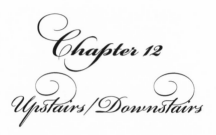

Chapter 12

Upstairs/Downstairs

There was no sound in the room, save the gasp that escaped from a very shocked Jane Bennet. Darcy's incredulous gaze took in his beloved's face and manner. He could not believe his ears. His response was on his lips, when there was a noise from the corridor without. Instinctively, the pair drew apart before the door was thrown open.

Mr. and Mrs. Gardiner were all concern. "Girls, what has happened? The parlor maid—Mr. Darcy! You are here, too?"

Mr. Gardiner took in the countenance of his nieces and turned on the gentleman. "Sir, I must ask you to explain yourself."

"Please forgive me, sir. Bingley and I came upon your nieces just as they received some distressing news from home. I have only remained until your return, and I will leave these ladies to your most excellent care. I shall intrude no more, but, sir, if I might have a few moments of your time when your business with your relations is completed, I would be grateful."

Gardiner, angry as he was, was no fool. He saw the earnest look in Elizabeth's eye. "Very well, sir."

"Excellent. I shall be in the public room below." With that, he took his leave.

Mrs. Gardiner then spoke to her nieces. "My dears, what has happened?"

DARCY FOUND BINGLEY PACING THE public room. He would not allow him to speak, but took his friend's elbow and led him to the table in the furthest corner of the room.

Bingley could be silent no longer. "What is this? What are we waiting for?"

Darcy glared at his friend. "Will you hold your tongue, Bingley? Do you wish all of Lambton to know the Bennets' business?"

Bingley collected himself. "Quite, quite. But I do not understand this delay. You do mean to go with me, do you not?"

"Charles," Darcy began carefully, "you are an admirable fellow, to be sure, but I must say that there is no reason for you to be involved in—"

"No reason!" he hissed. "Darce, do you mean to help or not?"

"I was speaking of *you*, Charles, not me."

"I cannot see that you have any interest in this affair that is superior to mine."

Darcy sighed. He would have to reveal what he knew. Concealment had been his downfall, and Darcy supposed he would have to get used to being more forthcoming with his friend.

"I am afraid I do have a connection to this, Charles. I am well acquainted with Wickham's infamous character, but I chose not to reveal it to the world at large. I had my reasons—foolish reasons—but they are such that I will not share with you now, not in this public place. Be assured that I will tell you all later. It is because I would not take the trouble to expose Wickham that this incident has occurred. I am responsible. I must make amends. But *you* have no injury—"

"Injury enough for a gentleman!"

"Keep your voice down," Darcy growled. "You speak of Miss Bennet? Do you have an understanding, then?"

Bingley looked down. "No, but I shall not see her in distress if it is in my power to relieve her of it. Besides, I do not think I am alone in my admiration of the Bennet sisters." He looked up, and at Darcy's alarm, Bingley laughed. "You are quite transparent, Darce. But do not despair. It is my opinion that the lady does not look upon you with disfavor."

No, she did not, Darcy knew, but he wondered if it was for the right reasons. Pushing those thoughts aside, Darcy returned to the issue at hand. "Charles, is it your wish to aid me in this endeavor?"

"If you mean to be of service to the Bennets, then, yes, with all my heart."

He looked hard at his friend. "I will not say that I do not want your help—indeed, it would be a comfort. But I must make myself clear. This is *my* task. The fault is mine and so must the remedy be. I will brook no interference from anyone, no matter how dear they might be to me. If you wish to help me, then you must be ruled by me. You must agree to follow my instructions to the letter, without question. This is absolute. You must agree now, or we must go our separate ways in this matter."

Bingley sat back. "You speak strongly, Darcy."

Darcy's voice became softer, more reasonable. "Charles, I *know* Wickham. I know his character. I know where he will flee. I know what motivates him—what will work with him. You, with no knowledge of the man, do not. You will never find him and neither will the Bennets. I have the only chance at success in this matter."

Bingley wore a perplexed expression. "You say you know where he is?"

"I know where he will go, rather. If he is not there, he soon will be."

"How is this? How do you know him so well?"

Darcy looked down. "This is not the first time I have had dealings with that…gentleman." His fists were clenched tight.

Nodding, Bingley said slowly, "Very well, Darce, it shall be as you say. Here is my hand upon it."

Darcy grasped the offered hand heartily. "You are too good. Thank you, my friend."

The other man sat back, his usual easiness returning. "So, my captain, what is our first step?"

"We must speak with Mr. Gardiner before we do anything else."

Bingley looked at the stairs. "That might take some time, Darce. What say you to a porter while we wait?"

THE GENTLEMEN HAD HARDLY TOUCHED their drinks before Mr. Gardiner descended. It took him but a moment to discover Darcy's table and move towards it. He took the offered chair with a tired grunt.

"Would you care for anything?" offered Darcy.

"I believe something stronger than porter would not be unwelcomed, sir." Bingley caught the girl's attention and soon a glass of acceptable port was before Mr. Gardiner. "Well, sirs," be began after taking a sip, "it seems you both are aware of our troubles."

"It was quite unintentional, sir," Darcy apologized.

"That is my understanding. What I do not comprehend is your intention to involve yourselves in this matter."

"Sir," cried Bingley, "as gentlemen, we feel it our duty to offer what assistance we may."

Gardiner looked at the both of them closely. "So you say. You must admit that it is unusual for men of your station to become a party to such unseemliness—unless there are other motivations?" He put down his glass. "Come, sirs, let us not bandy about. What is your interest in this? Do either of you have an understanding with one of my nieces?"

Darcy spoke almost immediately, hoping to stop the blush he was sure was covering his face. "Mr. Gardiner, both Mr. Bingley and I admire your nieces. There are no understandings of *that* nature to report, however. Our interest in this affair comes from another quarter."

Darcy then explained his history with Wickham, leaving out only the events at Ramsgate. "There are other examples of Wickham's wickedness which I cannot speak of here. If you require to know more, I will be willing to relate all to you in a more private setting. However, I feel it is due to my lack of judgment in not exposing Wickham to the world's scorn that," he looked around, "the lady in question was not protected from that man."

Gardiner was taken aback. "Sir, you take too much upon yourself."

The two fell into an earnest discussion, to which Bingley was a silent witness. Eventually, Mr. Gardiner gave way.

"I say, you are intent upon your purpose! It seems I cannot do anything but welcome your assistance and your friend's, too."

"I thank you, sir. May we call on you when you reach London?"

"That would be satisfactory. Here is my card. I take it you gentlemen plan to leave directly?"

Darcy glanced at his friend, who nodded. "As soon as we make our excuses at Pemberley. We shall leave before nightfall." He picked up the card. "Gracechurch Street. A lovely part of town."

Gardiner seemed surprised. "You are familiar with it, sir?"

"I have been through that part of London. That is where Beltbeck lives, Bingley."

Gardiner laughed. "That old thief? Surely you are paying too much for your wine, Mr. Darcy!"

Darcy offered a small smile. "Then I shall have additional business with you, sir."

Eventually all was packed, and the three ladies descended from the rooms upstairs. Elizabeth was grateful to see that Darcy had remained with her uncle to escort them to the carriage.

"Mr. Bingley is not here?" she asked for Jane's sake.

Darcy talked to Elizabeth but looked at Jane. "He has gone ahead to make our excuses to our people at Pemberley. He sends his most *earnest* compliments. I will join him directly and thence to London."

Mrs. Gardiner gave her husband an alarmed glance but said nothing.

Elizabeth turned to her uncle once they were out of doors. "Sir, might I have a few moments to speak with Mr. Darcy?"

Gardiner looked to his wife, who raised an eyebrow but uttered no objection. With permission given, the two young people walked about ten paces distance before the gentleman spoke.

"Miss Elizabeth, I must tell you—"

She interrupted him. "You must permit me to apologize for my... unseemly declaration in the upper rooms earlier." She closed her eyes; her mortification was so great. How could she say such a thing to him—to such a man—surely the best man in the world? "I am afraid I have embarrassed you...and dishonored your noble intentions. What you have volunteered to do for my family! We will never be able to repay—"

"Miss Elizabeth, please! If you will thank me, let it be for yourself alone. That the wish of giving happiness to you might add force to the other inducements which led me on, I shall not attempt to deny. But your family owes me nothing." He lowered his voice even more. "Much as I respect them, I believe I thought only of you."

Elizabeth was too much embarrassed to say a word.

After a short pause, he added, "You are too generous to trifle with me. If your feelings are still what they were last April, tell me so at once. Speak plainly and fear not. I shall not deviate from my intended course of action, no matter the answer. My affections and wishes are unchanged, but one word from you will silence me on this subject forever."

Elizabeth looked up at him, for the first time in perfect clarity. She beheld a tall, handsome man, graced by his Creator with a superb mind and understanding, clearly suffering fear and uncertainty. She knew her own feelings at last, and she knew that even a man as excellent as Fitzwilliam Darcy needed reassurance desperately. Only absolute truth would do for him. Elizabeth closed her eyes, and with all the courage she possessed, she answered him.

"Sir, I may give you pain with this undignified response. I am sorry, for you deserve better. But my character demands that I be forthright. I apologize for the *manner* of my statement above stairs. However, I cannot deny the *truth* of it. I meant every word I spoke. You *will* find them, soon, and I am yours, *now*…Fitzwilliam."

She opened her eyes, fearful of his response to her somewhat ill-bred answer to his question. She placed her trust in his affection, hoped he would be pleased, and thought she was prepared for a positive reaction—but she was so wrong.

Darcy did not touch her. He did not need to. His face glowed with wonderment, then joy, then contentment—all flashing across his countenance in succession. But his eyes grew so dark and intense that Elizabeth could feel her very soul burn with passionate feelings she never before experienced. She knew then she was lost and that her sanity, if not survival, depended upon being in his company again and very soon.

He pitched his voice very low, just for her ears. "I would move heaven and earth for you, Elizabeth, and I shall. I will not fail you."

She thrilled at the mention of her name and replied, "You cannot, Fitzwilliam. I do not say what I do because of *what* you pledge to do for me. I say it, instead, because you *want* to do it for me. I honor the man, not the deed."

At that, his face broke into a wide grin, and his body seemed to relax. "Thank you, Elizabeth, but my mind is determined. I will succeed."

She smiled in return, her eyes glowing. "I know." And, somehow, she did. She could not believe how easy it was to converse with him, now that all false illusions were gone.

He glanced up. "Your companions are eager to go, and I, too, must be on my way." In a louder voice, he said as he bowed over her hand, "I take my leave of you, Miss Elizabeth. I shall write to your mother."

She knew all he did was right and proper, but she felt a pang of disappointment that he did not sweep her up in his arms. By the time they returned to the carriage, she had recovered her senses and was able to observe him complete his leave-taking with composure and pride. Soon the party was in the Gardiner carriage, and Darcy was astride his horse.

"Farewell and safe journey! Mr. Gardiner, until London!" With a wave, Darcy rode away.

The carriage had been moving for several minutes before Mrs. Gardiner broke the pregnant silence. "Do you have any news for us, Elizabeth?"

"Not today, Aunt," she replied, "but perhaps one day soon."

"He is a fine man to be sure—"

"He is the *best* of men, as he will prove in the days to come," she stated with pride. "And Mr. Bingley, too." She grasped Jane's hand as she spoke.

"Yes," said Jane in a low voice as she gazed out the window, "and Mr. Bingley, too."

Mrs. Gardiner knew she would get no further information from her nieces, so she turned to her husband. "Mr. Gardiner, would you please tell me how Mr. Darcy and Mr. Bingley became involved in this business?"

WHEN BINGLEY RETURNED TO PEMBERLEY, he found Georgiana and his sisters in the music room. Waiting until Hurst could be found and brought to him, he informed the group of his intention to leave for London immediately with Darcy. Georgiana was distressed, but asked no questions. She and Mrs. Reynolds went to see about Darcy's packing.

Caroline was not so circumspect. "Charles what has happened? Why must you leave so abruptly?"

"I have told you, Caroline. Urgent business calls me to London—and Darcy, too."

"But you tell us nothing!"

"I told you all you need to know." He sighed. "Georgiana asks nothing. She just sees to her brother's things."

Caroline looked aghast at the censure in her brother's words. Louisa leapt to her defense. "Charles, that is unfair—"

Bingley could stand for no more. "How is pointing out your duty being unfair?"

"You cannot talk to me in that manner!" cried Caroline.

Bingley was silent. He turned, strode out of the room, his complaining sisters in his wake. Despite their entreaties, he would say nothing. Soon he entered the billiards room, where he found Hurst lining up a shot.

"Hurst," he cried, "can you do nothing with these relations of ours?"

The man looked up incredulously. "What do you expect *me* to do with them?"

"Anything! Take them to Scarborough, lock them in the Tower, put them on a boat to Australia! Just keep them from bothering me!"

Hurst considered. "I do not think the Regent with allow me use of the Tower."

"Mr. Hurst!" cried his wife.

"Oh, hush, Louisa!"

"Perhaps you can bully my sister," Caroline said as she pushed around her brother, "but I will not stand for it! No one will tell me to hold my tongue!"

"Caroline…" said Bingley dangerously.

"This is all very singular! You and Mr. Darcy ride into Lambton to retrieve those...ladies from Hertfordshire, and you later return exclaiming your intention to remove to Town instantly and without your family! What has happened? I know it has to do with those Bennet creatures!"

A horrified Louisa whispered, "Caroline, *stop!*"

"I will not stop! I will have my say! Does someone have need of a special license, I wonder? Has someone been caught by arts and allurements?"

"To whose *arts and allurements* do you refer, Miss Bingley?" came a voice from behind her. "Arts and allurements—are you speaking of your own, madam?" asked Mr. Darcy, dusty from just riding from Lambton. "You would not be so crass as to speak in such a manner of either of the Miss Bennets in my house, would you?"

Caroline paled and attempted a reply, but it died on her lips.

"I see that I will have to make something clear to you all. The Bennet family is under my protection now." Darcy moved into the billiards room, his hands clasped behind his back.

"And mine!" added Bingley.

"Just so, Charles. And as that good and honorable family is under my protection, I will not brook any malicious remarks or unsubstantiated rumors within my hearing or in any house I own. This is absolute. Any violation of these most reasonable requirements will subject the person responsible to my *displeasure*." He walked over to Caroline. "We would not want that, would we?"

Caroline was so horrified she could say nothing.

"I will make something else clear. There is *nothing* to announce—either for myself or for Charles. The Bennets and the Gardiners are our *friends*, nothing more, and I take friendship *very* seriously." Again he turned to Caroline. "It is my earnest hope that nothing *untoward* is spread abroad regarding those fine people. For if I do hear of such things, it would be most unfortunate for the one spreading such stories. They would lose my good opinion, and as you know, once my good opinion is lost, it is lost *forever*."

Staring down his nose at a dismayed Caroline, Darcy added, "Are you ready to leave, Charles?"

"I shall just see to it, old boy. I should not be a moment." With a grin to his sisters, Bingley left the room.

"Excellent. Hurst, can you manage without us?"

Hurst looked Darcy in the eye. "We shall leave for Scarborough immediately."

"There is no need for haste."

"Perhaps not, but I think it proper. You will excuse us, I trust?"

"Mr. Hurst!" cried his wife again.

"Louisa," Hurst replied, "see to our things. Now. Caroline, how soon can you be packed?"

"I...I cannot leave Georgiana!" she cried.

"Bah!" he said to her. "Georgiana is safe here with Mrs. Annesley and the Pemberley staff. She has lived here for weeks at a time while Darcy was in Town. You had no objections then. Your place is not here. And if you wish to continue to reside with me, you had best see to your packing!"

The sisters saw defeat when it was before their eyes, and they quit the room directly.

"Well said, Hurst," said Darcy in surprise. "Please excuse me. I must go to Georgiana now."

"As you will," the man replied as he lined up a shot.

CAROLINE BINGLEY WAS IN A fury over her brother's treatment of her. She stewed as the maid packed her things. It was obvious to her that something disastrous had happened to the Bennets. Why her brother and Mr. Darcy were involved was no mystery to *her*. It had to be for the oldest reason in the world—Elizabeth Bennet had somehow managed to be compromised by Mr. Darcy before *she* could.

Well, there was more than one way to get what she wanted.

"You, girl—is there pen and paper in that desk?"

"Aye, ma'am, there is," she answered. *Of course there is, you witch! Where do you think you are? This is Pemberley!*

Caroline smiled tightly, a plan coming to her. "Continue packing. I must write a letter."

"I have been thinking, girls," said their aunt, as they drove through the countryside, "and upon serious consideration, it appears to me so very unlikely that any young man should form such a design against a girl who is by no means unprotected or friendless and who was staying with his colonel's family, that I am strongly inclined to hope the best. Could Wickham expect that Lydia's friends would not step forward? Could he expect to be noticed again by the regiment after such an affront to Colonel Forster? The temptation is not adequate to the risk. It is too great a violation of decency, honor, and interest for him to be guilty of it. I cannot think so very ill of Wickham. Can you believe him capable of it, Lizzy?"

"Not perhaps of neglecting his own interest, but of every *other* neglect I can believe him capable! Why should they not go on to Scotland if that had been the case?"

"In the first place," replied Mrs. Gardiner, "there is no absolute proof that they are not gone to Scotland."

"But their removing from the chaise into a hackney coach is such a presumption! And, besides, no traces of them were to be found on the Barnet road," said her husband.

"Well, then—supposing them to be in London," continued Mrs. Gardner, "they may be there for the purpose of concealment and for no more exceptionable purpose. It is not likely that money should be very abundant on either side, and it might strike them that they could be more economically, though less expeditiously, married in London than in Scotland."

"But why all this secrecy?" Jane said uneasily. "Why any fear of detection? Why must their marriage be private?"

Elizabeth interrupted. "No, no—this is not likely. His most particular friend, you see by Kitty's account, was persuaded of his never intending to marry Lydia. Wickham will never marry a woman without some money. He cannot afford it."

Mr. Gardner shook his head. "All that Mr. Darcy has told me corroborates this. And what claims has Lydia? What attractions has she beyond youth, health, and good-humor that could make him forego every chance of benefiting himself by marrying well? As to what restraint the apprehension of disgrace in the corps might throw on a dishonorable elopement with her, I am not able to judge. But as to your other objection, my dear, I am afraid it will hardly hold good. Lydia has no brothers to step forward, and Wickham might imagine from her father's past behavior that he would do as little about it as any father could do in such a matter."

Mrs. Gardner tried again. "But can you think that Lydia is so lost to everything but love of him as to consent to live with Wickham on any other terms than marriage?"

"It does seem so," replied Jane with tears in her eyes, "and it is most shocking indeed. But I know not what to say. Perhaps I am not doing her justice."

"Lydia is very young," Elizabeth said. "She has never been taught to think on serious subjects, and for the last twelvemonth, she has been given up to nothing but amusement and vanity! She has been allowed to dispose of her time in the most idle and frivolous manner and to adopt any opinions that came in her way. Since the ——shire were first quartered in Meryton, nothing but love, flirtation, and officers have been in her head, and we all know that Wickham has every charm of person and address that can captivate a woman."

"But you see that Kitty does not think so ill of Wickham as to believe him capable of the attempt," Mrs. Gardiner said.

Elizabeth rolled her eyes. "Kitty! When has Kitty ever felt Lydia did anything wrong? But Jane knows, as well as I, what Wickham really is. We both know that he has been profligate in every sense of the word. He has neither integrity nor honor. He is as false and deceitful as he is insinuating!"

"How harsh you are, Lizzy! And do you really know all this?" cried Mrs. Gardiner.

"We do, indeed," replied Jane. "We told you the other day of his infamous behavior to Mr. Darcy. And you yourself, when last at Longbourn, heard in what manner he spoke of the man who had behaved with such forbearance and liberality towards him." She glanced at Elizabeth. "And there are other circumstances which I—which are not worthwhile to relate. But his falsehoods about the whole Pemberley family are endless. From what he said of Miss Darcy, I was thoroughly prepared to see a proud, reserved, disagreeable girl. Yet he knew it was a lie. Wickham knew she was amiable and unpretending, just as we have found her."

Mr. Gardner then spoke of his conversation with Mr. Darcy.

"But does Lydia know nothing of this?" asked his wife. "Can she be ignorant of what you all seem so well to understand?"

"Oh, yes!" said Elizabeth. "That is the worst of all. When we were in Kent, we saw so much of both Mr. Darcy and his relation, Colonel Fitzwilliam, but we were ignorant of the truth ourselves. And when we returned home, the ——shire was to leave Meryton in a short time. As that was the case, neither Jane nor I thought it necessary to make our knowledge public, for of what use could it be to anyone that the good opinion which all the neighborhood had of Wickham should then be overthrown? And even when it was settled that Lydia should go with Mrs. Forster, the necessity of opening *her* eyes to his character never occurred to me. That she could be in any danger never entered my head. That such a consequence as this should ensue, you may easily believe was far from my thoughts."

"When they all removed to Brighton, therefore, you had no reason, I suppose, to believe them fond of each other." said her uncle.

"Not the slightest," said Jane. "I can remember no true sign of affection on either side. When first Wickham entered the corps, Lydia was ready enough to admire him, but so we all were."

Elizabeth sighed. "Every girl in or near Meryton was out of her senses about him for the first two months, but Wickham never distinguished Lydia by any particular attention. Consequently, after a moderate period of extravagant and wild admiration, her fancy for him gave way, and others of the regiment, who treated her with more distinction, again became her favorites."

"This is a puzzlement that bodes ill," said their aunt. All in the coach knew of what she meant: Without affection, how was Wickham to be convinced to marry Lydia?

Darcy embraced his sister. "Do not cry, Georgiana. I will write from London."

"Be careful, Brother," she sobbed. "I…I hate him, you know."

"He will never bother you again, Georgie. I swear it."

She kissed his cheek. "All my love to Miss Elizabeth." Darcy said nothing but hugged his sister tighter.

"Are you ready, Darcy?" called Bingley from his saddle.

Without an answer, Darcy mounted his horse. From upon it, he saw the Hursts and Miss Bingley move towards their carriage.

"Godspeed, Fitzwilliam!" cried Georgiana.

Darcy tipped his hat, and the pair was away towards London.

Chapter 13

An Appointment in London

M r. Thomas Bennet was having an exceedingly bad day. He had planned to leave his rented rooms in London after breakfast and take a hired carriage to Gracechurch Street, but the innkeeper, having left the premises for an errand, kept him waiting for his meal over two hours. Then no hackney cab could be secured until another hour had been lost. On top of that, it began to rain. So it was that a damp and aggravated Mr. Bennet entered his brother-in-law's lodgings in Cheapside. After greeting his relatives and recounting his tale of woe, he was shown into Mr. Gardiner's study for a bit of brandy.

"What news, Brother?" asked Gardiner after Bennet had enjoyed his first sip.

Bennet rolled his eyes. "Colonel Forster might be a fine commander of militia, but as a hunter and guide, he is as bereft of ability as he is as a guardian! We have found no trace of Lydia or that scoundrel! I must admit I am glad to see you, for I am at my wit's end."

"Patience, Thomas, they will be found."

"Found? In the largest city in the world? I must wonder at your confidence, sir, for I have none. No, I have not the least expectation that Lydia will be discovered. In any case, I expect it is too late. I am sure Wickham has already achieved his purpose. She is ruined, Edward, and all my girls with her."

"You do not know that, Thomas. Do not despair. Have faith in your daughter."

Bennet cried, "I know she is lost; she is like her mother! I blame her mother for this!" At Gardiner's pained expression, he added, "Forgive me, Edward. That was unseemly."

"I know well my sister's failings, but you must hold your tongue. We have guests coming."

Bennet started. "Guests? At a time like this?" He raised his glass to his lips.

"Yes, Thomas, they are—"

At that moment, the door of the study was opened by the butler. "Mr. Bingley and Mr. Darcy to see you, sir."

Bennet choked on his drink.

"Sir!" cried Bingley to Mr. Bennet. "Are you well? May I get you something for your relief?" Without waiting for leave, he crossed over to the gagging man and began pounding him on the back.

"Bingley," said Darcy dispassionately, "might I suggest you stop beating the man before you injure him?"

"Oh, of course! I beg your pardon, Mr. Bennet!"

Bennet soon recovered from his coughing fit and Bingley's remedy. "It…it is quite all right, young man. I must admit I am surprised to see you here, and my astonishment is redoubled at *your* attendance, Mr. Darcy."

Bingley gave the gentleman a slight bow. "We are here to offer our services to you!"

A nameless dread crept into Bennet's bones. "What services are those, sir? I fail to understand your meaning."

Darcy glanced at Gardiner in confusion. That momentary pause prevented him from stopping Bingley from replying, "Why, to help find Miss Lydia!"

"WHAT?" He spun upon his brother-in-law. "Are these gentlemen aware of our troubles? Why in heaven's name did you tell them? You are mad, Gardiner!"

"Mr. Bennet!" cried Darcy. "I will explain all, but you must control yourself, sir!" As Bennet continued to babble, he added, *"Sit down, sir!"*

The power of Darcy's personality hit the older man like a force of nature. Before he knew it, Mr. Bennet was seated back in his armchair.

Darcy took breath. "Inadvertently, Mr. Bingley and I learned of your family's misfortune. As you know, I have had dealings with Mr. Wickham before. Due to my superior knowledge of that…man's habits and tendencies, I offer my talents and those of my friend to help recover your daughter and to protect your family's honor."

"You know where he is?" the distraught father asked.

"No, sir, I do not. However, I am confident that I can find him."

Bennet looked at Darcy with a suspicious eye. "How is it that a man of your standing would acquire such knowledge?"

Darcy hesitated, but he knew this time would come. In a calm voice, he relayed his history with Wickham, including the reprobate's attempt to seduce Georgiana. Bingley had heard the tale during their trip from Derbyshire, but the story was new to the older gentlemen, and their astonishment was great. They did not doubt the veracity of his account, as they could not imagine a man like Fitzwilliam Darcy inventing such a tale.

Bennet held his head in his hands. "Hopeless—it is hopeless." As Gardiner tried to comfort his brother-in-law, the gentleman raised his face to Darcy. "Such a man, such a lack of scruples! How is he to be worked on? Mr. Darcy, thank you for your offer—and you too, Mr. Bingley—but there is nothing to be done. My daughter is ruined, whether she is recovered or not, and all that remains is to call that rascal out and leave my wife a widow."

"There is a way to end this matter in a…somewhat satisfactory manner," offered Darcy.

"Do not toy with me, sir," begged Bennet. "I know you have little reason to love me. I have not been kind to you. But I ask you to take pity on me."

Darcy kneeled down, "Could you bear Wickham as a son-in-law?"

He grimaced. "I would bear anything to preserve my family's honor."

"Then all is settled. I shall see them married."

"How? Wickham hates you!"

"There is something Wickham loves above all else—money."

Bennet snorted. "I have not been sitting on my hands, Mr. Darcy! I have been making inquiries here and in Meryton. Colonel Forster has quite an accounting from Brighton, as well. Wickham's debts are more than I could hope to pay."

"Do not be concerned about that issue, Mr. Bennet."

"What do you mean?" Astonishment overcame his countenance. "Mr. Darcy, surely you are not—"

"The fault is mine, and so must the remedy be. Leave Wickham to me." Darcy's words were like ice.

"Mr. Darcy! You take too much on yourself!"

"Nevertheless, I shall have it. I shall not be swayed. My mind is determined."

"Do not bother to argue, Thomas," advised Gardiner. "I have tried, and Mr. Darcy is resolute if nothing else."

"Indeed, sir," added Bingley. "I cannot remember any time in our acquaintance that Darcy was persuaded away from his purpose."

Bennet shook his head. "But this makes no sense! I can understand your interest in the matter, Mr. Bingley," he said as he gestured to that gentleman, "as I assume you have come to your senses and are here for Jane's sake. By the way, we must have a conversation about your abandonment of Hertfordshire last autumn.

"But what is *your* concern, Mr. Darcy? Why should you care about my family, unless—" His face went white. "Oh...oh no, no, no!"

"Sir?" asked Darcy.

"Not Lizzy! Not my Lizzy!"

Mr. Bennet's day had definitely gotten worse.

A VERY FINE CARRIAGE ROLLED through a notorious part of the British capital in the early evening. Up and down narrow lanes it traveled, until it stopped by a darkened alley off a small street. Five gentlemen descended from the vehicle, all carrying weapons, and they took in their surroundings.

"Is my Lydia here?" a shaky voice was heard to utter.

"No," said another.

Instructions were given to the driver and his companions. After the gentlemen were satisfied that their servants were alert, the five moved quietly down the lane, never glancing at the denizens of the neighborhood as they traveled through. Within moments, they were knocking at a certain door.

"Who is it?" came a challenge.

"Mick sent me," was returned. "God save th' King."

Satisfied with the password, the door was unlocked. At that instant, the men charged the door, forcing it open and overpowering the large guard inside the vestibule.

"Quickly," cried a man used to giving orders. "That door! Stop for nothing!" An instant later, the group had forced the second door as well and found themselves in a hallway confronting an ill-dressed housemaid.

"Very well, Darcy, you are in charge now," said Colonel Fitzwilliam.

"You, girl," Darcy demanded the maid, "where is Mrs. Younge? Be quick, or it will go badly for you."

The frightened servant hastily took the group to a third door, but before they could knock, it opened. "Ah, Mr. Darcy, I thought I heard your voice," said a middle-aged woman who wore too much rouge and too little clothing.

Colonel Fitzwilliam jumped in front of his cousin, drawing his pistol on the woman. "Aye, Younge, and not alone! Drop that gun, or by heaven, you will not see the sunrise!" Bingley and Gardiner brandished their arms as well.

Mrs. Younge smirked and dropped her muff pistol. "You haven't changed, have you, Colonel?"

"It is why I am still alive, Mrs. Younge." He pushed by her and quickly searched the room. "It is safe to come in, gentlemen."

"Won't you come in, Mr. Darcy?" Mrs. Younge spoke in a mocking tone. The company entered the cheaply over-done sitting room. Their nostrils were filled with the exotic smells of illegal substances. "You gentlemen too," she added to the group's back. "May I offer you something? I believe I have what you're looking for."

Darcy turned to her. "If it is information you offer, Younge, yes, you do. As for what else you are peddling, I believe we shall decline."

"Information about what?"

"Where is Wickham?"

Her face closed up. "I don't know what you're talking about."

"Come, madam!" cried Mr. Bennet. "Tell us what you know! He has my daughter. Surely you see we are desperate?"

Younge's eyes glinted with malice. "And what is that to me?"

"I can have you taken up, you know." Darcy picked up a vase. "Do you think I have forgotten this piece? It has been missing from my townhouse for over a year."

Hate emanated from the woman's countenance. "Go ahead, sir, do your worst! Miss Georgiana gave that to me! My word against yours!" She laughed. "As if you would suffer your precious sister to testify in public!"

Before Darcy could reply, Bingley stepped in. "You are right, Mrs. Younge. Darcy has misused you, has he not?"

"Aye, he did. Underpaid and underappreciated, I was!"

Bingley gave her a tight smile. "Yes, I know how he can be. Do you know he told me not to marry my love?"

Younge nodded. "Yes, that's him all right."

Darcy flushed but said nothing. The other gentlemen remained silent as they followed Bingley's lead.

Younge's eye was caught by the gold guinea that had suddenly appeared in Bingley's fingers. It glittered in the candlelight as he twirled it about.

"Yes," he went on, "but we know what can make it better. *This* can, can it not?" Seductive was his voice. "Mr. Bennet will give me permission to court his daughter if we recover her sister. Now, I know you would not stand in the way of true love." A second guinea followed. "You want to help me, I am sure." She snatched at the coins, but he pulled away. "No, no...the address first."

She licked her lips. "You won't give me up to the magistrate?"

"You have my word. Twenty of these for the address. A like amount mailed to you upon our success."

"What if he's left already?" she whined.

"Then you best be quick about it."

"Where in the world did you learn that coin trick, Bingley?" asked Colonel Fitzwilliam once the group had returned to the carriage.

"I learned at school. I never dreamed it would become useful in a situation like that." Bingley turned to Darcy. "I do apologize for what I said back there." He leaned across the carriage, hand outstretched in friendship.

Darcy wasted no time in grasping it. "Think nothing of it," he said.

"You would have gotten her to tell us what she knows eventually, but it came to me that this approach might serve and in an expedited manner. And I thought she would be more amenable to someone she thought had a grudge against you, as she obviously does."

"It matters not, old man. We got the information we need. Besides," Darcy looked down, "you were not far wrong. My interference in your matters was beyond disgraceful."

Mr. Bennet could no longer hold his tongue. "I must interject, sirs, as you seem to be speaking about my daughter. Was there truth in what you said to that jade back there?"

Before Darcy could explain, Bingley said, "A misunderstanding, Mr. Bennet, nothing more, and one that has been forgiven. I must disagree with my friend's statement, however. Darcy's judgment is of the highest quality. I hope you are not offended by my claim to that woman, but it was the only thing I could think of at the time. I am most exceedingly sorry to have mentioned your daughter."

Bennet patted Bingley's knee. "Mr. Bingley, I would be honored to have you court my daughter."

Lt. George Wickham was awakened from sleeping off a night of drink and debauchery by an insistent knocking on the door of his rented rooms. Not one to trust anyone who knocked on any door he found himself behind, Wickham's first inclination was to ignore it. However, the noise awoke Lydia, and she had no scruples against calling out.

"Who is it?"

Stupid chit!

"There be some gentlemen wantin' to speak ta Mr. Wickham, ma'am," called the keeper of the disreputable lodgings in which they found themselves. "They got a business proposition fer 'im."

That perked up two sets of ears. "Did you hear that, Wickie? Now you can settle your business, and we can be married!"

Marriage to Lydia was not high on Wickham's list—going to fight Napoleon one-handed and blindfolded won by a factor of three—but she was a jolly and willing sort, and she caught on fast to the sorts of games Wickham enjoyed, so he intended to keep the girl around for a while.

"Excellent, my dear. Go into the dressing area and make yourself presentable while I see to the door. And remember…"

"Yes, yes—keep quiet. I know."

He gave her a grin. "Business can be *so* tiresome. Off with you." She squealed as he gave her a slap on her most agreeable bottom, and she dashed into the other room.

"Be right there!" Wickham called out as the knocking resumed. He pulled on his clothes and walked over to the door. "Who is it?"

"Younge sent us," came a response. It was the right one. Wickham took off the chain and opened the door to see—

"What the deuce? *Darcy!*"

"Wickham." The furious master of Pemberley stood without, and he was not alone.

"Good morning, Wickham. Surely you have not forgotten me," came another unwelcomed voice.

"No, I have not. It has been a long time, Colonel."

The rest of the party entered without waiting to be invited.

"Wickham," began Darcy, "this is Mr. Gardiner, Miss Lydia's uncle, and I believe you know Mr. Bingley. We would have words with you. First, where is Miss Lydia?"

Wickham was confused. He understood Gardiner's interest, but he had no idea why the other three were there. To buy time he tried to brazen it out. "Miss Lydia—Miss Lydia Bennet? I do not know what you are talking about. Is she missing? She is not here, as you can see."

A lady's chemise was carelessly draped on the lone chair for all to see. "Blackguard!" cried Bingley. "Tell us this instant what you have done with her!"

"Wickie?" came a female voice. "Is that Mr. Bingley?"

Bingley lost all control. "You cur! You have taken advantage of a mere child!" He stripped off one of his gloves and raised it high as he moved toward the cornered man. "You shall pay for this, you—"

He did not finish as a lightning-fast fist shot out and connected with his chin. Bingley fell to the filthy floor, insensible to all around him.

"Sorry about that, Darcy," said Fitzwilliam as he drew back his aching hand. "I thought you wanted to handle this."

"I did—good work, Fitz."

"Mr. Bingley!" cried Lydia as she emerged from the dressing room. "Why is he on the floor? Is he ill?"

The other four men blanched at her entrance for varying reasons. At least the girl had respectable clothing on.

Mr. Gardiner started to open his mouth, but Darcy interrupted. "Yes, he has just taken ill, Miss Lydia. Would you help your uncle take him downstairs for aid?"

"I cannot pick him up. I am a lady!" she cried. "You carry him, Mr. High-and-Mighty Darcy! Or are you too good to do it?"

This was not the place to argue. Mr. Bennet was waiting below, as planned.

"Very well. Mr. Gardiner, your assistance please. Miss Lydia, we will need your help downstairs." The two seized the now woozy Bingley by his arms and half-carried him out of the room, Lydia trailing behind. The room was empty, save for Colonel Fitzwilliam and Lt. Wickham.

"Well," sneered Wickham, "you got what you came for, so why not just clear off?"

"Wickham, you should be more grateful," replied Fitzwilliam easily. "We have just saved you a world of trouble."

"Trouble? What do you mean?"

"Surely, even a man of your limited intellect could see that Bingley was going to challenge you to a duel."

Wickham laughed. "That fool? You need not have bothered. I could have beaten him one-handed!"

A very distinct sound brought realization to Wickham's mind. He just recalled that most of the men present had walking sticks in their hands—the type that concealed thin blades. It was common for gentlemen to carry such weapons in Town for their protection. Colonel Fitzwilliam had no such stick in his hands, however. He did not have need of one, as it turned out. The next sound he heard was that of a cavalry sword being drawn from its scabbard; the same sword was now an inch from his throat.

Fitzwilliam shook his head sadly. "Wickham, Wickham, Wickham—will you ever learn? No one will have the chance to kill you before I do. You only live because I suffer that you do."

Wickham looked into the deadly serious eyes of the colonel. "I get your...point, Colonel."

"Fitz! What is this?" cried Darcy as he reentered.

"I was trying to decide the best way to filet this baggage, Cuz," Fitzwilliam eyed Wickham speculatively.

"Peace, Fitz. Let us give Wickham his last chance."

The colonel hesitated before re-sheathing his blade. "You always spoil my amusement, Darcy."

Wickham steeped back and laughed nervously. "Do not sport with me, gentlemen. Strike down an unarmed man, outnumbered three-to-one? You would not dare! You would be taken up for it."

"Do not be so sure, Mr. Wickham," said Gardiner as he came back into the room. "You, a steward's son, have misused the daughter of a gentleman. He, on the other hand, is an officer and the son of an earl. Do you really think he shall be held responsible?"

"A bit of scandal—what is that to me?" observed Fitzwilliam with his arms crossed.

Wickham was shaken. "And...and the Bennet family? Do you care nothing for them?"

Darcy assumed his most disinterested air. "They are not my family, Wickham."

"Mr. Gardiner, surely you can see the damage such a scandal would do to your nieces!" cried the desperate man.

Gardiner's rage was no play-acting. "Are they not already ruined by your actions? It seems to me your destruction would lessen that disgrace. Why, it might be forgotten in a twelve-month." He paused. "Let us get down to cases, Wickham. As Mr. Darcy said, you have one last chance. He is here on my behalf as my friend and business partner. He has kindly agreed to negotiate for my family."

It was not true—yet—as they had not had time to completely discuss the future business dealings they had mentioned in past conversations. But Wickham did not need to know Darcy's true motivations, and Gardiner could lie much better than Darcy.

"I am all attention, my good sirs."

"Sit down, Wickham," commanded the master of Pemberley. "This is how it will be."

Within a half hour, the party was on their way back to Cheapside. In one carriage were a distraught father, a disgusted uncle, and a foolish, newly engaged girl of fifteen. In the other, rode an embarrassed Bingley with his two companions.

"I am sorry about striking you, my good fellow," Fitzwilliam said as he patted Bingley's back.

"Come, say you forgive him," begged Darcy.

"Oh, I already have. Do not be alarmed, Colonel." He shook his head sadly. "Did I do it again, Darcy?"

"I am afraid so, old man." Darcy grinned to himself.

"It is just as well you never got to call Wickham out, Bingley," said Fitzwilliam. "We could not have him sticking you, now could we? Miss Bennet would never forgive us."

Bingley wore a hurt expression on his face, but it was Darcy who answered. "You might be wrong on that score, Fitz."

"What do you mean, Darcy? You cannot doubt Miss Bennet's affection now, can you?"

"How do you know about that?" cried Bingley.

Darcy frowned. "It matters not, as I have already told Charles that I was in error. I do not know your source of information, Cuz, but I would advise you to keep a better hold on your tongue lest Bingley makes you regret it."

Fitzwilliam laughed. "Forgive me, my dear Bingley, but I have seen you fence."

Darcy said, "Not lately. You mistook my meaning earlier, Fitz. What you are wrong about was Bingley's skill with a blade. He has been my fencing partner this last half year, and he has progressed very well. I believe he could thrash Wickham easily."

Bingley grinned. "It is nice for you to say so, Darce, but I have yet to beat you."

Not many have. "Ah, but I have also fought Fitz, and I would observe that there is not much difference between the two of you. No, you would be very well matched."

Fitzwilliam began chuckling at this. Darcy gave his friend a significant look, jerking his head at his cousin.

"Care to meet me, Colonel?" asked Bingley.

"All right, old boy. I was never one to back away from a challenge. What say you to tomorrow afternoon?"

Bingley smiled, which unnerved the colonel further. "The day following would be better. Would eleven o'clock at the fencing club suit you?"

"Done!" Fitz shook Bingley's hand, wondering what he had gotten himself into.

Darcy smiled. *This should prove to be entertaining.*

As THE CARRIAGES STOPPED BEFORE the Gardiner house on Gracechurch Street, Darcy took his farewell. To his surprise, Mr. Bennet handed over his daughter to Mr. Gardiner and approached him.

"Mr. Darcy," said the weary man, "I must thank you and your companions for everything you have done for me and my family."

"Think nothing of it, sir. We were happy to have been of service."

"Ah—the very subject I wished to raise with you. May I have the opportunity to speak with you tomorrow?"

Darcy frowned. "I have business with my banker tomorrow morning."

"No doubt," Bennet said dryly.

"Hmm, yes. But I am at my leisure afterwards." He handed Bennet his card. "Shall we say two o'clock?"

Bennet looked at the card. "I am honored, but I did not mean to invite myself to your home."

Darcy smirked. "It is not St. James's Palace, sir. I shall see you then."

Chapter 14

Tidings That Will Give Satisfaction

The carriage made good time from Derbyshire, and two days after leaving Lambton, it arrived at the steps of Longbourn. Mr. and Mrs. Gardiner tarried but an hour before gathering up their children and pushing on to Town, to Mrs. Bennet's dismay. But to no entreating would the couple attend. They were expecting distinguished company at Gracechurch Street.

Mrs. Bennet was all that Kitty had described and more. She flailed about, alternately blaming her distress on everyone but herself and making herself hysterical over fears that Wickham would make her a widow in the inevitable duel.

"If I had been able," said she, "to carry my point of going to Brighton with all my family, this would not have happened. Poor dear Lydia had nobody to take care of her. Why did the Forsters ever let her go out of their sight? I am sure there was some great neglect or other on their side, for she is not the kind of girl to do such a thing if she had been well looked after. I always thought they were very unfit to have the charge of her, but I was overruled, as I always am! Poor dear child! And now here's Mr. Bennet gone away, and I know he will fight Wickham and then he will be killed, and what is to become of us all? Mr. Collins cannot manage the estate, and if my brother is not kind to us, I do not know what we shall do!"

To the girls' peace of mind, she kept to her rooms, allowing the sisters to talk and console each other without interruption. Alone for the moment, they seized the opportunity to read the letter that had been received from Mary.

Sisters! Such distressing news you send me! Lydia run off with Mr. Wickham! Oh, why did no one pay heed to the warnings? How was it my father allowed a girl with such weak understanding to go to Brighton, where the temptations must have been overwhelming? This is a most unfortunate affair and will probably be much talked of. But we must stem the tide of malice and pour into the wounded bosoms of each other the balm of sisterly consolation.

Mr. Collins is very concerned and would go to Longbourn to offer succor, but I have convinced him to stay and attend to his duties. Alas! Be careful what you wish for! My husband took me at my word and went without delay to inform Lady Catherine of our distress. She is all concern, I am told, and advises us to write the wayward girl out of our lives this instant. Lady Catherine's kindness knows no bounds. Anne, of course, is truly concerned and sends her private condolences.

Mr. Collins has been advised on the poor choice he made in sharing our burden. He will feel it greatly, I have no doubt.

The only good news to come of this is that you tell me that Mr. Darcy and Mr. Bingley have offered their services. I, of course, have shared this intelligence with only Anne. She is as surprised and happy over this news as I, and she begs me to assure you both that Mr. Darcy is the cleverest of men and will soon see the matter set to rights, if any man can. I pray to Our Lord that her confidence is not ill placed and that more than one lady may win her happiness.

THE DAY AFTER SHE RETURNED, Jane was walking about the flower garden where she discovered Kitty in tears. Hurrying to her side, Jane embraced her sister while asking about the reason for her distress.

"Oh! I have just come from Meryton…I went for some lace…and was most cruelly cut by Mrs. Fairweather!"

"Oh, Kitty, are you certain? She has been our mother's friend for years."

"The cut direct, I say!" she cried. "I was coming out of the shop, and…and I saw Mrs. Fairweather and her daughter come out from the bakery across the lane. They had just begun crossing the street when I bid them hello. She…she saw me and turned on her heel and walked in the opposite direction, dragging her daughter with her!"

"Oh, my!"

"That is not all. I saw Lady Lucas and Maria on my way to the village. Lady Lucas was polite, as always, but I could tell she was uneasy. Oh, Jane, what shall I do if she decides I am unfit company for Maria? She is my only friend left." She broke down.

Jane tried to offer consolation, but Kitty would not hear of it. "No, Jane, I deserve it! I knew what Lydia was planning. I could have stopped it if I told. But I did not, and Father is so angry with me, and now all of Meryton is rising against me!"

"How much did you know, Kitty?"

"Lydia wrote to tell me that Mr. Wickham had been paying her exclusive attention in the last week before she—" Kitty dug into her reticule. "And Colonel Forster brought this note she left with them."

MY DEAR HARRIET,

You will laugh when you know where I am gone, and I cannot help laughing myself at your surprise tomorrow morning, as soon as I am missed. I am going to Gretna Green, and if you cannot guess with who, I shall think you a simpleton, for there is but one man in the world I love, and he is an angel. I should never be happy without him, so think it no harm to be off. You need not send them word at Longbourn of my going, if you do not like it, for it will make the surprise the greater when I write to them, and sign my name "Lydia Wickham." What a good joke it will be! I can hardly write for laughing.

Pray make my excuses to Pratt for not keeping my engagement and dancing with him tonight. I shall send for my clothes when I get to Longbourn, but I wish you would tell Sally to mend a great slit in my worked muslin gown before they are packed up. Good-bye. Give my love to Colonel Forster. I hope you will drink to our good journey.

Your affectionate friend,
LYDIA BENNET.

"Oh, thoughtless, thoughtless Lydia!" cried Jane, when she had finished it. "What a letter is this, to be written at such a moment! But at least it shows that she was serious in the object of her journey. Whatever Wickham might afterwards persuade her to, it was not on her side a scheme of infamy. My poor father! How he must have felt it!"

"I never saw anyone so shocked. He could not speak a word for full ten minutes. My mother was taken ill immediately, and the whole house was in such confusion!"

"Oh, Kitty," cried Jane, "was there a servant who did not know the whole story before the end of the day?"

"I do not know. I hope there was. But to be guarded at such a time is very difficult. My mother was in hysterics, and though I endeavored to give her every assistance in my power, I am afraid I did not do so much as I might have done!"

Jane stroked Kitty's forehead with concern. "Your attendance upon her has been too much for you. You do not look at all well. Oh, that I had been with you! You have had every care and anxiety upon yourself alone."

"It has been difficult. But what has Lydia done that was so bad? Is it not romantic to elope?"

Jane frowned. "Kitty, you must understand. Loss of virtue in a female is irretrievable. That one false step involves her in endless ruin. A lady's reputation is no less brittle than it is beautiful, and she cannot be too much guarded in her behavior towards the undeserving of the other sex."

Kitty bit her lip. "And *my* reputation, too?"

"Yes."

"Then it *is* my fault!" she wailed.

"It is no more your fault than it is mine or Lizzy's."

"How is this?" Kitty sniffed. "Did you know of Lydia's intentions?"

"No, but we knew Wickham's true nature."

"Then why did you not say something?"

"The information came from another. We thought it not our story to tell. In this, we were wrong. But you must see that this must be laid at Lydia's feet." She indicated the letter still in her hand. "She was not carried away. She *chose* to go with Wickham. We must now try to save her from herself, for she does not know what kind of man Wickham is."

"How can we? Father will never find them in London."

"There is no need. You must promise to keep this most secret, even from our mother." Kitty's eyes grew wide as her sister continued. "We have help. Mr. Bingley and Mr. Darcy, who we saw in Derbyshire, became aware of our shame by accident, and they have volunteered to help us. Mr. Darcy assures us he will be able to hunt down Mr. Wickham."

"Mr. Bingley and *Mr. Darcy*? Odious Mr. Darcy?"

Jane smiled. "Do not let Lizzy hear you say that."

"What do you mean?"

Jane recalled Elizabeth's outburst: *"Find them and I am yours."* Aloud she said, "We have discovered in Derbyshire that Mr. Wickham was not so admired, nor Mr. Darcy so disagreeable, as we had been lead to believe. Allow me to assure you that Mr. Darcy, rather than being proud and aloof, is the most kind and generous man. Wickham is his enemy, having done great injury to him in the past. Mr. Darcy feels he must protect his friends from Mr. Wickham."

"His injuries? But Mr. Wickham said—"

"All lies, my love. Everything Mr. Wickham said is untrue."

"And Mr. Darcy considers us his friends?"

"Us and the Gardiners, yes."

Kitty smiled. "It is agreeable to have such a friend, even if he is not an officer."

Jane laughed. "It is also agreeable to have you as my sister. You have done well here. Do not dwell overmuch on this sad business. Come, I would have you laugh again."

Kitty's eyes shone. A born follower, she copied Lydia because Jane and Lizzy had had no time for her, and Mary was ill suited to set an example. Now that Lydia was disgraced and Jane was paying her attention, it was but a moment's work for her to switch her alliance to her eldest sister, and by extension, to Elizabeth, too.

"MR. BENNET, SIR," THE BUTLER announced at the doorway of Darcy's study.

Darcy arose from his desk and greeted the older man. He offered his guest a chair, but the gentleman waved him off, lost in admiration of the owner's collection of books.

"This is a fine library, Mr. Darcy!" he said.

Darcy acknowledged the compliment and watched Bennet peer closely at the volumes. Seeing that all had been read, some numerous times, the master of Longbourn looked at the gentleman with new respect.

"I am glad you are not one of those who collects books for the color of the spines, sir."

Darcy hid a small smile. Clearly, he knew many who did just that.

"And does your home in Derbyshire have a like collection?"

Darcy shook his head. "This library has been my humble construction. It is nothing to Pemberley's; that is work of many generations."

Bennet sighed. He took a chair and sat, looking at Darcy. "I suppose you are wondering why I wished to speak with you."

"I must admit a curiosity," he replied as he took his own chair behind his desk.

"This has been a most unpleasant business and a puzzling one, too. I am the injured father, and I wish I had nothing to do with it. You, on the other hand, are a stranger. Yet you have announced that you will see my unfortunate daughter reclaim her respectability though lawful marriage—no matter the cost."

Darcy coughed. "Sir, I must insist—"

"No, no, there is no talking you out of it, I am sure. My question is: why? Why do you do it? Do you not know you are the kind of man I can deny nothing?"

Darcy started. "I do not have the pleasure of understanding you, sir."

"If you want to marry my Lizzy, why not ask me?"

Darcy leapt to his feet and crossed to the window, trying to settle his emotions.

Bennet watched him with glee. *I have you there, young man!*

After a moment, Darcy turned to him. "Mr. Bennet, I will not insult your intelligence by denying my feelings. I will say that I admire your second daughter—I admire her greatly, in fact. But I must make myself perfectly understood upon this matter. I do not do what I do in hope of thanks or reward. I expect nothing. Duty requires I set right what Wickham has done."

"Yes, yes, I remember your tale. Frankly, I would have let your cousin run the bugger through."

A smile tugged at Darcy's lip. "The thought had occurred to me."

Bennet was pleased to see that Darcy was human after all. "So you expect nothing, eh? Does Lizzy know of your involvement?"

Darcy blushed. "Yes, unfortunately."

"Why do you say this? Do you not want my daughter's gratitude?"

"Again, I must say I ask for nothing—"

"Yes, yes, let us stop beating around the bush. Do you have something to ask of me, Mr. Darcy?"

Darcy swallowed. "Mr. Bennet, may I have the honor of paying court to your daughter Miss Elizabeth?"

"Well, that was not so hard, was it?" Bennet said, all the while his heart sank with the reality of the situation. He knew this day would come, and he admired Darcy, but Lizzy was his favorite. "Have you any idea whether Lizzy would welcome your company?"

"Yes, I believe she would have no objection. I had not spoken before as, until recently, I had not earned Miss Elizabeth's favorable opinion. That I now have it, I am thankful. It was accomplished before this business with your youngest daughter, I must point out," Darcy quickly added.

"This is rather sudden. I know you were in her company while she and Jane were traveling with the Gardiners in Derbyshire."

"Yes. I also saw Miss Elizabeth in Kent. I was visiting Rosings while your daughters were visiting Mrs. Collins."

"Ah ha! And it was there you began changing Lizzy's opinion of you? It was rather low at one time, as I recall."

"Yes, I suppose that was the genesis of our better understanding. Sir, I must assure you that nothing untoward has occurred. Miss Elizabeth is one of the most unique and intriguing individuals I have ever met. I have for many months been impressed with her wit, understanding, and principals. I am well aware of the differences in our situations. Yet, she *is* a gentleman's daughter."

Bennet nodded.

"And I am a gentleman. So we are equal. I also wish you to know that I am a better man for knowing your daughter. Believe me when I say that I value Miss Elizabeth above anyone I know. She is on a par with my dear sister, for whom I would do anything."

Again, Bennet nodded.

"I am my own man. I answer to no one save my conscience. My good father raised me to know my duties and responsibilities. Should I be successful in my suit, I would look upon it as a great gift from my creator. Your daughter would want for nothing, be it comfort, respect, or affection." Darcy was blushing furiously.

Bennet, who had already received the same intelligence from Mr. Gardiner, decided to end his teasing game. "Then you have my permission to court Elizabeth, my boy. Now that that is over with, do you have any port? I could use a drink."

Darcy smiled and gave the older gentleman a glass of his best tawny. Grinning at the look of pure delight on his guest's face as he sipped, he asked, "Did you bring a carriage, sir?"

"What? No, I did not. I used a hired coach."

"Then we shall return to Gracechurch Street together. I am to sup there tonight along with Bingley."

"You are a glutton for punishment. There will be little suitable conversation with my youngest in the house."

"Perhaps. Might I interest you in a bit of entertainment tomorrow?"

"What have you in mind?"

"You must come to my fencing club. There will be a most interesting match. I think you will enjoy it."

As JANE AND KITTY WERE walking together behind the house a week later, they saw the housekeeper coming towards them and, concluding that she came to call them to their mother, went forward to meet her.

"I BEG YOUR PARDON FOR interrupting you, Miss Bennet, but I was in hopes you might have gotten some good news from Town, so I took the liberty of coming to ask."

"What do you mean, Hill? We have heard nothing from Town."

"Oh dear!" cried Mrs. Hill, in great astonishment. "Do you not know there is an express come from the master this half-hour? Miss Elizabeth has it."

Away ran the girls through the vestibule into the breakfast-room and from there into the library; Lizzy had been in neither room, and they were about to seek her upstairs with their mother when they were met by the butler.

"If you are looking for Miss Elizabeth, miss, she is walking towards the little copse."

Upon this information, Jane and Kitty instantly passed through the hall once more and ran across the lawn after their sister, who was on her way towards a small wood on one side of the paddock.

Jane, who was not so much in the habit of running as Kitty, soon lagged behind, while her sister, panting for breath, came up to Elizabeth.

"Oh, Lizzy—what news—what news? Have you heard from my father?"

"Yes, I have had a letter from him by express." Elizabeth's demeanor was cross.

"Well, and what news does it bring—good or bad?"

"What is there of good to be expected from this business?" She took the letter from her pocket. "But perhaps you would like to read it."

Kitty impatiently caught it from her hand, just as Jane came and stood beside them.

"Read it aloud," said Elizabeth, "for Jane's sake."

Gracechurch Street,
Monday, August 2.

MY DEAR DAUGHTERS,

At last I am able to send you some tidings of my wayward daughter and such as, I hope, will give you some little satisfaction. Soon after your Uncle Gardiner came to Town, I was fortunate enough to find out in what part of London Lydia and Wickham were residing. The particulars I will reserve until we meet. It is enough to know they are discovered. I have seen them both.

"Then it is as I always hoped," cried Jane; "they are married!"

"Keep reading, Kitty," growled Elizabeth.

I have seen them both. They are not married, nor can I find there was any intention of being so, but I hope it will not be long before they are. All that was required of me was to assure to your incredibly silly and irresponsible sister, by settlement, her equal share of the five thousand pounds secured among you girls after the demise of myself and your mother and, moreover, to enter into an engagement of allowing her, during my life, one hundred pounds per annum.

These are conditions with which, considering everything, I had no hesitation to comply. You will easily assume, from these particulars, that Wickham's circumstances are not so hopeless as they are generally believed to be. And if you believe that, I shall think you all are the great simpletons of the world. Without the aid of a certain gentleman from Derbyshire and his good friends, I doubt that even this melancholy event would have come to pass. The world is upside-down, my loves.

I command that you all stay quietly at Longbourn and depend on my diligence and care. I shall not further reward this sham of a holy event with your attendance or that of your mother. We have judged it best that my daughter should be married from this house, and I hope you will take comfort from that. I leave to you the task of informing your mother of the above. Tell her what you will.

I shall write again as soon as the deed is done.

Yours, etc.
THO. BENNET

"Is it possible?" cried Kitty, when she had finished. "Can it be possible that he will marry her?"

"My dear father, I congratulate you!" said Jane. "And have you answered the letter, Lizzy?"

"No, but it must be done soon."

"Let me write for you," said Jane, "if you dislike the trouble yourself."

"I dislike it very much," she replied, "but it must be done. Oh, Jane! Can you not see what has passed?"

Kitty asked, "What do you mean?"

"Kitty, Wickham was bribed to marry our sister, depend upon it!"

"Well, yes, Father settled some money on him. A hundred a year is not so bad—"

"No man in his senses would marry Lydia on so slight a temptation as one hundred a year!" cried Elizabeth.

"That is very true," said Jane. "His debts to be discharged and something still to remain! It must be our friends' doing! Good, generous men, I am afraid they have distressed themselves. A small sum could not do all this."

"No," said Elizabeth. "Wickham is a fool if he takes her with a farthing less than ten thousand pounds!"

Kitty gasped. "Ten thousand pounds! Heaven forbid! How is half such a sum to be repaid?" She stopped and thought about what Jane said. "And *who* must be repaid?"

Elizabeth took the letter from Kitty's hand and reread a portion of it. *"…without the aid of a certain gentleman from Derbyshire and his good friends, I doubt that even this melancholy event would have come to pass.'"*

Kitty gasped again. *"Mr. Darcy?"*

Elizabeth threw down the hated letter as tears formed in her eyes. "Yes! Fitzwilliam Darcy, the most honorable, the most worthy, the most generous man of my acquaintance, has paid a fortune so that the most *unworthy* man in England, his greatest enemy, will marry our fool of a sister!"

Jane was troubled, as well. "And they must marry! Yet he is such a man!"

Anger and shame battled over Elizabeth's expression. "Yes, yes, they must marry. There is nothing else to be done! But there are two things that I want very much to know: One is how much money Mr. Darcy has laid down to bring it about, and the other is how I am ever to repay him."

"What are you talking about, Lizzy?" cried Kitty.

"Never mind, Kitty. I have coin he will accept."

"Lizzy, do not speak so!" Jane grasped her shoulders. "Do not do this! I thought your exclamation in Lambton was due to your heightened emotions. You cannot have been serious! Oh, Lizzy, no matter what, do not marry without love!"

Elizabeth smiled through her tears. "Love and devotion *is* my dowry, Jane—and he shall have it all."

Jane looked at her sister. Then, seeing the truth in Elizabeth's eyes, she embraced her, breaking into tears herself.

Kitty still looked horrified. "Are you speaking of Mr. Darcy?" Lizzy nodded. Kitty continued, "Do you love him?"

"With all my heart and all my soul."

Kitty joined in the embrace. Soon their tears turned to laughter. "Mr. Darcy!" Kitty cried. "Who would ever believe it? And after what he said about you at the Assembly!"

"Kitty, that is all forgot!" cried Elizabeth with a smile. "I love him, and he has the perfect good sense to love me in return. That is enough for me. An Assembly—what nonsense! Indeed, in such cases as this, a good memory is unpardonable. This is the last time I shall ever remember it myself."

"Oh, what Mama will say!"

"No, Kitty! Nothing to Mama until this sad business is done!"

"I agree," said Jane. "Our thoughts must be with Lydia and Wickham now."

"And they are really to be married!" said Elizabeth once they separated. "How strange this is! And for this we are to be thankful. That they should marry, small as is their chance of happiness and wretched as is his character, we are forced to rejoice. Oh, Lydia!"

"I comfort myself with thinking that Wickham certainly would not marry Lydia if he had not a real regard for her," replied Kitty. "Though your kind friends have done something towards clearing him, I cannot believe that ten thousand pounds, or anything like it, has been advanced. How could even *he* spare half ten thousand pounds?"

"If we are ever able to learn what Wickham's debts have been," said Elizabeth, "and how much is settled on our sister, we shall exactly know what Mr. Darcy has done for them because Wickham has not sixpence of his own! The kindness of Mr. Darcy and Mr. Bingley can never be repaid, nor that of my uncle and aunt, either. Taking Lydia into their home and affording her their personal protection is such a sacrifice to her advantage as years of gratitude cannot enough acknowledge. If such goodness does not make Lydia miserable now, she will never deserve to be happy! What a meeting for her, when she first saw my aunt!"

"We must endeavor to forget all that has passed on either side," said Jane. "I hope and trust they will yet be happy. Wickham's consenting to marry her is a proof, I believe, that he is come to a right way of thinking. Their mutual affection will steady them, and I flatter myself they will settle so quietly and live in so rational a manner as may, in time, make their past imprudence forgotten."

"Their conduct has been such," growled Elizabeth, "that no one can ever forget! It is useless to talk of it."

Kitty stood silently for a moment then said, "May we take Father's letter to read to Mama?"

Jane nodded. "Yes, Kitty. It should be done instantly."

The sisters walked quietly to the house and went upstairs together. After a slight preparation for good news, the letter was read aloud—an edited version, of course. Mrs. Bennet could hardly contain herself. As soon as Jane had read Mr. Bennet's hope of Lydia's being soon married, her joy burst forth, and every following sentence added to its exuberance. Mrs. Bennet was now in an irritation as violent from delight as she had ever been from alarm and vexation. To know that her daughter would be married was enough. She was disturbed by no fear for her felicity, nor humbled by any remembrance of Lydia's misconduct.

"My dear, dear Lydia!" she cried. "This is delightful indeed! She will be married! I shall see her again! She will be married at sixteen! My good, kind husband! I knew how it would be. I knew he would manage everything! How I long to see her! And to see dear Wickham too! But the clothes, the wedding clothes! I will write to Mr. Bennet about them directly and ask him how much he will give her. Ring the bell for Hill, Kitty. I will put on my things in a moment. My dear, dear Lydia! How merry we shall be together when we meet!"

Jane endeavored to give some relief to the violence of these transports by leading her thoughts to the obligations which Mr. Gardiner's behavior laid them all under. "For we must attribute this happy conclusion," she added, "in a great measure to his kindness. We are persuaded that he has pledged himself to assist Mr. Wickham with money." The girls had decided to continue their omission of the involvement of Mr. Darcy and Mr. Bingley in the affair. Kitty, deeply distressed at her mother's antics, silently agreed to the scheme.

"Well," cried her mother, "it is all very right. Who should do it but her own uncle? If he had not had a family of his own, I and my children must have had all his money, you know, and it is the first time we have ever had anything from him, except a few presents.

"I am so happy!" she continued. "In a short time I shall have another daughter married. Mrs. Wickham! How well it sounds! And she was only sixteen last June. My dear Jane, I am in such a flutter that I am sure I cannot write, so I will dictate, and you write for me. We will settle with your father about the money afterwards, but the wedding clothes should be ordered immediately."

Mrs. Bennet then proceeded to list all the particulars of calico, muslin, and cambric, and would shortly have dictated some very plentiful orders, had not Jane, though with some difficulty, persuaded her to wait until her father was at leisure to write again. One day's delay, Jane observed, would be of small importance, and her mother was too happy to be quite as obstinate as usual. Other schemes, too, came into her head.

"I will go to Meryton," said Mrs. Bennet, "as soon as I am dressed, and tell the good, good news to my Sister Phillips. And as I come back, I can call on Lady Lucas and Mrs. Long. Kitty, run down and order the carriage. An airing would do me a great deal of good, I am sure. Girls, may I do anything for you in Meryton? Oh! Here comes Hill! My dear Hill, have you heard the good news? Miss Lydia is going to be married, and you shall all have a bowl of punch to make merry at her wedding."

Mrs. Hill instantly expressed her joy. Elizabeth received her congratulations along with the rest, and then, sick of this folly, she took refuge in her own room.

Poor Lydia's situation must, at best, be bad enough, but that it was no worse, Elizabeth had need to be thankful. Elizabeth felt it so, and though neither rational happiness nor worldly prosperity could be justly expected for her sister, in looking back to what they had feared only two hours ago, Elizabeth felt all the advantages of what they had gained.

Oh, Fitzwilliam, come quickly! I need you!

Jane proved to be right and wrong at the same time. Mr. Bennet did write again. In fact, more than one letter was delivered the next day—a public letter was sent to Mrs. Bennet, and private messages were sent to his two eldest daughters.

Jane's letter was an accounting of Mr. Bingley's actions during *la affaire Lydia*. Still of two minds about that gentleman, Jane was warmed to know that he had kept to his word and was instrumental in finding her wayward sister. But clouding her happiness was her guilt for hurting him so badly in the spring. Did she deserve his attentions, his services? She thought not.

She was confused, however, about one line in the letter.

Mr. Bingley continues to be a surprising individual with unexpected abilities, as Colonel Fitzwilliam discovered to his dismay.

Elizabeth's letter was far less teasing.

My dear Lizzy, may I say how much I like your Mr. Darcy? Ha, I have shocked you, I think. He and I have had a long talk about many things, and I would like to share our conversation with you when I return home—that and a small request.

"STOP FIDGETING, DARCY!"

"I am certainly *not* fidgeting, Fitz. I just wish this to be over."

Darcy, Fitzwilliam, and Bingley stood in the pews of St ——, the Gardiner's church, watching Wickham and waiting for the bride to arrive. Finally, a quarter-hour past her time, the doors opened and the Gardiners entered the church.

"Aww, too bad, Wickham," teased the colonel. "She is here."

"My apologies, Darcy," said Gardiner. "Lydia had to change her gown three times."

Four young men rolled their eyes.

"Are we ready now?" asked the curate.

The signal was given, and the bride was escorted down the aisle by her father. All brides were lovely, but this one's insistent giggling ruined the illusion.

"You still have your sword, Fitzwilliam?" asked the groom from the side of his mouth.

"Sorry, Wickham, you missed your chance," returned the colonel.

Chapter 15

An Unwelcome Party Arrives

The women of Longbourn gathered in the front parlor, awaiting the expected arrivals. Mr. Bennet's letter had stated that he and the happy couple would set off for Hertfordshire immediately after an abbreviated wedding breakfast. Mrs. Bennet did not take her eye off the road for more than two minutes once the hour-long vigil commenced.

"A carriage! No! It is only the curate! Hateful man! Can he not stay at home rather than riding about the parish?"

"Mother, it is Mr. Goulding's duty to call upon the sick and unfortunate."

"That is all very well, Jane, but must he do it today? Wait…Yes! I see him! Your father's carriage and another behind! Wait…it is passing him? Who…LYDIA! I see her! Look! She is waving from the other coach! Oh, how fine it is! My darling girl is here!"

Mrs. Bennet dashed to the door, her daughters following behind at a more measured pace. The coach-and-four stopped before the house in a cloud of dust, but Mrs. Bennet paid it no mind. She could only think of her dearest daughter.

"Lydia!" she squealed.

Mrs. Wickham descended from the coach and ran to her mother, laughing out loud. Her mother stepped forwards, embraced her, and welcomed her with rapture. She gave her hand with an affectionate smile to Wickham, who followed his lady, and wished them both joy with an enthusiasm that showed no doubt of their happiness.

The gentleman's new sisters greeted him with far less warmth. Their thoughts flew to their father. Mr. Bennet removed himself from his carriage with a firm look at his son-in-law.

"I do beg pardon, sir," said a grinning Wickham, "but Lydia had a mind to race."

"That is understandable," replied Bennet as he beat the dust from his clothes, preventing his remaining daughters from embracing him. "Lydia was always fast."

Wickham blinked at the comment, which sounded suspiciously like a double entendre.

Bennet was attacked by his daughters.

"Oh, Papa, what you have borne!" whispered Elizabeth.

"Say nothing of that!" Mr. Bennet replied in a like manner. "Who should suffer but myself? It has been my own doing, and I ought to feel it."

"You must not be too severe upon yourself," replied Jane.

"No, Jane, let me once in my life feel how much I have been to blame. I am not afraid of being overpowered by the impression. It will pass away soon enough." He said in a louder voice, "Good day, Kitty. Any other officers skulking about?"

"Let them, Papa; I care not. I am only happy to see you home!" She hugged her surprised father tightly.

"A fine coach-and-four, sir," observed Elizabeth with no little resentment. "Courtesy of Mr. Darcy?"

Bennet smirked. "No, that is Mr. Bingley's contribution to this farce—a hired team. Your sister and her husband will continue their journey in more conventional transportation."

"Where will they go, Papa?" asked Jane.

"A commission in the Regular Army has been purchased for His Majesty's newest lieutenant. He and Mrs. Wickham are to Newcastle—far enough north that even your mother will not wish to visit."

"Mr. Bennet!" cried his wife. "Come welcome your daughter and new son!"

"And have I not been in their constant company this last week, Wife?" he said as he moved over to the group. "Lydia, Wickham—welcome to Longbourn."

"Only think of its being three months since I went away!" Lydia cried. "It seems but a fortnight, I declare, and yet many things have happened in the time. Good gracious! When I went away, I am sure I had no more idea of being married until I came back again! Though I thought it would be very good fun if I was." Her sisters blanched at the unfeeling stupidity in her words. "Does not everything seem so small, Wickham?"

"Everything is as it was—as pleasant as ever!" Wickham simpered. "And my new family even pleasanter. I had none of my own, but now my loss is richly compensated!"

A single thought raced through the minds of Bennet and his three other daughters— *I believe I shall be ill now.*

Lydia gaily continued. "Oh! Mama, do the people here know I am married today? I was afraid they might not, and we overtook William Goulding in his curricle, so I was determined he should know it. So I let down the side-glass next to him, and took off my glove and let my hand just rest upon the window-frame, so that he might see the ring, and then I bowed and smiled like anything."

Mrs. Bennet began herding them all in. "Come in, my loves! Dinner is on the table!"

Lydia, with anxious parade, walked up to her mother's right hand and said to her eldest sister, "Ah, Jane, I take your place now, and you must go lower, because I am a married woman!"

Elizabeth closed her eyes. *Give me strength!*

Elizabeth closed the door to her father's library behind her. "You wished to see me, sir?"

Mr. Bennet looked at her from over his glasses. "You did not enjoy dinner, Lizzy. Have you no appetite?"

"I have stomach enough." *But not for our company!*

Bennet chuckled as his daughter's expression. "Sit down, my dear, and tell me of Lambton." As Elizabeth opened her mouth to begin, he admonished her, "Everything, if you please. Recall that I have spoken to Mr. Darcy."

Elizabeth gulped and started again. She told her father of the trip to visit Pemberley, of Mr. Darcy's unexpected return, of the introduction to Miss Darcy, of the invitation to Pemberley, and of the accidental discovery by Mr. Darcy and Mr. Bingley of Lydia's elopement.

"Lizzy, I am aware of the events you have relayed. What I wish to know is not the *what* but the *why*. Mr. Bingley's motivation in helping us recover Lydia is clear enough. He is as enamored of Jane as much as he ever was. But what of Mr. Darcy?"

Elizabeth was blushing furiously. "He—Mr. Darcy said he felt responsible for Wickham. He said he should have revealed Mr. Wickham's character to the world."

"Yes, so he says. He has honored me with a full accounting of his past interactions with my unfortunate son-in-law."

Elizabeth was open-mouthed. "*All* of them?"

Bennet smiled without mirth. "He was *quite* thorough."

Elizabeth fought the tears that threatened to erupt. She was so mortified on her beloved's behalf. "Papa, how much money did Mr. Darcy lay down to convince Mr. Wickham to do his duty?"

"It is not for me to say." At her look, he leaned forward. "Even I do not know, but if I did, I would not tell you. *He* would not have it."

Elizabeth was happy at this evidence of friendship between her father and her suitor, but she did not like that they were keeping secrets from her. "I do not understand."

"Do you not? Hmm, you are a clever girl—or at least I have always fancied that you were. Can you not guess at his motivation?"

She would not look at her father for the world. "I have not the least idea."

"Do you believe he admires you, my dear?"

The tears did start. "I believe he does, Papa."

"And you?"

How can I tell you my heart will break if I do not see him? "How can anyone not admire so great a man?"

"Is that all you have to say?"

Elizabeth dried her eyes. "I have nothing of import to say, Papa. Did...did Mr. Darcy say otherwise?"

"No, but I believe there is more to this."

Darcy had declared his love, but had not proposed again, and Elizabeth would say nothing until he did. "Mr. Darcy is very kind."

"Yes, yes. But what passed between you both in the street before the Lambton inn?" At Elizabeth's shocked expression, he added, "Your aunt reports you were both quite transparent, my love."

Lizzy's tears started again.

"Do you have an understanding with Fitzwilliam Darcy, Elizabeth?"

Elizabeth screwed up her courage and admitted, "Not in the usual manner. But he knows that he has but to ask...and—"

"And you would accept him?"

In a small voice, she answered, "Yes."

"Lizzy," said Mr. Bennet, "do you know what you are doing, to be accepting this man? Have not you always hated him?"

How earnestly did Elizabeth then wish that her former opinions had been more reasonable, her expressions more moderate! It would have spared her from explanations and professions, which it was exceedingly awkward to give but were now necessary. So with much passion and earnestness, she assured her father of her attachment to Mr. Darcy.

"He is rich, to be sure, and you may have many fine clothes and fine carriages. But will they make you happy, Lizzy?"

"I care not about that!"

"I know that you could be neither happy nor respectable unless you truly esteemed your husband—unless you looked up to him as a superior. Your lively talents would place you in the greatest danger in an unequal marriage. My child, let me not have the grief of seeing you unable to respect your partner in life."

"I do, I do respect him!" she replied, with tears in her eyes. "I love him! Indeed, he is perfectly amiable! You cannot know what he really is if you say that! Pray do not pain me by speaking of him in harsh terms!"

"Lizzy," said her father, giving up his test, "I do indeed know him and have given him my consent."

"Consent?"

"Consent to court you, for the usual purpose, I assume." He chuckled at Elizabeth's transparent relief. "He is the kind of man, indeed, to whom I should never dare refuse anything which he condescended to ask! If this be the case, if you truly love him, he deserves you. And he is a truly good man."

He spoke at length of Darcy and Bingley's efforts to recover Lydia, including the recruitment of Colonel Fitzwilliam. Lizzy could not hear enough good things about her lover and listened in joy and longing.

"I can safely say that, without Mr. Darcy's efforts, we never would have found them. I never will meet with a better man, I dare say. I could not have parted with you, my Lizzy, to anyone less worthy."

Elizabeth's heart was full, but still her smile was weak. When her father inquired about it, she said, "But the money, sir! How mortifying for him to do this for Wickham!"

"Darcy did everything—made up the match, gave the money, paid the fellow's debts, and got him his commission! But if you think he did this for any silly reason such as pride or duty, I shall be very disappointed in you! He has only one motivation, and you should know it if you take the trouble to think on it."

At Elizabeth's happy blush, Mr. Bennet laughed again. "So much the better. It will save me a world of trouble and economy, you know. Had it been your uncle's doing, I must and would have paid him, but these violent young lovers carry everything their own way. I shall offer to pay him again when next we meet. He will rant and storm about his love for you, and there will be an end of the matter."

Elizabeth grew wistful. "Did Mr. Darcy say when we would see him again?"

Mr. Bennet looked at Elizabeth. "You cannot expect him while *he* is here," he said with a jerk of his thumb.

Elizabeth sighed. "I know. These next ten days will go very slowly, sir."

Mr. Bennet thought of his wife, reunited with her favorite. "Indeed.

I do have a request of you, Lizzy."

"Yes, sir?"

"I understand Pemberley's library is very grand. Might I hope for an invitation at your earliest convenience, Mrs. Darcy?"

"Papa!"

ANOTHER LETTER ARRIVED FROM HUNSFORD.

So Lydia and Wickham are married. Well, it is for the best, I suppose, and I wish them joy. But I am not fool enough to expect marital felicity from that quarter. God have mercy upon them!

Anne sends her best wishes and reminds you that she was correct in her estimation of our friend from Derbyshire's abilities.

Mr. Collins sends his prayers for their union, but this is the last acknowledgement Mr. and Mrs. Wickham may expect from him. He has decreed that they shall never cross the threshold of any house in which he resides and wonders at my father's acceptance of them in his. In this, I shall not try to persuade my husband otherwise, for I must admit I quite agree with him. My sister and her husband have violated both God's law and man's, and they feel not the least sorry for it. I must forgive them as a Christian, but I cannot and will not accept them until they repent of their sins. I pray that will be soon.

There is other news you need to know. The involvement of our friends in this matter may have become known to Lady Catherine. Anne tells me a letter from Derbyshire arrived that sent her ladyship into spasms of outrage. Lizzy's name, in particular, has been taken in vain. We know not who sent the message, except they meant no good by it.

A advises us to bide our time until the storm blows over. We do so with concern in our breasts. It is not inconceivable that our situation is hereby endangered. Do not fret, my loves, but send us your prayers.

*On a happier note, it seems that we shall be blessed with an addition
to the parsonage. Mr. Collins is beside himself, and Lady Catherine is
full of advice. It is well that I like the name Catherine, but there will
be some discussion over the name Lewis.*

Your loving sister,
MARY

"Ohh! That Caroline Bingley!" cried Elizabeth.

"Lizzy! You do not know it was she who sent the letter," advised Jane.

"Who else that was in that county wished us ill? You know
it was she!"

Jane colored. "Until I have proof positive, I shall not condemn her,
Lizzy, and neither should you."

"Jane, you are too good!"

Jane touched her sister's hand. "No, I am not." *Otherwise, I would
not have hurt Mr. Bingley so.*

ELIZABETH SOON FLED TO THE sanctity of a bench in the gardens. The
contents of Mary's letter cast her into a flutter of spirits, in which it
was difficult to determine whether pleasure or pain bore the greatest
share. That her sister and her friend were aware of and approved of
Mr. Darcy's actions in Town were very satisfying, yet Lady Catherine
being informed of his involvement could lead to nothing good. Could
Mr. Collins be in danger? Could Mary lose her home? Heaven forbid!

How did Caroline Bingley come to learn of it? Elizabeth thought
furiously, for she had no doubt as to the identity of the informer.
*Could Mr. Bingley have been so careless as to tell his worthless sister all?
Of course he told her!*

No, she could not condemn Mr. Bingley! He, too, raced to Lydia's
aid, and he could not know of Miss Bingley's talent for treachery. She
was his sister, and he loved her. She would not judge Charles Bingley.

To ease her mind, she turned to more pleasant prospects. Mr.
Darcy was everything wise and good. He had followed Lydia and
Wickham purposely to Town. He had taken on himself all the trouble

and humiliation attendant on such a research, and he was reduced to meet—frequently meet, reason with, persuade, and finally bribe—the man whom he always most wished to avoid and whose very name it was punishment to pronounce. He had done all this for a girl whom he could neither regard nor esteem. Lizzy's heart cried out with joy that he had done it for her.

But to be the brother-in-law of Wickham! Every kind of pride must revolt from the connection. Mr. Darcy had, to be sure, done much. Elizabeth was ashamed to think how much. They owed the restoration of Lydia, her character—everything to him.

Oh, how heartily did she grieve over every ungracious sensation she had ever encouraged, every saucy speech she had ever directed towards him. For herself, she was humbled, but she was proud of him. Proud that, in a cause of compassion and honor, Mr. Darcy had proven himself the best of men.

Elizabeth thought over her father's commendation of Mr. Darcy again and again. It was hardly enough, but it pleased her. She was roused from her seat and her reflections of just how she would reward her dear Fitzwilliam by someone's approach. Before she could strike into another path, she was overtaken by Mr. Wickham.

"Do I interrupt your solitary ramble, my dear sister?" said he, as he joined her.

"You certainly do," Elizabeth replied with a smile, "but it does not follow that the interruption must be unwelcome." She would be polite for her sister's sake.

"I should be sorry indeed if it were. We were always good friends, and now we are better."

"True," she lied. "Are the others coming out?"

"I do not know. Mrs. Bennet and Lydia are going in the carriage to Meryton." The two walked the gardens of Longbourn, commenting on the flowers, before Wickham got to his purpose of seeking out Elizabeth. "And so, my dear sister, I find from our uncle and aunt that you have seen Pemberley."

She replied that she had.

"I almost envy you the pleasure, and yet I believe it would be too much for me, or else I could take it in on my way to Newcastle. And you saw the old housekeeper, I suppose? Poor Reynolds, she was always very fond of me. But, of course, she did not mention my name to you."

"Yes, she did."

"Oh? And what did she say?"

"That you were gone into the army, and she was afraid you had not turned out well. At such a distance as that, you know, things are strangely misrepresented." Elizabeth's eyes glinted as she was able to slip the dagger home.

"Certainly," he replied, biting his lips.

Elizabeth hoped she had silenced him, but he soon afterwards said, "I was surprised to see Darcy in Town last month. We passed each other several times. I wonder what he can be doing there."

Odious man! You know full well why he was there! "Perhaps meeting with his banker," said Elizabeth. "It must be something particular to take him there at this time of year."

"Undoubtedly. Did you see him while you were at Lambton? I thought I understood from the Gardiners that you had."

"Yes, and Jane, too. He introduced us to his sister."

"And do you like Miss Darcy?"

"Very much."

"I have heard, indeed, that she is uncommonly improved within this year or two," he said offhandedly. "When I last saw her, she was not very promising. I am very glad you like her. I hope she will turn out well."

That did it! It was bad enough that he snidely referred to Darcy, but to thus attack his own victim was too much to bear. "I dare say she will. She has got over the most *trying age*." Elizabeth sneered.

Wickham was insensitive to it. "Did you go by the village of Kympton?"

"I do not recollect that we did."

"I mention it because it is the living which I ought to have had. A most delightful place! Excellent parsonage house! It would have suited me in every respect."

"More than three thousand pounds?"

Wickham stopped short. He gasped, "Pardon me?"

Elizabeth turned and looked at him, completely silent. Unconsciously, in her stance, her visage, she assumed the haughty look and attitude of a certain gentleman of Derbyshire, but had she been aware of it, she would not have repined. "I know *everything*, Wickham," Elizabeth warned him coldly.

"Darcy? He told you—"

In pure anger, Elizabeth said between her teeth, "Ramsgate."

Wickham staggered back. The enormity of this intelligence would take a moment to digest. He considered the facts before him—added two and two—and slapping his forehead cried, "Damn me! Darcy has taken you for his mistress! Oh, but if I had known of it! I settled for too little!"

Elizabeth laughed at the insult. "And I thought you an evil genius! You are nothing but a selfish man. Not everyone is driven by all-consuming, animal lust! Oh, but if I were a man, I should call you out for that! Be thankful my champion is an extraordinary gentleman, else you would have been dancing on his cousin's blade in London!"

"You…you know about that, too?"

"I do. And if you think that Mr. Darcy has offered me *carte blanche*, you do not know his character any more than you know mine since you believe I would accept such an arrangement!"

"You do not mean to tell me that Darcy and you—impossible! His family would never consent!"

"Mr. Darcy's intentions are his own, and they are certainly not your concern. As for his family, if they are anything like Colonel Fitzwilliam, they are sensible people who would have only Darcy's happiness in mind. Your vilification is a comfort, *dear Brother*, given the exactness of your descriptions of Miss Darcy and Miss de Bourgh. Since everything you say is contrary to reality, I am content indeed."

They were now almost at the door of the house, for Elizabeth had walked faster to be rid of him. But unwilling, for her sister's sake, to further provoke him, she only added with a good-humored smile, "Come, Mr. Wickham, we are brother and sister now, you know. Do not let us quarrel. In future, I hope we shall be always of one mind."

He took her hand and bent to kiss it with affectionate gallantry.

"Do not kiss my hand if you value your teeth."

He paused, bowed over her hand, and they entered the house.

"THANK YOU FOR COMING TO see me, Jane," said her father as she entered his study. "Please close the door behind you."

She did so and sat in front of Mr. Bennet's desk. "What did you wish to talk to me about, Father?"

"A matter that I believe you will find diverting. You know, of course, that Mr. Bingley was in London with Mr. Darcy."

Jane's insides turned into tapioca pudding, but she maintained her patented calm expression. "Yes, I believe he was very helpful in the matter of Lydia and her new husband, or so your letter led us to believe."

"He was instrumental, my dear—as vital to our success as Mr. Darcy. I must admit that I had underestimated him. Mr. Bingley is a charming gentleman. Anyone with eyes can see that, but in this matter, he proved to have a quick wit and undoubted courage. I like him very much."

"I am glad that you are friends, Father. There is much to admire in Mr. Bingley."

"I am glad you think so, for he will surely come to call when he returns to Netherfield."

"Indeed?"

"Jane, my love, I have given him my permission to call upon you."

"Did he...did he ask to do so?"

"Not in so many words, but he was pleased with the invitation, I have no doubt."

Jane had numerous doubts, but she kept them to herself. "It will be pleasant to see him again."

"Yes," he grinned, "I was sure you would think so. We talked a little about last autumn, and I am satisfied with his explanation which, I believe, he has already shared with you." Despite her quiet demeanor, Jane was extremely agitated—agitated for Jane, that is.

He continued. "I have another matter I wish to raise with you, and

I would appreciate your counsel. Since this unfortunate event—oh, let us just call it what it is—this *farce* involving Lydia, I had determined to keep a tighter hold onto Kitty. She and Lydia are as alike as two peas in a pod! I firmly intended to forbid Kitty any balls, dances, or assemblies unless she stands with at least two of her sisters and to allow no officers to darken my door for the foreseeable future. I have not raised my family as I should, and I wish to give Kitty all the benefit of my recognition of my failures as a father and the improvements I mean to institute.

"Yet, Kitty seems astonishingly improved since I went to Town. I truly feared how she would react with Mrs. Wickham in residence, but Kitty has surprised me. She spends very little time with her former favorite. In fact, she seems to be *your* shadow now, Jane."

Jane welcomed the change of subject. "Father, I have spent much of my time recently with Kitty. She has done remarkably well dealing with Mother during this crisis. She is a good sort of girl; she only wants proper guidance. I have taken her under my wing, and she will turn out well. Father, trust her."

"That is much to ask, Jane, but I do trust *you*. It shall be as you request, as long as you take responsibility for her."

Jane was taken aback, but she really had no choice. "Very well, Father."

"Excellent!" Bennet was pleased. It wasn't *complete* selfishness on his part, for he truly expected Jane to become Mrs. Bingley in a short time. It was traditional for younger girls to spend time with their married siblings, and as he would never allow Kitty within a dozen leagues of Mrs. Wickham's house, and he had doubts that the otherwise admirable Mr. Darcy would not blanch at entertaining the last remaining unmarried Bennet daughter, the obvious choice was Mrs. Bingley.

And his house would be that much quieter.

Yes, this was a good morning's work.

THE NEXT FEW DAYS CRAWLED by. Wickham often found entertainment by using his father-in-law's horses for riding about the neighborhood or by forming shooting parties with Sir William Lucas and his son. He stayed far away from Elizabeth, and the lady was very agreeable to that arrangement.

Lydia found herself with her mother, which suited her, as Mrs. Bennet continued her years-long spoiling of the girl. They remained upstairs in Mrs. Bennet's room, looking over the lace they had purchased that morning in Merton and gossiping.

A week had passed since the invasion of Longbourn, and Mr. Bennet, not long being able to stomach Wickham's attentions, rode to Meryton. Jane decided on a stroll to Oakham Mount. Elizabeth and Kitty volunteered to go with her, but company was declined. Her thoughts were troubled, and Jane sought solitude to sort them out.

So it was that Elizabeth and Kitty were in the sitting room, one with her embroidery, the other with a sketching pad, when Mrs. Hill came into the room.

"Miss Elizabeth, Lady Catherine de Bourgh is here to see you."

Chapter 16

Lady Catherine Attacks

Lady Catherine de Bourgh entered the room with more than her usual ungracious air, made no other reply to Elizabeth's salutation than a slight inclination of the head, and sat down without saying a word. Elizabeth had mentioned her name to her sister on her ladyship's entrance, though no request of introduction had been made.

Kitty, all amazement, though flattered by having a guest of such high importance, received her with the utmost courtesy.

After sitting for a moment in silence, Lady Catherine spoke stiffly to Elizabeth.

"I hope you are well, Miss Bennet. That lady, I suppose, is one of your sisters."

"Yes, madam," said Elizabeth. "She is my youngest sister but one."

"You have a very small park here," returned Lady Catherine after a short silence.

"It is nothing in comparison of Rosings, my lady, I dare say."

"This must be a most inconvenient sitting room for the evening in summer; the windows are full west."

"We have not found it so. May I take the liberty of asking your ladyship whether you left Mr. and Mrs. Collins well?"

"Yes, very well. I saw them the night before last."

Elizabeth sat quietly. She would force the old dragon to begin.

"Miss Bennet, there seemed to be a prettyish kind of a little wilderness on one side of your lawn. I should be glad to take a turn in it, if you will favor me with your company."

So you wish for privacy? Elizabeth obeyed and attended her noble guest out of doors. As they passed through the hall, Lady Catherine opened the doors into the dining parlor and drawing room, and after pronouncing them after a short survey to be decent looking rooms, walked on.

Her carriage remained at the door, and Elizabeth saw that her waiting-woman was in it. They proceeded in silence along the gravel walk that led to the copse, and Elizabeth was determined to make no effort for conversation with a woman who was now more than usually insolent and disagreeable.

How could I ever think her like her nephew? But for *his* sake, Elizabeth would deal with this harridan with composure. She did not wish to be the reason for rupture within Darcy's family if she could help it.

As soon as they entered the copse, Lady Catherine began speaking. "You can be at no loss, Miss Bennet, to understand the reason of my journey hither. Your own heart, your own conscience, must tell you why I came."

Elizabeth looked with a neutral expression. "Indeed, you are mistaken, madam. I have not been at all able to account for the honor of seeing you here." *But I have my speculations.*

"Miss Bennet," replied the lady in an angry tone, "you ought to know that I am not to be trifled with! But however insincere you may choose to be, you shall not find me so. My character has ever been celebrated for its sincerity and frankness, and in a cause of such moment as this, I shall certainly not depart from it! A report of a most alarming nature has reached me. I was told that not only your sister was on the point of being most advantageously married, but that you, that Miss Elizabeth Bennet, would in all likelihood, be soon afterwards united to my nephew—my own nephew, Mr. Darcy! Though I know it must be a scandalous falsehood, though I would not injure him so much as to suppose the truth of it possible, I instantly resolved on setting off for this place, that I might make my sentiments known to you."

"If you believed it impossible to be true, I wonder you took the trouble of coming so far. What could your ladyship propose by it?" *Is that what Caroline wrote? Odious woman!*

"At once to insist upon having such a report universally contradicted."

"Coming to Longbourn to see my family and me," said Elizabeth with a small smile, "will be rather a confirmation of it, if indeed such a report exists."

"If! Do you then pretend to be ignorant of it? Has it not been industriously circulated by yourselves? Do you not know that such a report is spread abroad?"

"I never heard that it was."

"And can you likewise declare that there is no foundation for it?"

"I do not pretend to possess equal frankness with your ladyship. You may ask questions which I shall not choose to answer."

"This is not to be borne! Miss Bennet, I insist on being satisfied. Has he—has my nephew made you an offer of marriage?"

You wish to play? Very well. "Your ladyship has declared it to be impossible."

"It ought to be so, it must be so, while he retains the use of his reason. But your arts and allurements may, in a moment of infatuation, have made him forget what he owes to himself and to all his family. You may have drawn him in!"

That sounds remarkably like Caroline! "If I have, I shall be the last person to confess it."

"Miss Bennet, do you know who I am? I have not been accustomed to such language as this. I am almost the nearest relation he has in the world and am entitled to know all his dearest concerns."

"But you are not entitled to know mine, nor will such behavior as this ever induce me to be explicit."

"Let me be rightly understood. This match, to which you have the presumption to aspire, can never take place. No, never! Mr. Darcy is engaged to my daughter. Now what have you to say?"

Does she ever talk to Anne de Bourgh? "Only this—that *if* he is, you can have no reason to suppose he will make an offer to me."

Lady Catherine hesitated for a moment, and then replied, "The engagement between them is of a peculiar kind. From their infancy, they have been intended for each other. It was the favorite wish of his mother as well as mine. While in their cradles, we planned the union, and now, at the moment when the wishes of both sisters would be accomplished in their marriage, to be prevented by a young woman of inferior birth, of no importance in the world, and wholly unallied to the family! Do you pay no regard to the wishes of his friends, to his tacit engagement with my daughter? Are you lost to every feeling of propriety and delicacy? Have you not heard me say that from his earliest hours he was destined for his cousin?"

"Yes, and I had heard it before. But what is that to me? If there is no other objection to my marrying your nephew, I shall certainly not be kept from it by knowing that his mother and aunt wished him to marry Miss de Bourgh. You both did as much as you could in planning the marriage. Its completion depended on others." *Including your own daughter, you witch!* "If Mr. Darcy is neither by honor nor inclination confined to his cousin, why is not he to make another choice? And if I am that choice, why may not I accept him?"

"Because honor, decorum, prudence—nay, interest, forbid it. Yes, Miss Bennet, interest! For do not expect to be noticed by his family or friends if you willfully act against the inclinations of all. You will be censured, slighted, and despised by everyone connected with him. Your alliance will be a disgrace; your name will never be mentioned by any of us."

"These are heavy misfortunes, indeed," replied Elizabeth sarcastically, hiding her smile again. "But the wife of Mr. Darcy must have such extraordinary sources of happiness necessarily attached to her situation that she could, upon the whole, have no cause to repine."

"Obstinate, headstrong girl! I am ashamed of you! Is this your gratitude for my attentions to you last spring? Is nothing due to me on that score? Let us sit down." The grand dame took a place on a bench before Elizabeth could respond. "You are to understand, Miss

Bennet, that I came here with the determined resolution of carrying my purpose, and I will not be dissuaded from it. I have not been used to submitting to any person's whims. I have not been in the habit of brooking disappointment."

Elizabeth remained standing. "That will make your ladyship's situation at present more pitiable, but it will have no effect on *me*."

"I will not be interrupted! Hear me in silence. My daughter and my nephew are formed for each other. They are descended, on the maternal side, from the same noble line, and on the father's, from respectable, honorable, and ancient—though untitled—families. Their fortune on both sides is splendid. They are destined for each other by the voice of every member of their respective houses. And what is to divide them—the upstart pretensions of a young woman without family, connections, or fortune? Is this to be endured? But it must not, shall not be. If you were sensible of your own good, you would not wish to quit the sphere in which you have been brought up!"

Elizabeth could almost pity the foolish, deluded woman, but recalling the suffering Anne must endure by living with such a mother, her heart hardened. "In marrying your nephew, I should not consider myself as quitting that sphere. He is a gentleman. I am a gentleman's daughter. So far we are equal."

"True. You are a gentleman's daughter. But who was your mother? Who are your uncles and aunts? Do not imagine me ignorant of *their* condition."

"Whatever my connections may be," said Elizabeth, wearying of the game, "if your nephew does not object to them, they can be nothing to you."

"Tell me once and for all. Are you engaged to him?"

Though Elizabeth would not, for the mere purpose of obliging Lady Catherine, have answered this question, she could not but say, in all truthfulness, after a moment's deliberation, "I am not." *Yet.*

Lady Catherine seemed pleased. "And will you promise me never to enter into such an engagement?"

Elizabeth smiled widely. "I will make no promise of the kind."
Take that!

"Miss Bennet I am shocked and astonished. I expected to find a more reasonable young woman. But do not deceive yourself into a belief that I will ever recede. I shall not go away until you have given me the assurance I require."

"And I certainly never shall give it! I am not to be intimidated into anything so wholly unreasonable." Elizabeth's resolve to be polite to her beloved's unpleasant aunt was weakening. "Your ladyship wants Mr. Darcy to marry your daughter. But would my giving you the wished-for promise make their marriage at all more probable? Supposing Mr. Darcy to be attached to me, would my refusing to accept his hand make him wish to bestow it on his cousin? Allow me to say, Lady Catherine, that the arguments with which you have supported this extraordinary application have been as frivolous as the application was ill judged! Do you truly speak for your daughter? You have widely mistaken my character if you think I can be worked on by such persuasions as these. How far your nephew might approve of your interference in his affairs, I cannot tell, but you have certainly no right to concern yourself in *mine*. I must beg, therefore, to be importuned no farther on the subject." Elizabeth hoped, rather than believed, that this would be an end to the discussion.

Her hopes were dashed. "Not so hasty, if you please! I am by no means done. To all the objections I have already urged, I have still another to add. I am no stranger to the particulars of your youngest sister's infamous elopement. I know it all—that the young man's marrying her was a patched-up business at the expense of your father and uncles. And is such a girl to be my nephew's sister? Is her husband, the son of his late father's steward, to be his brother? Heaven and earth! Of what are you thinking? Are the shades of Pemberley to be thus polluted?"

At this, Elizabeth became furious. She was already unhappy over Mr. Darcy paying out large sums to bribe Wickham. To have him unknowingly attacked was more than she could bear. "You can now have nothing further to say! You have insulted me in every possible method. I must beg to return to the house."

At that, she turned and saw a tall man walking quickly

across the lawn.

"Here!" cried Darcy. "What is this?"

"Nephew!" cried Lady Catherine. "You are here! Then it is true! You have betrayed your family!"

In her heightened emotional state, the last person Elizabeth wanted to see was the man she was trying to discreetly protect and defend. Her outrage was at Lady Catherine's hateful pronouncements that were unjustly directed toward her *intended* intended—as she thought of him in her mind, having no other title for him. How dare his proud unworthy family attack hers so? Elizabeth walked quickly towards him but disregarded his hand as he reached for her.

"Elizabeth?" he said uncertainly.

She gave him a fierce look. "I believe your aunt wishes a few words with you, Mr. Darcy." Ignoring his gasp, she fled into the house, just as her eyes filled with angry tears.

ELIZABETH RAN PAST AN ASTONISHED Kitty to her bedroom, slamming the door behind her. At that moment, she was ready to throw Fitzwilliam Darcy and all of his relations into Meryton Pond. As she paced her room, she could not help but glance out her window. She knew her bedroom faced the little copse, and she could plainly see Darcy in intense discussion with his aunt.

Lady Catherine raised her stick, and for an instant, Elizabeth was afraid she was going to strike Darcy with it. A moment later, it was obvious that she was only gesturing to make some point, but the fear that flared in Elizabeth's heart cooled her resentment. She looked at the scene with her newfound understanding of the man she loved and saw that he was struggling valiantly to restrain his anger.

And I fled from him! He is only defending me. He needs and deserves my encouragement.

A splash of water on her heated face, a pat from a towel, and she was out the door.

NEVER BEFORE IN HIS LIFE had Darcy wished to strike a woman. His anger at his aunt and his confusion over Elizabeth's behavior had brought him to his breaking point. He was on the verge of losing control.

"Ah! I see your little minx returns!" Lady Catherine sneered.

Darcy was so amazed at her crude words he forgot to be insulted. He turned and beheld his beloved walking across the lawn with what he now recognized as deceptive calm. He paid no attention to the ranting of his aunt as the lady grew closer.

To his immense relief, Elizabeth gave him a slight nod and mouthed, *"Forgive me"* before taking her place beside him, raising her hand to take his arm. As she did, Darcy noted that she displayed a haughty and seemingly disinterested air—an expression he had never seen Elizabeth exhibit before. For an instant before turning back to his aunt, he wondered whether he appeared as cold when he assumed such an appearance.

"So, it is true! You are then resolved to have him?"

Elizabeth answered in an unemotional voice. "I have said no such thing. I am only resolved to act in that manner which will, in my own opinion, constitute my happiness, without reference to you or to any person so wholly unconnected with me." As she finished speaking, Elizabeth slightly squeezed Darcy's arm.

Lady Catherine was highly incensed. "You have no regard, then, for the honor and credit of my nephew! Unfeeling, selfish girl! Do you not consider that a connection with you must disgrace him in the eyes of everybody?"

Darcy had begun to growl a retort when Elizabeth interrupted him. "Lady Catherine, I have nothing further to say. You know my sentiments."

"You refuse, then, to oblige me. You refuse to obey the claims of duty, honor, and gratitude. You are determined to ruin him in the opinion of all his friends and make him the contempt of the world!" The old biddy turned to her nephew. "Darcy, what of your family? Your cousin Anne? Where is your duty there?"

"Neither duty, nor honor, nor gratitude," replied Darcy, "have any possible claim on me in the present instance. No principle would be violated by my marriage to Miss Bennet, should such a marriage take place. As I tried to make plain to you, I am not attached to my cousin Anne, or she to me. On this, we are in perfect agreement. I would suggest you speak *to* your daughter before presuming to speak *for* her.

"And with regard to the resentment of my family or the indignation of the world, if the former were excited by Miss Bennet marrying me, it would not give me one moment's concern—and the world in general would have too much sense to join in the scorn.

"I would add, Aunt, that I have been exceedingly generous to allow such an interview. I cannot speak for Miss Bennet, but *my* patience is at an end! Allow *me* to be rightly understood, madam. I will brook no further interference by you into my personal affairs, or into anyone that is closely connected to me. By that I mean any relations I may have in the future."

Lady Catherine's eyes grew wide at this, but she was not permitted to interrupt. "The family of the companion of my future life *is* my family, and thus falls under my protection. Do not be so foolish as to fall foul of my good graces! You know my power."

Lady Catherine blanched. "You would not dare."

"Do not tempt me, madam."

At this, Elizabeth's reserve cracked momentarily. "Lady Catherine, shall I show you to your carriage?"

In the manner displayed previously, Lady Catherine talked on until they were at the door of the carriage when, turning hastily round, she added, "I take no leave of you, Miss Bennet. I send no compliments to your mother. You deserve no such attention. I am most seriously displeased!"

Elizabeth said nothing as the footman closed the door of the carriage, and it drove off down the lane. She felt, rather than saw, Darcy approach her from behind.

He was very close when he said, "Elizabeth, I must beg your forgiveness. You have done nothing to deserve such treatment from my family."

She turned and faced him. "I am sure she meant well."

With a look of open astonishment on his face, he said, "Meant well? How can you defend her so? I have a right mind to banish her from—" The twinkle in her eye gave her away, and he laughed in a relieved manner. "You are teasing me, I see. It is well you can take the matter so." She walked into his open arms. "I am not so merciful, I fear. I have not your kind heart. A failing—forgive me."

"It would be wrong of you, sir, to think I am untouched by what has happened today," she said into his coat as she happily snuggled close. "But I recall that this dream of Lady Catherine's is of distant creation and of long duration. I fear it will take no little time for her to reconcile herself to the destruction of all her hopes. In time we may be, if not forgiven, at least tolerated. I pray that Anne or the Collinses will not have to suffer her wrath in the meantime."

"They will not, if Lady Catherine does not wish to provoke my displeasure."

She looked up. "You are before your time, sir. I had not expected you to Longbourn while my sister and her husband were in residence."

He looked down at her with an ardent expression. "You are correct to think that it was not my wish to spend any more time in *their* company than I already have, but to own the truth, I could not abide to be apart from you any longer, Elizabeth."

"So, you have come to collect your reward, Mr. Darcy?"

Confusion showed on Darcy's face. "Elizabeth, I told you, I expect nothing for my actions. It was an honor to be of service to your family. It is my fault that—"

"Ask me."

"—Wickham was free to—I beg your pardon?"

"Fitzwilliam, ask me."

Darcy's eyes darkened. "Miss Bennet, would you do me the very great honor of accepting my hand in marriage?"

Instead of answering, she threw her arms about his neck and kissed him full on the mouth. It took a moment for an amazed Darcy to respond, but when he did, he returned his lady's affections ten-fold. The passion in their kisses stirred him, and only with the greatest of efforts was he able to push away.

"I see I shall have to be careful of you, sir," Elizabeth shakily uttered into his chest.

"Elizabeth, I cannot say I am sorry, but I must control myself. Have I embarrassed you?"

She still could not look him in the face and smiled into his shirt. "I assure you I am unharmed. Do not be uneasy, Fitzwilliam. You did not do anything I did not desire."

"So you are not displeased?"

She blushed. "No, in fact, it is rather comforting."

"Good, for after we are married, I shall spend much time demonstrating how *comforting* I can be, my love," he said roguishly. "May call you 'my love'?"

She kissed his chest. "If you do not, I shall be most *seriously displeased*."

Darcy chuckled. "Oh, you are clever!" Her reward for her wit was another kiss. "Should I go to your father now?"

Elizabeth seemed to consider the question for a moment. "Fitzwilliam, would it be too much to ask to wait until our guests are gone? I would much rather not deal with their false congratulations."

Darcy sighed. "As much as I want your father's blessing, I must agree with you. The less time I spend with *them* the better."

Elizabeth released him. "I do not believe my father will withhold his blessing, dearest. You are quite his favorite now. He cannot wait to invade your library at Pemberley."

Darcy smiled. "If that is the price for having you as my wife, then I will pay it gladly."

She took his hand. "Then come, let us sit in the garden. Mama is busy with Lydia, and her husband is hunting with the Lucases. No one will disturb us. I have much to ask."

"What of Miss Catherine?" he asked as they walked arm-in-arm.

"Kitty?" Elizabeth frowned. "I suppose she is with Mama." When they reached the bench in the garden, she asked, "Thank you for defending my sister and Mr. Collins, my love, but I am full curious about something. You said something to Lady Catherine—that she knows your power. Would you tell me what you meant by that?"

"I have no objection to telling you, my dear. Have you never wondered why Colonel Fitzwilliam and I journey to Rosings each year?

We are caretakers for the management of the estate. Lady Catherine's household allowance is determined by us."

"Are you really? That is too amusing!"

"Yes. Anne will inherit Rosings from her father's estate only after Lady Catherine's death; it does not belong to her mother. The management was left to my father and my uncle, the Earl of Matlock. The living at Rosings is her gift, to be sure, but I can make things very unpleasant for her, should I chose to do so."

"Then Mary and her husband are safe! I thank you, Fitzwilliam."

"They will be my family. It is my duty to protect them and my pleasure to please you."

"You do that, sir." She kissed his hand. "Are you here by yourself?"

"No, Bingley rode with me. We are staying at Netherfield."

"But where is he?"

Darcy grinned. "We saw Miss Bennet walking towards Oakham Mount. I believe Bingley is with her now."

Elizabeth's eyes flew open. "You left them unchaperoned? Mr. Darcy, of what could you be thinking?"

His smile only grew wider. "I am thinking I shall soon have another brother. Aye, and a more pleasant one."

JANE AND BINGLEY WALKED SLOWLY along the lane between Meryton and Longbourn in silence, she with her hands clasped before her, and he holding his horse's reins as the creature trailed behind. They had not said ten words between them since exchanging self-conscious greetings a quarter hour before.

Bingley was in a quandary. Since his first disastrous proposal, he had endeavored to prove to Miss Bennet that he was his own man, that he could be a husband, master, and provider without constantly seeking the advice and approval of others. He had accomplished his goal of helping the Bennet family during the Wickham matter, but he felt he failed, as well. He could not have succeeded if not for Darcy. He was sure that Jane knew all. There were no secrets between her and Elizabeth. How could he secure his future happiness if Miss Bennet still felt he was unworthy?

Bingley was afraid to begin, and how long they might have remained in this state no one could tell, had not the sound of a rushing carriage startled the pair out of their common misery.

"Miss Bennet! Watch out!"

Without another moment's hesitation, Bingley released his horse, seized the lady and pulled her out of the path of the oncoming vehicle. Rolling on the grass beside the road, they could barely make out a woman's cry of, *"Stupid farmers—out of my way!"* as the coach dashed past. The carriage did not stop, and by the time the couple was able to sit up, it was halfway to Meryton. Bingley's frightened horse was galloping back to Netherfield.

"Good heavens! Are you uninjured, Miss Bennet?"

"I am well, Mr. Bingley. I believe you have saved us from an unfortunate accident." Jane's hair had come undone, and her dress was dusty, but to Bingley's eyes, never had she looked more desirable.

"Thank God! Oh, Jane, had anything happened to you—I could not bear it!" His hands grasped her shoulders. Overwrought by his feelings, Bingley blurted out, "Oh, my dear, dear Jane! Have I any chance of succeeding? I know I am not much of a man, but I will try to be what you need, what you deserve. I vow to protect you always! Can you not give me some sign that you feel in any way kindly towards me?"

"Oh, Mr. Bingley! I am so sorry for the pain I must have inflicted upon you. Please forgive my wicked words. Oh, how they have haunted me! To say what I did—you have been so good, so kind—"

"Jane! Please, you must see—you must know how I adore you! Please say you will be mine! I swear I shall prove worthy of your trust!"

"How can you doubt the feelings I have for you? I love you, Charles!"

"Then you say yes? You will have me?"

"For forever and a day!" What else she meant to say was lost, as her mouth was more agreeably occupied.

"JANE!" CRIED ELIZABETH. "WHAT HAS happened to you?" She and Darcy hurried to the dusty and dirty couple as they approached Longbourn.

"We…err…we were forced to hurry off the road, as a carriage almost trampled us," explained Bingley.

Darcy and Elizabeth frowned. The redness on their friends' complexions did not seem to come from exertion.

"Where is your horse, Bingley?" Darcy asked.

Told that the animal in its fright had, in all probability, returned to its stall at Netherfield, Darcy further inquired to the description of the carriage.

"It seems that my aunt almost did you in, Bingley. Damned unneighborly of her!"

"Fitzwilliam! Your language!" teased Elizabeth. The other couple looked at one another at Elizabeth's use of Darcy's Christian name.

Bingley's habitual grin returned. "Am I to infer that your mission to Longbourn has been as successful as mine, Darce?"

The Bennet ladies' blushes only added to Darcy's mirth. "You may indeed—Brother!"

"Oh, I hoped it would be so!" cried a voice behind them. The four, startled, turned to see Kitty Bennet stepping from behind a tree, almost dancing with joy. "From the parlor window one can see much, you know!"

"Oh, lord!" Elizabeth cried, one hand over her heart. "And where is my mother?"

"Do not worry, Lizzy. She is upstairs in her room with Lydia. It faces the other side of the house."

Kitty was quickly sworn to secrecy and joined in the lovers' happy conversation.

THE GENTLEMEN TENDERLY TOOK THEIR leave of their ladies and began the long trek back to Netherfield, Darcy walking his horse, as Bingley had refused a mount from Mr. Bennet's stables.

"I must say, Charles, when we saw you and Miss Bennet come up the road, we thought the worst of it."

Bingley took the jibe with the good-natured spirit it was offered. "I can well believe that, Darce! We must have been quite the sight! I am glad, however, that Mr. and Mrs. Bennet were not witness to it. I think that conversation would have been awkward indeed."

"I am sorry about my aunt, Charles. I wish I could make amends for it."

"It is quite all right, old man. We are none the worse for it, save for a bit of dust. In fact, I believe she helped things along. In our relief of our safe delivery, we were rather…transparent with our feelings. I do not know what would have happened had that carriage not come along. Most likely I would still be stumbling about like a tongue-tied schoolboy."

Darcy grunted. "Lady Catherine would be pleased, then. She lives to be of use to people."

Chapter 17

Another Wedding

Mrs. Bennet's sorrow at losing her favorite daughter and her "dear Wickham" to the wilds of the north was soon all forgotten. For the very afternoon of the Wickhams' removal, Mr. Bennet received requests for private interviews from two of the most eligible bachelors in the empire.

Mr. Bingley's suit was no great surprise. Mrs. Bennet's only thought besides joy was why it took the man so long to come the point at last. *She* knew her Jane could not be so beautiful for nothing. However, Elizabeth's triumph quite took her mother's breath away. Ten thousand pounds a year and likely more! A house in Town! Carriages, jewels, two or three French cooks, everything that was delightful! She could say nothing for a full quarter-hour.

She made up for it, of course, when she did find her tongue. So much so, that the happy pair soon sought out the quiet of a walk. Jane and Charles, realizing that they could better tolerate Mrs. Bennet's indescribable elation, which she proclaimed again and again, insisted that Darcy and Elizabeth go by themselves while they entertained the happy matron.

The contented couple walked along the lanes of Longbourn, discussing their opinions of the upcoming nuptials. Between the day of the proposals and the day of the father's blessing, the future Darcys and future Bingleys had decided on a joint ceremony to be held in Hertfordshire as soon as may be. Darcy wanted a special license, but common sense soon prevailed, and a date six weeks hence was agreed upon.

Darcy was speaking of the warm and kind letter he had received from the Earl and Countess of Matlock—they, along with the Gardiners, had been let in on the secret—when his betrothed turned to him.

"Fitzwilliam." She stopped him. "You do know I would have accepted you if you had not succeeded in finding Lydia."

"You would have had me if I failed?" he jested.

"Of course. I love you."

"Ah, but that is a moot point, Elizabeth! For you see, I have never failed, nor will I ever, to secure anything that is *your* true desire. For your desire is mine." And he silenced her response with a kiss.

Elizabeth's spirits soon rose to playfulness again. She asked Mr. Darcy to account for his having ever fallen in love with her. "How could you begin? I can comprehend going on charmingly when you had once made a beginning, but what caused you to fall in love in the first place?"

"I cannot fix on the hour, or the spot, or the look, or the words, which laid the foundation. It is too long ago. I was in the middle before I knew that I had begun."

"My beauty you had earlier withstood, and as for my manners— my behavior to you was at least always bordering on the uncivil. I never spoke to you without rather wishing to give you pain. Now be sincere—did you admire me for my impertinence?"

"For the liveliness of your mind, I did."

"You may as well call it impertinence at once. It was very little less. The fact is that you were sick of civility, of deference, of officious attention. You were disgusted with the women who were always speaking, and looking, and thinking for your approbation. I roused and interested you because I was so unlike them. You thoroughly despised the persons who so assiduously courted you. There, I have saved you the trouble of accounting for it, and all things considered, I begin to think it perfectly reasonable." She reached up to stroke his face. "To be sure, you knew no actual good of me, but nobody thinks of that when they fall in love."

Darcy kissed her palm. "Was there no good in your affectionate behavior to Jane while she was ill at Netherfield?"

"Dearest Jane! Who could have done less for her? But make a virtue of it by all means! My good qualities are under your protection, and you are to exaggerate them as much as possible. And in return, it belongs to me to find occasions for teasing and quarrelling with you as often as may be, and I shall begin directly by asking you why you wished to diminish the kindness of your endeavor when you went to London in search of my unfortunate sister. Such a quest could do nothing but secure your lady's heart."

Darcy blushed. "That is indeed the point, Elizabeth. I did not want you to feel obligated to me—to feel that you owe me anything."

"This will never do! Did I not shamelessly promise myself to you? You are unchivalrous, sir! You threaten to disappoint the heart of a maiden raised on the tales of King Arthur and Sir Galahad! Who is to be my knight in shining armor, if not my husband? Shall I need to look elsewhere?"

Darcy embraced her. "The only place you may look for protection, Miss Bennet, is in these arms."

She smiled. "That is an agreeable prospect, sir. Tell me, Mr. Darcy, are there many suits of armor at Pemberley?"

"Aye, and lances, too," he said as he bent to kiss her again.

DEAR SIR,

I must trouble you once more for congratulations. Elizabeth will soon be the wife of Mr. Darcy. Console Lady Catherine as well as you can, but if I were you, I would stand by the nephew. He has more to give.

Yours sincerely, &c.
T. BENNET

"My dear! Mrs. Collins! Such a calamity that has befallen us! Oh, what shall we do?"

Mary Collins looked up from her needlework at her husband's outburst.

"Whatever is the matter, Mr. Collins?"

"Your...your—" He could not get the words out. "Your sister!"

Never had Mary seen her husband so upset. "Mr. Collins! What has happened? To which of my sisters do you refer? Oh, my nerves!" *My goodness, did I really say that?*

"Elizabeth—your sister Elizabeth is engaged to Mr. Darcy!"

In her relief, she could not help herself. "She is? Oh, how wonderful!"

Aghast would not sufficiently describe Collins's expression. "Wonderful? How can this news be wonderful? How can you think such a thing? Lady Catherine—oh, how she must feel it! Our noble patroness has long held to the sweet dream of uniting Miss de Bourgh with Mr. Darcy. It is not to be borne! She would not have it! Our sister does not know what she is about!

"We must write to her—nay, we shall go to her! We must counsel her to see the better of this improper action, to think the better of it. Mr. Darcy's duty is to honor our ladyship's desire of marrying her daughter—"

"Rather than becoming your brother, my dear?"

"Yes! I—what?" Collins lost the power of speech as the implications flowed over his rather limited brain. "Oh!"

Mary slyly continued. "It would be a feather in our cap to be attached to that august family, to be sure. But you are right, dear. How selfish of me! We must do our duty to Lady Catherine. I shall ring for the girl—"

"Girl? What for?"

"Why, to begin packing for Longbourn, Mr. Collins. To convince our sister not to marry Mr. Darcy."

Collins held up his hand. "Let us not be so hasty, my dear. We must consider this delicate matter for no little time. Only fools rush in where angels fear to trend, you know." He began to pace. "You have a close friendship with Miss de Bourgh. How do you think she will respond to this news?"

Mary assured her husband of Miss de Bourgh's indifference to Mr. Darcy and let him know of the lady's stated hope that her cousin and Elizabeth would come to an understanding. And she told him that she believed Miss de Bourgh's feelings went to another quarter entirely.

"But, my dear," said Collins, "not everyone may be assured of the marital felicity we enjoy! Those of the upper class have a duty to their station."

"That is true, and I cannot speak for my friend, but consider this. Is not the son of an earl superior in rank to a simple, landed gentleman, no matter his income?"

Collins gasped. "Colonel Fitzwilliam? Do they have an understanding?"

Not yet. "Husband, I said no such thing. I am sure that there is no skullduggery about. I suspect that Miss de Bourgh's opinion of her cousin is very high, that is all."

"I see." Collins thought about that for a moment. "A union between Rosings and Matlock would do as well as one with Pemberley, at least in stature. But I am certain that Lady Catherine will be displeased— highly displeased. Where does our duty lie?"

"Why, to help Lady Catherine admit the present situation. We must support her in her time of crisis. Surely, she will come to acknowledge my sister's marriage and grant her permission to another arrangement for Miss de Bourgh. No one can offer the counsel and guidance that *you* can, my dear."

Mary continued on in this vein, complimenting and persuading her husband towards this course of action. In their months of marriage, she learned how to thus manage her spouse. Vain and opinionated he was, but well intentioned too. Mary found that she had developed a talent for manipulation, though she would never call it such; she *convinced* her husband. Her friendship with Anne had taught her subtlety, a powerful combination that a man in possession of both self-importance and lack of understanding, as well as being besotted with his wife's charms, would find impossible to resist.

Once she was able to set in his mind that Anne's future resided in a union with Colonel Fitzwilliam, Mary only had to reinforce the notion that she had carefully built in his mind that, as Lady Catherine's most able advisor, it was his duty to help guide the formidable lady towards this solution to her distress. The task would take another hour before it was accomplished.

The job of convincing Lady Catherine would prove more daunting, but in time and with the assistance of Miss de Bourgh, the grand dame was persuaded that Colonel Fitzwilliam would make an acceptable substitute for the wayward Mr. Darcy—a superior alternative actually, since surely the good colonel would prove to be easier to manage than his proud and stubborn cousin.

Therefore, when Richard Fitzwilliam appeared at Rosings with the task of conveying Miss de Bourgh and the Collinses to Hertfordshire for the double ceremony in which Darcy and Bingley would gain their hearts' desires, he was unknowingly faced with the prospect of three ladies determined that he marry Anne de Bourgh.

He never stood a chance.

Colonel the Hon. Richard Fitzwilliam descended his family's coach refreshed, for he had stopped in London the night before. He jauntily ascended the steps into Rosings with his usual devil-may-care attitude, not knowing his fate was already sealed. The footman assured the colonel that his baggage would be seen to and informed him that Lady Catherine requested his presence in the front parlor. Upon entering the room, he saw that his aunt was in her usual chair—and quite alone.

"Nephew, you have made good time. That is well; punctuality was always insisted upon by my late father, the earl. It is good that some things do not change. My compliments to my brother for instilling the proper respect for duty and honor in you. At least *someone* takes care of such things these days."

After offering his greetings and delivering the usual compliments from his family, Richard awaited his aunt's pleasure. It was not long in coming.

"This is a sad business, this marriage of your cousin's! I tried to talk him out of it, to remind him of where his duty lies, but I am ignored. I always am! Darcy has proven as stubborn as his father, God rest his soul. There is nothing for it, it seems! The banns have been published, and it would be too much now, should anything unseemly happen to disrupt this unfortunate event. Indeed, that the ceremony should occur with as little fanfare as possible is the lesser of many evils!"

"Have you changed your mind about attending, then?"

"Absolutely not! I will not scruple to pretend that…that *woman* would ever be noticed by me! Why my brother attends is a mystery to me. It must be that wife of his!"

Fitzwilliam was well aware of the bad blood between his mother and his aunt. "I am thankful, then, that you have seen fit to allow Anne to go."

"I have ever been celebrated for my magnanimity, Richard. Anne wished to be of comfort to poor Georgiana. And Mrs. Collins has proven a good friend and companion to my dear Anne. At least one of the Bennet girls knows her place! She knew enough not to try to rise above the sphere where she was brought up. We should all know our rank, my dear Richard."

"Indeed, Aunt Catherine." Richard humored her.

"I am pleased that you agree with me. Your duty, therefore, should be as pleasing as it is obvious."

"Duty, Aunt?"

"Why, that you must take Darcy's place. You must marry Anne."

"Me? Marry Anne?" spurted Richard. "You want me to marry Anne?"

"Of course! Such an agreeable outcome should be apparent to you. Your eldest brother, the viscount, is already married. Your unfortunate younger brother, the sailor—well, the less said about *him* the better! As Darcy has betrayed his family, it falls to you to uphold the Fitzwilliam honor."

"But—"

"I agree your situation is not all that it should be—you, a second son. My brother has not laid much on you, has he? However, as a younger son, your pedigree is such that there will be little discussion of that! Where does avarice end and discretion begin? It matters not. Somewhere below fifty thousand pounds, I dare say. I am sure that all right-thinking people would understand that it is natural to seek a union of Matlock and Rosings. And Anne is undeniably improved this last year, is she not?"

"Umm, yes, but Aunt, how does Anne feel about this?"

"Anne? Do not be concerned on that score. Anne will do her duty."

"I am shocked…and surprised. I must speak to Anne about this!"

Lady Catherine's smile suspiciously resembled a leer. "To court her, I suppose. Very well, off with you. You young lovers must have everything your own way. In my day, such things were unnecessary. My father chose Lewis de Bourgh for me. It saved much inconvenience. The less an engaged couple meet before the wedding the better. Unpleasant news can always wait."

Richard turned as he reached the door. "Lady Catherine, I am two and thirty. I am hardly young!"

"A ripe age—young enough to wish to marry without being too set in your ways, too old to be much of a bother as a husband. Yes, an excellent age!"

With no answer to that, Richard quit the room. He was soon in the main hall and approached the butler to find out Anne's whereabouts.

"I was told that, should you enquire about Miss de Bourgh, I should direct you to Mrs. Parks's room," the butler said with absolutely no emotion. "If you will follow me?"

She is at her music lessons with Mrs. Collins, Richard thought. *I must find her and let her know of her mother's newest obsession.*

The pair walked the length of Rosings, down a hall, and around a corner before stopping before the housekeeper's room door.

"Shall I announce you, sir?"

"No, no, I will see to it, my man," Richard dismissed the butler. He opened the door and entered to find Mrs. Collins at the pianoforte—and quite alone.

"Colonel Fitzwilliam! I am honored, sir."

"Mrs. Collins! Forgive me, madam, but I was led to believe that Anne—Miss de Bourgh was here. Do you know where she is?"

"Come in, sir, and have a seat."

Richard chose not to question the lady from the doorway. He left the door ajar and took a seat on the sofa in the room. "I thank you, Mrs. Collins, but I must ask again. Do you know where my cousin may be found?"

Mary brought her hand to her chin in concentration. "That would be hard to say, Colonel. This announcement of the marriage between my sister Elizabeth and Mr. Darcy has affected her greatly."

"What?" Richard started. "But she said—Mrs. Collins, it was my understanding that Anne, I mean, that Miss de Bourgh was indifferent to her cousin. Was I misinformed?"

"Oh, do you think she is distraught over Mr. Darcy's joy? Let me assure you that Miss de Bourgh is quite delighted for her cousin and wishes my sister and him all happiness. No, I believe I spoke carelessly. My meaning was that this event has reminded Anne that she has not the accomplishments that the granddaughter of an earl should have. For her to attract proper suitors, she needs to apply herself."

"Suitors? Apply herself?"

"Oh, yes! As Miss de Bourgh has undoubtedly informed you, I have been teaching her the pianoforte. Her success at this endeavor has inflamed her desire to do more. She is drawing; singing is out of the question, you know. She already handles her dog cart very well. She has engaged one of the grooms to teach her to ride—"

"Anne *ride?*"

"She is determined, Colonel. The young man assigned to the task promises to be most attentive."

"Young man? *What* young man?"

"A delightful and handsome yeoman, sir." Marry giggled. "He is quite the favorite of the under-maids, I understand." She sighed.

Richard's countenance darkened. A young and handsome groom? Laying hands on his Anne? He would not have it!

"Mrs. Collins! Thank you for this intelligence. It has been most enlightening, but I must insist you tell me this instant where Anne is!"

Mary hid her smile. "Well, I cannot know for certain…but you may wish to try the billiards room."

"The billiards room?"

"Indeed. She has found the game most enjoyable."

Richard jumped to his feet. "I thank you, Mrs. Collins. Please excuse me. My best wishes for your health. I will see you tomorrow." With that he dashed from the room.

Mary dissolved in giggles.

Richard ran down the halls, disregarding the open looks of astonishment from the housekeeping staff. Grasping a banister, he whirled around and down the flight of stairs to the lowest level. In another moment, he had reached that symbol of male sanctuary, the billiards room. There he found the most disconcerting image: Anne, facing the door, leaning over to line up a shot, her décolletage shown to great advantage in her low-cut neckline—and quite alone.

"Good day, Richard." She sniffed and struck the cue ball with her stick, sending another ball into the corner pocket. "When did you arrive?"

The colonel was speechless as he shut the door absentmindedly behind him, many improper thoughts racing through his head.

"Did you have a good trip?" she inquired as she scanned the table for her next shot.

Richard was temporarily struck dumb. He could only observe Anne move gracefully about the table. "Umm, yes. Quite a nice journey... *Oh God!*"

Anne had bent over again, her posterior revealing itself to be most enticing. She tried a bank shot and failed.

"Oh, fiddlesticks!" she cried. "Well, Richard, I suppose it is *your* turn to play." She walked over to him and handed him the stick.

Richard took it without a thought but was taken aback by Anne's hands lingering on his. He could feel the heat radiating from her touch. He felt as uncomfortable, as un-cousinly, as he had last spring in that very room.

Finally, his confused mind began to work. *Anne is flirting with me!* He grasped her hand with his, holding the stick in his left, and demanded of her, "What kind of game are you playing at, my girl?" Anne's eyes grew wide, and Richard wondered how it was that he had never before noticed how pretty they were.

"What game, Richard?"

"This! You have obviously played billiards before. You could not have become so proficient without many months of practice. Yet you led me to believe that you needed my assistance when last I was here."

She looked at him square in the eyes. "I thought you could teach me things."

"Stop it! Do you know what your mother is saying? She says I should take Darcy's place!"

Anne frowned. "Did she?"

"She did!"

"I do not believe Miss Elizabeth would care for that."

"What? Miss Eliza— Anne, I mean that Lady Catherine demands that we marry! You and I!"

"Oh. And this distresses you?"

"No, I did not say— Anne, your mother...your mother is meddling again! She wants a union of Matlock and Rosings in the place of her disappointment over Pemberley. Anne, what I mean to say— Oh, Anne, what do *you* want?"

"I see no difficulty in a union of Rosings and Matlock."

Before Richard could digest those words, the door to the room flew open.

"Colonel Fitzwilliam, I am requested by my honored patroness— Oh! Oh, my goodness! Pardon me, I did not wish to interrupt! But this is unseemly, sir! Single people alone behind a closed door! It will not do!"

"BE SILENT, MAN!" Richard pointed the cue stick like a cavalry saber at Mr. Collins. The officer turned to the lady. "You have no objection?"

"No, Richard."

"Really?"

She looked at him through her lashes. "No, none at all."

Richard looked at Anne for long moments, considering her statement. "Then...shall we give it a go, my girl?"

Anne's smile was breathtaking. "Very well—I will 'give it a go.'"

Without a thought, Richard raised Anne's hand to his lips to seal the understanding. Once his lips touched her skin, he was loath to release her. "I suppose I should go to your mother now, Anne."

"That will not be necessary, Richard." Lady Catherine swept into the room, followed by Mary. "Are you satisfied with his proposal, Anne?"

"It will do, Mother," Anne responded with a twinkle in her eye.

"Excellent. I do not understand all this carrying on about proposals. However, I am sure your late father would have given an excellent one, had he had the choice of the matter. Now, come along, Anne. We have planning to do. Kindly release my daughter, Richard. You will have plenty of time to court on your way to Hertfordshire."

Richard let go of Anne's hand. "Umm, of course. Planning?"

Lady Catherine gave him a withering stare. "For the wedding, of course! We cannot leave these things to chance, you know. The union of our houses requires a ceremony equal to our stature. Months of preparation are needed! Is your education that bereft? It is your mother's doing, I dare say."

The three women turned and left the room, talking over each other.

"Your husband shall officiate, of course, Mrs. Collins, but I will have my part of the conversation about the sermon."

"Shall you make an announcement at the wedding breakfast, Anne?"

"Of course, she shall! We must have our share in the entertainment! I shall entrust this to you, Anne."

"Oh, what shall I wear? Shall it be blue or yellow?"

"You do not know all the best shops, Anne. I will guide you."

"Oh, she would look divine in blue!"

"As long as it is not white! Why anyone would marry in white is beyond me."

As the voices faded with distance, Colonel Fitzwilliam looked at Mr. Collins in confusion. "Pardon me, Mr. Collins," said the officer. "Perhaps you will be kind enough to enlighten me. What just happened here?"

Collins started and then closed his mouth. He struggled, and then with an apologetic look said, "My dear colonel, it has been my experience that it is well not to think overmuch at times like these. It is best that the ladies get their way. Hearken to me when I advise you that it works out for the better in the long run if one…just goes along."

"I am engaged, though?"

"Yes, you are."

"I see. Well, that is well." Colonel the Hon. Richard Fitzwilliam, a newly engaged gentleman of two and thirty, sighed. "Apparently the ladies will be occupied until dinner. Mr. Collins, what say you to a glass of port and a game of billiards while we wait?"

Caroline Bingley sat in the pew of the Meryton Church trying to understand what was going on. There, before the altar was her brother, Charles, a participant in a wedding ceremony. Jane was his bride. This was not unusual—Caroline had come to the regrettable conclusion that she must suffer Miss Bennet as her sister-in-law, which was not a bad thing, really. Jane was a sweet, lovely girl. Yes, Charles could have done better, but he also could have done much, much worse.

Like the other participant of the wedding. The other groom. Mr. Darcy. Who was being married. To Elizabeth Bennet.

What has happened?

Three months ago, Caroline was enjoying the company of Mr. Darcy, Charles was safe from Miss Bennet, and all were securely away from Hertfordshire. Now her brother was making Jane her sister, and Darcy was marrying the impertinent Eliza Bennet. And all of the Darcy family, except Lady Catherine de Bourgh, was in attendance! In spite of her letter—in spite of everything!

What has happened? No, this is wrong. I should be the one getting married to Mr. Darcy. Perhaps this is a dream. Perhaps if I close my eyes very tightly and open them, this will all go away.

She tried. It did not serve.

Mr. Darcy was repeating his vows. "With this ring, I thee wed. With my body, I thee worship."

I believe I shall be ill now.

The breakfast finally over, the Darcys made their escape to the townhouse in London. The pair could hardly restrain their passions, but as the carriage carried two coachmen and two footmen, it would not do to begin their married life by scandalizing the help. Within a few hours, they were safely delivered, and they found themselves in their private apartments as soon as propriety allowed.

"My love, my love," Darcy murmured as he undressed his bride, "how I have longed for this moment, to make you mine in all ways."

Elizabeth shuddered in delight as she trailed kisses along the line of his jaw down his strong neck. *Who knew gentlemen were so agreeable without cravats?* "Husband, I must ask a favor of you."

"Anything, my heart."

"Oh, Fitzwilliam, I adore the pet names you have for me."

He chuckled. "Then it shall be my agreeable task to dream up a hundred for you, my own." He began trailing kisses over her rapidly revealing flesh.

"But...oh, that is nice! But you must—Fitzwilliam! Stop, or I shall grow distracted!"

"I thought that was the point of all this."

"Teasing, teasing man! I have something important to say!"

"Very well, Elizabeth, what do you wish of me?"

"You must promise me, most firmly, that you will NEVER, EVER call me Lizzy-kins!"

Darcy looked at his half-dressed wife. "Lizzy-kins?"

"Swear! Or I shall leave you forever!"

"Doubtful."

"Fitzwilliam, please—I beg you!"

Darcy shook his head. "It is easily done, as I would never call the queen of my soul such a name as—"

"DO NOT SAY IT!"

"My lips are sealed, Mrs.—"

Elizabeth found a way of quieting him.

Chapter 18

The Business of Happily Ever After

Who could doubt the happiness that followed? Mr. and Mrs. Darcy would retire to Pemberley after a week's visit to London. Georgiana would follow after another month's stay at Matlock, to the delight of all involved. Kitty, now Miss Bennet, would join them in time to prepare for the Season, where the spirited pair would make quite the impression. Both would eventually marry well in the years to come.

Of course, the *ton* was mostly interested in the new Mrs. Darcy, and if there were any unkind words mentioned about that lady, it was confined to the young women and their mothers who had for years set their caps on the master of Pemberley. Those without such interest would proclaim Darcy's bride a most excellent match, charmed as they were by her beauty, wit, and graciousness.

However, jealous of their privacy, the Darcys would cause a small scandal by removing to Derbyshire when the Season was only half over, there to begin the process of delivering five more Darcys into the world.

Mr. and Mrs. Bingley's happiness was almost as great. One could say that distance from Longbourn played a deciding factor. Mrs. Bennet despaired of Jane fulfilling her duty to produce a Bingley heir, a concern that justified her daily presence at Netherfield.

Bingley was a very even-tempered and considerate man. It took a twelve-month before he came to the conclusion that a new estate was necessary to his position in life. To Mrs. Bennet's disappointment, a suitable place could not be found closer than Derbyshire. Jane's mother was consoled by the loss of the society her eldest daughter by the news six months later that Jane had conceived the first of what were to be four children. It would never cross her mind that there was a connection between their removal and the Bingleys' domestic bliss.

Mr. and Mrs. Collins's position at Rosings was enhanced by the marriage of Colonel Fitzwilliam to Miss Ann de Bourgh. Mr. Darcy was instrumental in the decision of his aunt and his cousin to make substantial improvements to the living at Hunsford. Therefore, Mr. Collins was not of a mind to request a better living from his brother-in-law in Derbyshire. This pleased Mrs. Collins, for she and her children would not lose the company of her close friend, Mrs. Fitzwilliam, and her offspring. Mr. Collins was constantly occupied by attending to Lady Catherine and puttering about in his gardens, which became legendary in Kent.

Lydia Wickham's happiness would last but two years before her unfortunate Wickie was shot by an enraged husband while fleeing a married woman's bed. Darcy established the Widow Wickham in a hat shop in London, which promptly went bankrupt. Lydia was only saved from debtor's prison by marrying an embezzler sentenced to transport to Australia.

Caroline Bingley was kidnapped by pirates, or gypsies, or some such group—no one could be certain. She ultimately was discovered in Paris after the war, ensconced there as the mistress of a wealthy French noble.

And as for Charlotte Lucas…

SIX MONTHS HAD PASSED SINCE Fitzwilliam Darcy irritated half of the mothers in London by marrying Miss Elizabeth. As wonderful as married life would prove, Derbyshire was rather north of Mrs. Darcy's friends and relations. It was expected that she would request female company—not that there was anything lacking in Miss Darcy, mind you.

So it was, on that summer's day, that Miss Charlotte Lucas found herself exploring the grounds of Pemberley. It was warm, and her frock was rather thinner than her usual wear, but as there was no one about, she thought little of it.

The last week at Elizabeth's new house was everything delightful, and she was a little sad that a gentleman was to join them today, a Captain Tilney. Charlotte enjoyed being with Lizzy again, and she was loath to share her. While at Pemberley, she could forget her unsettled state.

For Miss Lucas was uneasy and had felt that way for some time. Something was amiss, but she could not determine what it was. Coming to a wooden footbridge over a stream, the lady crossed halfway and took in the aspect of the great house.

Yes, she had been uneasy for over a year, ever since learning of Mary's engagement to Mr. Collins. Not that she had any claims on that gentleman—she hardly knew him. It just felt...wrong, somehow, as if the Universe itself had changed. And this was to affect her destiny in ways Charlotte could not know.

Distracted, she paid no mind to the creaking of the boards beneath her feet. It was not until she leaned against the railing that she remembered Mr. Darcy's warning that the footbridge was scheduled to be replaced because it was rotting.

Oh, bother! she thought as the railing gave way and she fell into the stream.

CAPTAIN FREDERICK TILNEY WAS LATE for his visit to Pemberley, as usual, but this time it was not his fault. His father, General Tilney, had pressing business with him back at Northanger Abbey—to berate his eldest son for his lack of a wife and heir.

Blast the old sot! Tilney raged as he rode the back roads into Pemberley. *I believe he was placed upon this Earth to bedevil me! Are not Henry and Catherine enough to keep him entertained?*

Passing through a stand of trees, he beheld a figure emerging from the stream nearby. His first inclination was to ride closer and offer aid, but at second glance, he thought better of it. He was not called Eagle-Eyed Tilney for nothing.

Zounds! The way her thin dress clings to her—it is as if she was wearing nothing! Who could that beauty be? 'Tis not Mrs. Darcy—too tall, or Miss Darcy—not blonde. Another guest at Pemberley?

Reaching down, he quieted his horse while watching the woman walk towards the manor house. He told himself that he was being polite, for it would not do to intrude upon the lady in her current state. He convinced himself that he only watched her out of concern, to make sure that no further misfortune befell her. The enticing movement of her hips and bottom was just an unintended reward for his gallantry.

"OH, CHARLOTTE! I AM SO sorry! Mr. Darcy warned me of that bridge."

"Lizzy, I am well," Charlotte assured her. "It is a warm day. I am not chilled. I am mortified but not harmed."

"Well"—the mistress of Pemberley grinned—"we shall just fix you up. Come with me." Minutes later, the two ladies were in Elizabeth's dressing room, her abigail attending them.

Charlotte cried, "I cannot wear this gown! It is too—"

"Nonsense! It looks lovely on you."

"I believe I shall fall out of it!"

Elizabeth laughed. "No, you shall not, my dear friend. Now, about your hair…"

CAPTAIN TILNEY HAD EASED HIMSELF into an armchair in the sitting room, and he was enjoying a bit of wine with Mr. Darcy when the ladies made their appearance. Jumping to his feet and bowing to them, Tilney's eyes never left the lady standing next to Mrs. Darcy.

Her face cannot be called beautiful, he thought, *but it is handsome enough. The way she fills out that gown makes up for much.* He recalled the first time he beheld the lady, wet and exposed, and grinned.

A few moments' conversation showed that Miss Lucas had a sharp mind. She was different from the usual girls with whom Tilney wasted his time. *They* were lovely and boring. The intelligence behind Miss

Lucas's eyes stirred him.

Watch out for the plain, quiet ones. Their gratitude for attention will astonish you, he had been warned. He felt a need to put that that adage to the test. As dinner was announced, Tilney made his way to Miss Lucas's side as quickly as he could.

"May I escort you in to dinner, Miss Lucas?" He held out his arm.

Charlotte blinked in confusion, surprised that he was addressing her. "Yes, that would be delightful, Captain Tilney."

Three months later, he successfully proposed. And the old saying proved most accurate, at least in this case. But that is another story.

THEREFORE, IT WAS ONLY WITH a slight qualification that Mrs. Bennet could exclaim to her husband as he prepared for yet another unannounced visit to Pemberley and its vast library, "Oh, Mr. Bennet! God has been so good to us—save for that part about Lydia. Oh, my poor nerves!"

THE END

Coming in 2015

CRESCENT CITY

The epic series by
JACK CALDWELL

January 2015
The Plains of Chalmette

May 2015
Bourbon Street Nights

July 2015
Elysian Dreams

September 2015
Ruin and Renewal

WHITE
SOUP
PRESS

Made in the USA
Lexington, KY
21 February 2014